Damsels In Distress

Damsels In
Distress

Nikita Lynnette Nichols

www.urbanchristianonline.com

Urban Books, LLC
97 N18th Street
Wyandanch, NY 11798

ISBN 13: 978-1-60162-717-9
ISBN 10: 1-60162-717-3

First Trade Paperback Printing April 2014
Printed in the United States of America

10 9 8 7 6 5 4 3 2 1

*This is a work of fiction. Any references or similarities
to actual events, real people, living or dead, or to real
locales are intended to give the novel a sense of reality.
Any similarity in other names, characters, places, and
incidents is entirely coincidental.*

Distributed by Kensington Corp.
Submit Wholesale Orders to:
Kensington Publishing Corp.
C/O Penguin Group (USA) Inc.
Attention: Order Processing
405 Murray Hill Parkway
East Rutherford, NJ 07073-2316
Phone: 1-800-526-0275
Fax: 1-800-227-9604

Damsels In Distress

by

Nikita Lynnette Nichols

Titles by Nikita Lynnette Nichols

None But The Righteous

A Man's Worth

Amaryllis

Crossroads

A Woman's Worth

Lady Elect

Contact the author:

kitawrites@comcast.net

Twitter: @nikitalynnette

Facebook: Nikita Lynnette Nichols

nikitalynnettenichols.blogspot.com

www.nikitalynnttenichols.com

Acknowledgments

My parents, William and Victoria Nichols, you are my lifeline, the air I breathe. I must, I shall, I will take this time to say thank you to my lovely editor, Joylynn Ross. She keeps me on the bestseller list. I love you, Joy!

Chapter 1

Am I My Sister's Keeper?

It was the third Saturday evening in April. The spring rain fell hard. Heavy thunderstorms accompanied by dangerous lightning blasted throughout the Windy City. Chicago had been given that nickname, decades ago, for its angry winds. The sewers overflowed on South Ada Street: the same street where twenty-seven-year-old Ginger Brown modeled a royal blue two-piece satin suit inside her house. Her best friends, Portia Dunn and Celeste Harper, encouraged her to sashay and turn then turn and sashay. Ginger had recently purchased the suit at Macy's. The following Sunday would be Women's Day at church and as the emcee for the afternoon program, Ginger had planned on looking good.

Portia and Celeste were seated on opposite ivory chaise lounge chairs in Ginger's immaculate living room. White Berber carpet and white stone cocktail and end tables matched the white plantation shutters that covered the floor-to-ceiling bay windows. Ginger had broken a strict rule. She had been warned that no one, not even herself, who owned the house, was ever allowed to step a foot inside the sterile living room. Ginger, her live-in boyfriend, and guests must enter the house through the back door, at all times. But her significant other, Ronald, who enforced the rule, was not home. Therefore Ginger felt bold enough to entertain her friends in what she considered to be the most beautiful room in her home.

The thirty-two-inch space between the women seated served as a catwalk for Ginger to strut. "All right, Ginger, girl. Show us what you're working with," Celeste encouraged her.

Ginger unbuttoned the suit jacket, slipped it off of her arms, then swung it over her left shoulder to reveal the silver-gray satin camisole she wore underneath. She turned away from Portia and Celeste, then strutted back to her starting point just at the archway that separated the living room from the dining room.

As Ginger walked away, Portia's smile quickly vanished when she noticed black and blue bruises on Ginger's right shoulder, next to the spaghetti strap of her camisole. She sat straight up on the chaise chair. "Ginger, what the heck is that on your shoulder?"

Portia's outburst startled both Ginger and Celeste.

Ginger had no clue that the boxing match from the previous night with Ronald was evident. She was usually extremely careful not to allow any bruises to show. Had she known the marks were visible, Ginger never would've taken off her jacket. "Oh, girl, it's nothing." She quickly put the jacket back on. "Ronald got a little high last night. Y'all know how he gets."

Ginger's poor excuse for being a punching bag was for her own benefit. Truth be told, she was quite embarrassed. How could she have been so careless and allow anyone to see the bruises?

When Ronald came home the evening before with his eyes glazed, Ginger knew he had brought trouble home with him. She was in the kitchen, standing at the stove, frying pork chops.

Ronald approached Ginger reeking of marijuana. He lifted the lid of a pot that sat on the stove. "What is this?" he asked. His speech was slurred and his voice was just above a whisper.

Nothing infuriated Ginger more than when Ronald asked her a question that he already knew the answer to. She hated when he asked stupid questions. Anyone in their right mind could see that the pot was half filled with white rice. Evidently smoking weed had taken Ronald's common sense away. Ginger exhaled a loud sigh of frustration.

"It's rice, Ron. I'm gonna make gravy to go with it."

Ronald placed the lid back on the pot then turned to walk away. Ginger thought the conversation was over but was mistaken when Ronald spun back around. He slammed his open palm against Ginger's face and with all the strength he had, Ronald pushed Ginger backward. He sent her flying down but on the way to the floor, Ginger's right shoulder connected with the edge of the marble-top kitchen table. She screamed out in pain.

"Who are you huffin' and puffin' at? Huh?" Ronald stood over Ginger, glaring down at her. He drew his leg back in preparation to kick Ginger in her abdomen but stopped short. "I told you about catching an attitude every time I ask you a question."

Ginger lay on the kitchen floor moaning and wincing in pain. Her right shoulder was on fire.

"I don't want rice and gravy," he spat. "Throw that garbage out and make me some corn." With that being said, Ronald exited the kitchen.

Celeste stood, went to Ginger, and forcefully pulled the jacket off her shoulders to get an up-close and personal look at the marks. Portia came and stood next to Celeste. The bruises were blue, black, and purple. They stopped just above Ginger's right elbow.

It wasn't the first, second, or third time Celeste and Portia witnessed bruises on Ginger. They had been begging Ginger to end her abusive relationship with Ronald ever since she moved him into her home three years ago.

Last month Ginger showed up at church with a swollen busted lip that she tried to hide with lipstick. Portia and Celeste were so angry that they wanted to go to Ginger's house and confront Ronald, but just like all the times before, Ginger had begged them not to interfere. Now the three best friends stood in Ginger's living room facing the issue again for what seemed like the one hundredth time.

"Is that fool still pounding on you, Ginger?" Celeste asked.

Ginger's heart raced as tears began to run down her chocolate-colored face. "Celeste, please understand," she pleaded.

Portia frowned. "Understand what, Ginger? That fool is out of control and you need to get away from him."

"I'm calling the police." Celeste returned to her chair for her purse. Her cell phone was inside.

Ginger was quickly on Celeste's heels. As soon as Celeste pulled her phone from her purse, Ginger snatched it out of her hand. "No, Celeste."

Celeste placed her right hand on her hip and shifted all of her weight onto one leg. "No? What the heck do you mean no? Ronald needs to be locked up and you need to be institutionalized for allowing him to beat on you."

By the expression on Ginger's face, Portia knew Celeste's words had hurt her. Celeste had basically accused Ginger of being crazy. Portia came and stood next to Ginger. "Celeste, I know you're upset but—"

"Upset?" Celeste cut Portia's words off. "Furious is what I am, Portia. And why are you so doggone calm about this? We've been dealing with this crap for three years. Did you get a good look at her back?"

Ginger placed her face in her hands and cried. Not only was she embarrassed, but if a call was made to the police and Ronald found out about it, Ginger knew she'd be in even more trouble with him.

Portia wrapped her arms around Ginger. "It's okay, sweetie. We're gonna get through this. We'll work it out."

Celeste couldn't comprehend Portia's attitude about the situation Ginger was in. "How do you suppose we work this out, Portia? Huh?"

Portia guided Ginger to one of the chaise chairs and sat her down. "I don't know, Celeste. Let's talk about it."

In Celeste's mind, talking with Ginger wasn't necessary. The only talking that needed to be done was on a 911 call. She hastily left the living room and walked toward Ginger's bedroom. "You and Ginger talk. I know what I'm gonna do." In Ginger's bedroom, Celeste opened the closet door. She found a small suitcase and threw it on the bed. She snatched blouses, dresses, and pants off of racks and threw them on top of the suitcase. Ginger and Portia came into the bedroom and saw Celeste on a rampage. Just as Celeste was headed for the dresser, Ginger ran and stood in between it and Celeste.

"What are you doing, Celeste?" Ginger asked her.

"I'm helping you get through this. That's what I'm doing. Get out of my way."

More tears ran down Ginger's face. "Ron apologized. He promised to never hit me again."

"That's what he said the last time and the time before that, Ginger," Portia interjected from the doorway. "When are you gonna learn that Ronald is sick?"

Ginger looked at her best friends through teary eyes. "Y'all just don't understand. He told me . . ." She couldn't finish her sentence as she choked back tears.

Celeste placed her hands on her hips again. "He told you what?"

Ginger knew that if she revealed what Ronald had told her years ago, all heck would break loose. She hesitated. She wondered how she could pacify this situation and calm Portia and Celeste down.

"He told you what?" Celeste's outburst startled Ginger.

Ginger opened her mouth and spoke softly. She looked into Portia's eyes because she didn't want to see the expression on Celeste's face. "Ron once told me that he'd kill me if I ever left him."

Both Celeste and Portia's eyes grew wide. "What?" They screamed at the same time. Celeste became enraged. She was even more eager to pack Ginger's clothes and get her out of that house. "Move out of my way, Ginger."

Ginger pleaded with Celeste to calm down. "Celeste, please understand."

"Why do you keep saying that, Ginger? What is it that you want us to understand? You ain't married to that fool. Ron won't even give you his last name. He's too darn lazy to get a job. All he does is smoke weed all day. He's living in your house while you go to work every day. You pay the mortgage, utilities, and you buy the groceries. Ron has you so twisted that he makes you ask his permission to go to church. Plus he's ugly. I don't see how you can stand to look at him let alone sleep with him. You deserve better, Ginger. So, since you don't have enough brains to pack your bags, I'm gonna do it for you." Celeste pushed Ginger aside and opened the top dresser drawer, then grabbed a handful of bras and panties and threw them on the bed.

Ginger grabbed her underwear from the bed and brought them back to the dresser. "Stop it, Celeste."

Celeste ignored Ginger and proceeded to another drawer. She grabbed another handful of clothes and took them to the bed. On her second trip, she looked at Portia standing in the bedroom doorway. "What the heck are you just standing there for? You should be helping me."

Portia didn't move. She was torn. She knew Celeste was doing the right thing by packing Ginger's clothes and of course she should be helping Celeste. But Ginger just said that Ronald would kill her if she left him. Portia watched as Celeste transferred clothes from the dresser to the suitcase; then she watched Ginger transfer clothes from the suitcase back to the dresser. Portia knew Celeste was out of control but, then again, enough was enough.

Ginger was crying and begging Celeste to stop trying to pack her clothes. Celeste forcefully took the clothes from her hand and looked at her. "Look, Ginger. I'm sick of this crap. Now, either we pack your clothes and you come home with me, or we pack Ron's clothes and set them out on the curb. One of you is getting the heck out of here tonight. Now, since this is your house, I'll let you decide. Because if he touches you again, I'm gonna pay somebody to touch him. So, who's leaving, you or Ron?"

Ginger didn't answer Celeste. She stood in the middle of her bedroom crying. Celeste waited five seconds then threw the clothes on top of the suitcase and proceeded to the dresser to grab more. Ginger reached out to try and stop Celeste, but lost her balance and fell. She managed to grab a hold of Celeste's left leg. Celeste stumbled but was able to deliver the suitcase's deposit. Ginger begged and cried for Celeste to stop packing her clothes. "Celeste, please. Please, Celeste."

Celeste dragged Ginger from the dresser to the bed as she continued to pack her clothes. "Portia, get her off of me."

Portia had a decision to make. She could only pray that Ginger would eventually forgive her and Celeste for doing what had to be done. She went to Ginger and pulled her arms from around Celeste's legs. "Ginger, we gotta do this."

Ginger stopped fighting. She knew that her friends were relentless and they were not going to let her stay in her home as long as Ronald resided there also. But Ginger also knew that she needed to come up with a plan to get Portia and Celeste to leave before Ronald got home. "Okay. Okay, I'll go to the police station." She told them what they wanted to hear.

Portia released Ginger's arms. "You will?"

"Now you're talking like you got some common sense, Ginger." Celeste said. She grabbed the suitcase by the handle. " You're coming home with me after we leave the police station."

"Okay." Ginger didn't argue. She wanted them to leave. She had a plan.

Celeste, Ginger, and Portia rode in silence to the police station. It was when Celeste drove into a parking spot and put the gear in park that Ginger said from the back seat, "I'm not doing it."

Both Portia and Celeste turned around and looked at her. Celeste was furious. "What the heck you mean you're not doing it?"

Ginger turned her head away from her friends and looked out of the window. "I've changed my mind."

Portia looked at Celeste and exhaled loudly. "Now what?"

Without a word Celeste removed her key from the ignition. "I'll be right back." She opened the door and got out of the car. Celeste shut the door and pressed a button on her remote. The feature that Celeste had on her car was the same feature that the police use as car bait. Once a button is pressed on the remote, the car can't be opened from the inside. Because the windows were raised, Celeste couldn't hear the foul names Ginger called her as she ran, through the rain, inside the police station.

Five minutes later Celeste returned to her car with an African American female. Celeste felt that a black lady cop would be better suited than a man to convince Ginger to press criminal charges against Ronald and leave him for good.

The rain had lightened up to a drizzle. Celeste pressed the button on her remote again and opened the passenger door. "Ginger is the one sitting in the back seat," she told the female officer.

The lady cop knelt and looked in the back seat. She asked Portia to get out of the car. Portia exited the car and stood next to Celeste on the sidewalk.

With Portia out of the way, the lady cop sat in the front passenger seat and faced Ginger. "Are you Ginger Brown?"

Ginger sat in the back seat with her mouth shut.

"I'm Sergeant Phyore Montgomery. I'm here to help you. Have you been abused?"

Not a word from Ginger. *What kind of name is Phyore?* she wondered.

Celeste stuck her head inside the car. "Open your darn mouth, Ginger."

Sergeant Montgomery patted Celeste's arm. "Mrs. Harper, please calm down. Give her time."

Celeste rolled her eyes at Ginger and walked away.

Sergeant Montgomery saw tears streaming down Ginger's face. "Miss Brown, I've been on the force for twenty-three years. I've dealt with all kinds of abuse. Nine times out of ten, domestic abuse turns into murder because the victim is too afraid to report it. Your friends brought you here because they love you and want to help you."

Ginger looked through the rear passenger glass window and saw Portia and Celeste standing on the sidewalk glaring at her. "They kidnapped me. Isn't that a crime? Can I file charges against them for bringing me here against my will?"

Ginger had just lied to Sergeant Montgomery. Back at her house she had agreed to come to the police station just to get Portia and Celeste to leave before Ronald arrived home. Ginger had gotten into Celeste's car voluntarily. Telling Sergeant Montgomery that she had been kidnapped by her best friends was Ginger's anger speaking. Celeste and Portia were constantly meddling in her personal business. It would serve them right if Sergeant Montgomery slapped handcuffs on both of them.

Sergeant Montgomery had already gotten the full story from Celeste why she and Portia had brought Ginger to the police station. "They brought you here to save your life." She didn't entertain the thought of allowing Ginger to press charges against her best friends. "Have you been abused?" she asked Ginger again.

Ginger turned her head in the opposite direction. Tears ran down her face. She refused to answer the question.

"Miss Brown, I can't help you if you don't talk to me," Sergeant Montgomery said. "Your friend, Celeste, said that your boyfriend threatened to kill you if you told that he physically abused you. Is that true? If it is, I will personally see to it that you're placed in protective custody. I can have him picked up tonight."

Nothing from Ginger.

Portia became frustrated. "Ginger, tell her about the time when you were five months pregnant and Ron kicked you in the stomach. That caused you to miscarry."

Sergeant Montgomery gasped. Her eyes grew wide and her mouth fell open. "Is that true?" she asked Ginger.

A tear dripped from Ginger's chin. "I really don't wanna be here," she said.

Sergeant Montgomery pleaded with her. "The only way to stop this is to press charges. If you don't press charges, it won't stop. He's not worth your life. No man is. I know you're afraid but you have to admit to me that he put his hands on you."

Ginger focused on someone walking across the street. Sergeant Montgomery sat in silence for a few seconds. "You are a beautiful black woman. Learn to love yourself. It hurts me deeply to get called to a house and find one of my black sisters unresponsive from domestic abuse. And I'm gonna tell you something, Miss Brown. Eventually he will kill you. It happens like that all the time. So, get out while you can."

Sergeant Montgomery waited another twenty seconds for Ginger to confess. She then got out of the car and walked over to where Portia and Celeste were standing. She looked at them both. "I can't do anything without a complaint from her."

That didn't please Portia. "This is bull crap. Look at her shoulder."

"I understand but I can't make an arrest unless she files a formal complaint."

"So, what are we supposed to do?" Celeste asked.

Sergeant Montgomery shrugged her shoulders. "There's nothing anyone can do. Miss Brown has to help herself first."

"But what if we say that we actually saw her boyfriend hit her?" asked Portia.

Sergeant Montgomery sighed. She understood Portia and Celeste's frustration. But she couldn't take a false statement. Neither of them had actually seen Ronald put his hands on Ginger. They had only seen the marks he left behind.

"If Miss Brown is not willing to file a complaint, according to the law, to heck with what anyone else says."

Celeste stormed around to the driver's side of the car, got in, and slammed the door. Portia sat in the passenger seat. Sergeant Montgomery watched Celeste's tires burn rubber as she pulled away from the curb.

"This is absolutely ridiculous," Celeste said angrily as she sped away. She drove back to Ginger's house so that Portia could get her car. Celeste pulled into the driveway and parked next to Ronald's car. "The fool is home. Hurry up and get out, Portia."

Ginger yelled from the back seat, "Let me out, Celeste!" She knew Celeste was gonna try to take her home with her.

"No!" Celeste yelled back at Ginger.

Portia looked at her friend. "Celeste, Ginger is a grown woman. We can't make her do anything she doesn't want to do. Look what just happened at the police station."

"I don't care. If you hurry up and get out, I can drive off."

Ginger yelled again. "Celeste, I wanna get out of this car."

Celeste switched the gear to park, took her foot off the brake pedal, then turned her upper torso around to face Ginger. "You know that if you go in there with your suitcase, Ron's gonna go off."

"Well then keep the darn suitcase, Celeste. I'll get it from you tomorrow."

"If you live that long," Celeste commented.

Ginger couldn't believe what her friend had just said to her. "You know what, Celeste? Just because you live in a fairy tale world with the perfect husband and the perfect job don't make you any better than anyone."

"What the heck are you talking about, Ginger? I'm trying to keep this fool from killing you. You better wake up and realize who really loves you. I'm tired of begging you to save your own life. If you wanna let Ron knock your brains out, then that's on you 'cause I'm through with it." Celeste opened her door, got out, and then pressed the seat forward.

Ginger climbed out of the back seat. Portia exited the passenger seat and walked around to the driver's side where Ginger and Celeste stood.

Ginger looked at both of them. "I love y'all. I will see you at church in the morning."

Portia hugged Ginger. "I love you too, honey."

Ginger let go of Portia and looked at Celeste. "I'm sorry for yelling at you. I know you love me."

Celeste made no effort to hug Ginger. She was angry. "Yeah, whatever. I gotta go." She got in the car and slammed the door shut. She backed out of the driveway.

"You know Celeste is a hothead," Portia said to Ginger when they were left alone in Ginger's driveway. "But she only wants what's best for you. We both do."

"Portia, I love Ronald. And I know that he loves me too." Ginger made the statement as though she was simply telling Portia what time of day it was.

It saddened Portia that Ginger may have actually convinced herself of that lie. "Ginger, is he loving you when he's bouncing you off the walls?"

Ginger lowered her head and didn't respond. Portia proceeded to her car and drove off.

Ginger walked to the garage door and stood before the security panel mounted just beneath the security light. She keyed in the four digit code and the garage door lifted. Once inside the garage Ginger walked to the interior door that led to the breezeway. She pressed the CLOSE button on a different panel and went inside.

Ginger walked through the kitchen. On the way to her bedroom she saw Ronald lying on the sofa in the living room, watching a basketball game. The same white, sterile living room that Ginger was forbidden to enter. Ronald was wearing a pair of gray jogging pants and a white ribbed tank T-shirt known as a wife beater. Ginger wondered if Ronald was dressed to beat her.

Ronald had heard Ginger come in. He knew she was standing at the archway to the living room. He looked up at her. "What did I tell you about leaving this house with dirty dishes in the sink?"

Ginger became nervous. "I'm sorry, baby, I forgot."

Ronald looked at the suit she was wearing. "Why do you have on a suit and where have you been?"

Ginger nervously looked down at her attire. "I went to see a lady from the church. She's a seamstress. I needed to get my skirt hemmed for church tomorrow." Ginger's lies to Ronald had become more and more effortless.

Ronald repositioned himself on the sofa. "You went to church last Sunday. You ain't going tomorrow."

Ginger started to panic. Her name was on the church programs. She'd been looking forward to emceeing the annual Women's Day program for the past three months. In preparation for the service, Ginger had been walking around the house pretending to hold a microphone in her hand, practicing her speech. What would happen if she didn't show up at church? Folks were depending on her to be there. Ginger had to be at church, she just had to.

She walked to Ronald and knelt down to kiss his lips softly before heading to the kitchen to wash the three glasses and saucers that she, Portia, and Celeste had drunk tea and eaten cookies from.

"Next time, I'm not gonna ask any questions about dirty dishes being left in the sink, Ginger. If you're gonna act like a two-year-old, then I'll treat you like one."

"It won't happen again," Ginger said over her shoulder.

"Make me a sandwich," Ronald ordered.

Five minutes later, Ginger brought Ronald a bacon, lettuce, and tomato sandwich on a small wooden lap dinner tray. Next to the sandwich was a glass of grape Kool-Aid.

"Where is my napkin?" Ronald asked. "And you know I like ice in my Kool-Aid."

Ginger quickly returned to the kitchen for a napkin and to put ice cubes in the glass of Kool-Aid. "Can I go to church tomorrow?" she asked when she returned from the kitchen with the napkin and Kool-Aid.

Ronald looked at her. "I said 'you went last Sunday'. So, you ain't going tomorrow."

"But tomorrow is the annual Women's Day celebration. I've been asked to be the mistress of ceremonies. Had I known that you wouldn't have let me go to church two Sundays in a row, Ron, I would've missed last week just so that I could be there tomorrow."

Ginger stood in the middle of her living room, looking at an unemployed man who was not her husband lie on her sofa and watch the television she paid for, praying that he would allow her to go to church. It dawned on Ginger that Celeste was right. Ronald was very ugly. His face was oily, his French braids were long overdue to be braided again, and he needed to shave. The hair on Ronald's chin was nappy and it looked like taco meat.

Ronald drank from the glass and swallowed. He took a bite of his sandwich. "I shouldn't let you go anywhere 'cause I'm tired of telling you about leaving dirty dishes in the sink."

"Portia and Celeste stopped by this evening. We had tea and cookies. I modeled my suit for them and that's when Portia suggested that I get my skirt hemmed. She said it was way too long. So we had to leave in a hurry to get to the seamstress's house before it got too late. I had totally forgotten about the cups and saucers."

"You're gonna have to start entertaining those broads outside of this house. They don't like me and the feeling is mutual."

The hatred Ginger's friends felt toward Ronald was not unknown to him. The very first time Ginger told Portia and Celeste that Ronald had slapped her face they drove to Ginger's house and confronted him. They threatened to kill Ronald if he touched her again. Ronald told Ginger that if her friends insisted on interjecting themselves in their personal relationship then they would be banned from the house altogether. From that moment on Ginger had rarely invited the girls to her home and if she did it was always at a time when she knew that Ronald would be out of the house.

Ginger didn't respond to Ronald's latest demand. If he didn't want Celeste and Portia to visit then she would see to it that they didn't. With her suit still on, Ginger sat next to Ronald and pretended to be into the basketball game he was watching. When he had finished his meal and drunk the last of his Kool-Aid, Ginger took the plate and glass into the kitchen and washed them.

She turned the kitchen light off then came and stood nervously by the sofa. "Honey, I know you're into the game but I was wondering if you've decided to let me go to church."

Ronald ignored Ginger for a long thirty seconds while he continued to watch the game before he looked up at her and asked, "What's in it for me?"

Ginger didn't say a word. She knew what to do next. Right there in the living room, she stripped naked then knelt before Ronald. He grabbed Ginger by the back of her head and guided her face toward his lap.

Celeste walked in the front door and slammed it shut behind her. Her husband, Anthony, was talking on the telephone with their pastor. He watched as Celeste threw her purse and keys on the sofa next to him and stormed toward the rear of the house.

"It was good talking with you too, Pastor. Celeste and I will see you at church in the morning." Anthony disconnected the call and went to find his wife. He found her in the master bathroom sitting at her vanity, removing makeup from her eyes with a cotton ball.

In the mirror, Celeste saw Anthony leaning against the doorframe watching her. She didn't acknowledge him but by how far Celeste's lips were poked out, Anthony sensed that she was upset.

Celeste tossed the cotton ball toward the trash can but missed. Anthony picked it up from the floor and threw it in the trash can, then came and sat next to her. Celeste inched over to allow him more room.

Anthony faced his wife. He exhaled. "Let me guess. Ginger and Ron, right?"

"Yep, you guessed it." Ginger opened the cabinet next to her left leg and grabbed a bottle of Sea Breeze astringent. She soaked a cotton ball with the blue liquid and began rubbing it all over her face.

Anthony extended his legs and crossed his ankles. He leaned backward and placed his elbows on Celeste's vanity. "What did that punk do this time?"

Celeste threw the cotton ball into the trash can. "He hit her again, Tony. You should see her shoulder. Bruises are all the way down her arm."

"She showed them to you?" Anthony asked.

"No. Evidently, Ginger didn't know the marks were there. Portia and I saw the bruises while she was modeling the suit she's wearing to church tomorrow; that is, if Ron even allows her to go to church."

Anthony could only imagine how Celeste behaved when she saw Ginger's bruises. "You didn't freak out did you, Celeste?"

Celeste was applying moisturizer to her face when she stopped and looked at her husband. "Heck yeah, I freaked as I should have. What would you do if your best friend was getting his butt whipped all the time?"

"Look, baby. You and Portia have to come to the conclusion that Ginger is an adult. You can't live her life or make decisions for her, nor can the two of you fight her battles. Yeah, Ron is a punk. But until Ginger decides that she's had enough of his crap, there's nothing you, Portia, or anyone else can do." That wasn't the first time that Anthony had to remind Celeste to stay out of Ginger's business. "My concern is you," Anthony stated. "You're my wife and I don't want you to have a stroke or develop ulcers over Ginger and Ron's issues. The only thing you can do for Ginger is pray for her and be there when she needs you."

Tears ran down Celeste's face. "Portia and I took her to the police station but she wouldn't even get out of the car. I went inside and got a female cop, a sister, and brought her to Ginger but she sat in the back seat and wouldn't open her mouth. Portia and I looked like two fools."

Anthony grabbed Celeste's hand and kissed her open palm. "You and Portia have been going through this with Ginger for years. Nothing will change until she faces reality and realizes that it's up to her, and only her, to get away from Ronald. So let's change the subject. How did your doctor's appointment go this morning?"

Celeste wiped the tears from her eyes. "And that's another thing that's getting on my nerves, Tony. I'm sick of being disappointed every month. We try and try and try but I always get my period. Today Dr. Bindu took my temperature and gave me an ovulation predictor. He said that our best chances of becoming pregnant is between now and next Friday."

Anthony stood behind Celeste and massaged her shoulders. What he didn't know was that his loving wife, the wife he cherished, and the wife he desperately wanted to have a baby with, had just lied to him. Those were not Dr.

Bindu's words. He had sent Celeste home with bad news. The ovulation predictor was a purchase that she'd made at Walmart after her appointment. But she had wasted her money. Doctor Bindu told Celeste that her chances of conceiving a baby were slim to none.

"So, what are we waiting on?" Anthony asked.

Celeste dismissed Anthony's question and asked one of her own. "What am I gonna do about Ginger?" She was not in a rush to make a baby because a baby would never be made.

Anthony let out a loud sigh. "Celeste, I want you to let Ginger take care of Ginger. And I want you to come to bed so I can take care of you."

In her bedroom, Portia pressed the play button on her answering machine. She listened to her messages as she undressed.

"Hey, beautiful. What's up with you? It's me, David. I've been calling you all day. Hit me on my cell when you get in." Beep.

David insisted that Portia only called him on his cellular phone. She wasn't worthy of his home number. His wife could answer.

"Hi, Portia. This is Greg. I've been trying to hook up with you for two weeks. What's up? Are you missing in action or what?" Beep.

Every two weeks, like clockwork, when Gregory's wife got a headache, he wound up in Portia's bed.

"Portia, this is Richard. Why are you avoiding me? You think a brotha ain't got nothing else better to do than track you down?" Beep.

Three days ago, Portia received a dozen red roses at the car dealership where she worked as an administrative assistant. The inside card read:

My dearest Tamara, I love you always, Richard.

Portia did a little detective work and found out that Tamara was Mrs. Richard Clark. The fool had mistakenly written his wife's name on the card.

"Hey, beautiful. I'm in town for a few days. Let's get together. Give me a call at my mother's house. 555-3743. I would love to see you." Beep.

The last message was from Gary Stokes. He was stupid fine and had always been Portia's weakness. She returned his call.

Forty-five minutes later, Portia stood at her stove and unwrapped a king-sized milk chocolate Hershey's candy bar. She placed it into a small saucepan then added two pats of butter. She heated the saucepan on low then stirred the chocolate and butter until the mixture melted and blended well. On the sink next to the stove was a bowl of fresh, ripe, juicy, sweet strawberries. Portia removed the melted chocolate from the heat then dipped the strawberries, one by one, in the chocolate and laid them on a plate. She placed the plate in the freezer then showered while the chocolate hardened.

Fifteen minutes later, Portia removed the plate of strawberries from the freezer and set it on the sink next to an open bottle of Pink Moscato. She filled a syringe with the wine and carefully inserted the needle into each strawberry and emptied it. She smiled when she heard a soft knock on the front door. It was time to play.

She carried the plate of chocolate-covered strawberries into the living room with her. Portia greeted Gary wearing a white sheer teddy and a smile. "So glad you could come over."

Gary stood in the doorway looking as fine as he wanted to look. Retired from the National Football League, where he was a wide receiver for the Chicago Bears for nine seasons, Gary's broad shoulders, buffed arms, and thick neck were easy on Portia's eyes. Six feet three inches, and 260 pounds of solid muscle walked past Portia. He left a whiff of Usher cologne in the wind.

Portia shut the door and leaned against it. She admired Gary's smooth bald head. His goatee mended greatly with his mustache. His caramel-colored skin was as smooth as silk. "Umph, umph, umph. It's a shame your wife lets you travel alone."

Gary's mischievous smile melted Portia. "Why is that?"

"Because you don't know how to behave yourself."

"That's not true. I'm always on my best behavior when I'm away on business. It's only when I come back to Chicago that I get into trouble."

Portia walked to Gary and wrapped her left arm around his broad neck while holding the plate of chocolate-covered strawberries in her right hand. "Is that what I am, 'trouble'?"

He pulled Portia's body closer to his. "With a capital T. But you're the kind of trouble I don't mind getting into, if you know what I mean." Gary seductively bumped his torso against Portia's.

Portia picked up a chocolate strawberry from the plate and inserted it into Gary's mouth. He bit into it and when he tasted the wine, he smiled. "Umm, yummy."

Portia returned the smile. "You like?"

"I love," Gary answered sinfully.

She set the plate of strawberries on the cocktail table and stood on her tippy toes to kiss Gary's forehead, his left cheek, and his right cheek. Portia took her time and ran her tongue along his mustache from left to right. Gary picked Portia up and she wrapped her thighs around his waist. The married man carried Portia to her bedroom and there wasn't any shame in their game.

Chapter 2

He Loves Me Not

On Sunday afternoon Ginger stood behind the podium and introduced the speaker of the hour for the afternoon service. "Let's give a good and hearty 'God bless you' for Evangelist Yvette Shaw."

Ten minutes into Evangelist Shaw's sermon, the women at True Holiness Church were on their feet. She was no stranger there. For the past seven years Evangelist Yvette Shaw had been chosen to be the main speaker for the church's annual Women's Day celebration and she had brought the house down each and every time.

Evangelist Shaw wiped sweat from her brow with her hanky. She whooped and hollered as she strutted across the pulpit. "Women of God must understand that we are not to pick and choose our mates. Often we go against the will of God and plan our own lives, rather than submit ourselves to Him. That's when we end up on paths of self-destruction. Everything that looks good to us is not necessarily good for us. And how many of you know that everything that shines ain't gold?"

There were a bunch of amens to that comment. Portia, who sat next to Ginger, nudged her elbow and leaned into her. "Pay attention. She's preaching to you."

Ginger rolled her eyes at Portia. "Where's Celeste?"

Portia looked around the church but didn't see Celeste anywhere in the sanctuary. "I guess she decided to skip this Sunday."

Ginger was disappointed. "She knew I was hosting this program. She could've come to support."

"Ginger, she tried to show you support last night, we both did, but you didn't want it."

Evangelist Shaw started to pace the pulpit. "Ladies, you don't have to go to a lounge, sit at the bar, and wait for a man to come along and offer to buy you a drink." She spoke to the handful of men present in the sanctuary. "Men, you don't have to sign up for a step aerobics class and wait for a woman to commend you for not being intimidated by sweating with a bunch of women."

"Come on and talk about it. Tell the truth. You're in the house today," the congregation responded.

"When God brings your Adam or Eve to you, it will be totally unexpected. Women, he'll walk up to you and say, 'Excuse me, I've been watching you for weeks. I've been praying for the nerve to approach you. I want you to know that I love your praise. I saw you a few Sundays ago when you were on your knees engrossed in true worship while crying out to God and for some reason, I found that very attractive. I saw how you dismissed everything around you and concentrated on worship. I love it when a woman is not ashamed of letting her mascara run or is not in fear of ruining a pair of stockings.'"

The women in the sanctuary were on their feet. "All right, Evangelist. Teach it, teach the truth."

"Ladies, God knows your heart's desire and He sees you exactly where you are. But He wants to make sure that you're ready for the blessing before He sends him to you. If you're not faithful to God, how can He trust you to be faithful to your Adam? The man God has for you will never come to you in a nightclub and offer you a drink. The man sent from God will not proposition you to his bedroom after he buys you an expensive gift. A man sent from God will not share a home with you without giving you his last name."

Ginger looked around the church wondering who was looking at her. *Why did Evangelist Shaw have to put my business out there like that?*

After the benediction, Ginger raced out of the church toward her car. She couldn't speak to Evangelist Shaw and tell her how great her sermon was. Ginger couldn't stay and linger in the vestibule like everyone else. She turned down an invitation to go out to dinner and fellowship with a few of the women.

Ginger had a curfew to beat. The streetlights on Ada Street would be on at exactly 7:00 p.m. Before Ginger had left for church Ronald told her that she had to be home before the streetlights came on. Ginger worried that if she stepped foot inside the door at one second past 7:00 p.m., she would have hell to pay.

Driving home from church Ginger was on a spiritual high. She stopped at a red light and reflected on Evangelist Shaw's words. She really put something on Ginger's mind when she talked about breaking soul ties and being unequally yoked with a mate.

Ginger knew she had made a mistake sending for Ronald and allowing him to live in her home three years ago. It was Ginger's addiction to online chat rooms that brought Ronald into her life. At first it was harmless idle chat with various folks about various topics. But when Ronald chimed in and asked Ginger to send him a picture of herself, she went against her better judgment and obliged him. Soon after Ronald e-mailed Ginger and complimented her beautiful mocha skin, petite nose, and sultry lips. The next thing Ginger knew, Ronald had sweet-talked his way to a first-class one-way airplane ticket from New Orleans to Chicago, at her expense. It was only a week and four days into her forbidden living arrangement when it was revealed to Ginger what a monster Ronald was. She would never forget the first time Ronald smacked her across her face.

Ginger had just come upstairs from the basement after she had put a load of laundry in the washing machine. As soon as she reached the top step, Ronald was there waiting for her. By the expression on his face Ginger knew he was angry.

"What's wrong?" she asked.

"Did you use the toilet?"

Ginger didn't understand why Ronald would ask her that. "What?"

The frown on his face became even more evident. "Don't 'what' me." He stepped closer to Ginger and raised his voice. "Did you use the toilet?"

Ronald's body language threatened Ginger. She became uncomfortable in his presence. "Yes, I did. Why?"

With the back of his hand Ronald struck Ginger across the right side of her face. She lost her balance and fell into the doorway to the basement. Ginger grabbed the door handle to steady herself. She caressed her face where Ronald had hit her.

He moved closer to Ginger and pointed his finger in her face. "Don't you ever disrespect me."

In her mind Ginger tried to make sense out of what was happening. Was Ronald angry because she used the bathroom? How could that possibly be a sign of disrespect?

"You ain't the only one living here," Ronald stated. "Make sure to raise the toilet seat before you leave the bathroom."

The driver behind Ginger pressed the horn. Ginger snapped out of the daydream and stepped on the gas pedal. The digital clock on Ginger's dashboard read 6:49 p.m. She floored the gas pedal and raced west on Ashland Avenue toward her home.

At 6:57 p.m. Ginger lowered the garage door and stepped out of the car. No sooner did she insert her key into the lock on the door to the breezeway, than Ronald yanked it open and in a split second, punched Ginger in her left eye. Because she didn't see it coming, Ginger fell backward. Ronald reached down and grabbed Ginger's hair and dragged her into the house and kicked her in the stomach. Ginger screamed out in pain.

"What did I tell you, Ginger?" he yelled. His eyes were blazing.

She didn't know why Ronald was so angry. She had made it home with three minutes to spare. Her left eye was burning and already beginning to swell. "It's not seven o'clock yet, Ron."

"Don't play with me. You know what I'm talking about. And don't eyeball me." Ronald once told Ginger that women were inferior to men and should never look them in the eyes.

Ginger focused on the dark hardwood floor. She covered her sore eye with her hand. "I don't know what you're talking about. You told me to be home before seven. I'm home before seven."

Ronald gritted his teeth and balled up his fists. "You wanna play games? Huh? Are you playing with me, Ginger?"

Ginger looked up at Ronald standing over her then quickly averted her eyes to the floor. It was becoming difficult for her to see out of her left eye. "Ron, I swear to God. I don't know what you're talking about."

"Well, since you don't seem to know what I'm talking about, I'll show you." Ronald stood Ginger up by her hair. He forcefully pulled her into the kitchen and yanked open the cabinet over the sink that housed the can goods. "Look at this. Now do you know what I'm talking about?"

With her right eye, Ginger saw a can of whole kernel corn stacked on top of a can of string beans. That was a no-no.

Ronald grabbed the can of corn and tapped Ginger's right temple with it. "It's the stupid and careless crap you do that pisses me off, Ginger. You may be a dumb broad but you're not stupid. How many times do I have to tell you to stack corn on top of corn, peas on top of peas, and string beans on top of string beans? You're not in preschool. This ain't no romper room."

Tears ran down Ginger's face as she stood next to him. "I'm sorry. I swear I stacked them right, Ron. I swear I did."

"Ain't nobody living here but you and me. What are you saying? That I did this?" Ronald tapped her right temple again with the can of corn. "Huh? Is that what you're saying, Ginger?"

She opened her mouth to speak but decided that she should say nothing.

A can of cling peaches in light syrup, which sat on the top shelf in the cabinet, caught Ronald's eye. He set the can of corn on the counter and grabbed the can of peaches. "What the heck is this? You know I like my peaches in heavy syrup."

Fearful that he would hit her again, Ginger flinched at every gesture Ronald made. "I was gonna make a cobbler. This can must have been mixed in with the peaches in heavy syrup. I can still use it."

Ronald gripped the can tighter. "You can't make peach cobbler with this crap. You gotta have the heavy syrup. What's wrong with you? Do you like pissing me off? Do you enjoy getting knocked on your butt?"

Ginger focused on the bottle of Dawn dishwashing liquid next to the faucet as she spoke softly to him. "I thought I had bought the right kind. I'm sorry."

Ronald threw the can of peaches across the kitchen and it slammed against the wall. The sound of the can hitting the wall made Ginger scream out in terror. Ronald retrieved the dented can of peaches and set it on the counter in front of Ginger. "Open it and eat 'em."

Ginger didn't need to be told twice. With shaky hands, she slid open the utensil drawer. She saw a steak knife and wanted nothing more than to drive it straight through Ronald's heart. She found the can opener. As she turned the can, Ginger could hear Ronald's heavy breathing in her right ear. She snapped the lid off and contemplated sliding the sharp edge across Ronald's throat. Ginger laid the lid on the counter and reached in the drawer for a fork. Just as she was getting ready to insert a slice of peach into her mouth, Ronald turned the can over and poured the peaches on the counter. He grabbed Ginger by the back of her neck and slammed her face onto the counter. Ginger yelled out at the pain when her front teeth split open the inside of her top lip.

Ronald rotated her face in the peaches. "Eat 'em, eat 'em."

On Monday morning, Celeste sat behind the counter at Midway Financial Savings Bank and sighed. She looked toward the door and saw customers outside waiting for the clock to strike 9:00 a.m.

Celeste had awakened that morning with Ginger on her mind. She thought about the events that took place on Saturday evening. Celeste felt bad about the last words she'd spoken to Ginger that night. And to make matters worse, she didn't support Ginger's program at church the day before. Celeste knew that Ginger was so excited about hosting the Women's Day service because she had been obsessing over it for weeks.

Celeste glanced at the huge clock over the main door as her fellow bank tellers assembled behind the counter and readied themselves for business. Celeste had about a minute and a half to get a quick prayer in. She leaned forward, placed her elbows on the counter, lowered her head and closed her eyes.

Lord, I'm confused about something. I need you to help me understand why someone as beautiful and intelligent as Ginger has to go through this. Lord, I'm coming to you on her behalf. Please break the stronghold Ron has on her. And I need you to work on my temper, Father, because my mouth has gotten Ginger into trouble many a day. Show me what I need to do to be the friend she needs.

When Celeste opened her eyes and looked up, there was an elderly Caucasian woman standing on the opposite side of the counter smiling at her. "Good morning."

Celeste returned the smile. "Yes, it is. How may I help you?"

The woman set two two-and-a-half-pound Folgers coffee cans on the counter. She removed the lids from both cans. Celeste saw both cans were filled with pennies.

"Can you give me what this is worth in dollars?" the woman asked.

"Yes, ma'am, I can." Celeste took both cans to the coin machine. Most banks required customers to roll their coins. Celeste was excited that she got to operate the coin machine.

She returned three minutes later with a receipt and cash. "Thirty-four dollars and seventeen cents," Celeste said to the woman.

The elderly woman looked at Celeste. "You stole my money."

Celeste was sure she hadn't heard the woman correctly. "Excuse me?"

"There was at least one hundred dollars in pennies in those coffee cans. You bring me thirty-four dollars like I wouldn't know you stole my money."

The bank teller working next to Celeste heard the woman's complaint and called for their supervisor to come to the teller's station.

"Miss, I don't need to steal your money," Celeste said. "Those were pennies in those cans, not quarters."

The woman raised her voice. "I know what was in the cans. I had a hundred dollars' worth of pennies. Give me my money!"

Linda Marshall, Celeste's supervisor, appeared at her side. "Is there a problem, Celeste?"

The old woman spoke. "Yes, there is a problem. She stole my money. I came in here with two coffee cans full of pennies and she brought me thirty-four dollars and some change." The woman threw the money Celeste had given her on the counter.

Celeste was hot. That was the third time the woman accused her of stealing her money. "Look, old lady, I didn't—"

"Celeste, take a break," Linda interrupted.

Celeste looked at her boss. "But, Linda, I didn't steal her money."

Linda smiled at Celeste. "Take a break."

Without another word Celeste scolded the old woman with her eyes and walked away. She went into the break room, made herself a cup of tea, and lay on a lounge chair. The old woman had Celeste so wound up, she had to count from one to ten to calm herself.

She dismissed all thoughts of what had just happened and thought about her situation with Anthony. She could only hope that her intimate time with him over the weekend was beneficial to her womb but deep down inside Celeste knew it wouldn't be. She had been lying to her husband for so long that Celeste wondered how much longer she could get away with making Anthony believe they were really working on conceiving before he found out the truth.

The door to the break room opened and Linda entered. "You can go back to your station now, Celeste. The crisis is over."

"Oh, really? Did you give that woman more money?"

Linda chuckled. "Heck no. That old broad has pulled that stunt before. I think you were on vacation when she tried it last year. She came into the bank with two coffee cans filled with pennies. The teller gave her twenty bucks and a receipt. The old woman acted a fool claiming she had been cheated."

Celeste couldn't believe it. "Are you serious, Linda? What happened?"

"After she was shown the surveillance tape of the teller putting the pennies in the coin machine and the machine displaying in big, bold red letters that the total came to twenty dollars, she took her money and left."

Celeste shook her head from side to side. "That's a doggone shame, Linda. But you know what, I bet that old woman was just trying to make ends meet. It's hard out here. I blame the economy."

Linda shrugged her shoulders. "Celeste, the economy may be bad but that doesn't give that old woman or anyone else an excuse to try to scam a bank."

Celeste agreed. "That's true."

Linda left Celeste alone in the break room. Celeste leaned her head back and closed her eyes. Suddenly Ginger's face appeared in her mind. Celeste immediately jumped up and walked to the employee's closet to retrieve her cellular phone from her purse. She didn't know why her fingers were shaking as she dialed the number to the school where Ginger worked as a teacher.

"Good afternoon, Brainerd Middle School," the receptionist answered.

Celeste's heart was racing but she didn't know why. "Hello. I know Miss Brown is in class at the moment but may I please leave a message for her?"

"One moment please." As instructed, the receptionist transferred Celeste's call and all calls pertaining to Ginger to the principal's office.

"Brainerd Middle School. Principal Sanford speaking."

"Hey, Diane. It's Celeste."

"Hey, girl. What's up? I missed you at church yesterday."

"I wasn't feeling well," she lied. Celeste was still angry at Ginger from Saturday night. She purposely missed church to not support Ginger as the emcee for the afternoon service. But at that moment Ginger was all Celeste could think about. Celeste felt that something was terribly wrong.

"So, what's up?" Diane asked Celeste. "You wanna do lunch today?" Celeste's bank was only two blocks away from the school. She, Ginger, and Diane met for lunch often.

"Actually, I'm calling for Ginger. I want you to put a note in her mailbox to call me."

"Ginger is not here today, Celeste."

Celeste frowned. "She's not? I thought the students were taking their Iowa Tests this week."

"They are," Diane confirmed. "But I had to call in a substitute teacher for Ginger's class this morning."

"Did she call in sick?"

"She didn't call. Ronald did."

Celeste's heart started racing. "Ron called off for her?"

Working so closely with Ginger every day and attending the same church, Diane knew what Ginger was going through with Ronald. What Celeste didn't know, and Diane wasn't about to share, was that Ginger called off at least three times a month whenever Ronald got violent. "Yep. He called the school early this morning and said that Ginger wasn't feeling well. Then he said she may need the entire week off."

Celeste's palms were sweaty. "The whole week, Diane?"

"That's what Ron told me. I'm gonna give her a call this afternoon because I need to know if a substitute is definitely needed for her class tomorrow."

"Okay, Diane. Thanks a lot." Celeste disconnected the call with Diane and dialed Portia's number at work.

"Chevrolet on Pulaski, Portia speaking," she answered.

"Ginger didn't go to work today," Celeste stated.

"What do you mean she didn't go to work? The kids are taking their tests this week, aren't they? She has to be there."

"I just spoke with Diane, Portia. Ron called and told her that Ginger is sick and it's possible that she'll need the whole week off."

Portia's voice rose. "The whole week?"

"Yep. I woke up this morning with Ginger heavy on my heart. And to find out that she didn't go to work today bothers me," Celeste said.

"Yeah, and the fact that Ron called in sick for her bothers *me*."

"I'm thinking about taking the rest of the day off and going to her house. Can you get away?"

"Yeah, it should be no problem. Business is slow. Did you drive today?" Portia asked.

"No. Tony drove me this morning."

"Okay. I've got to type up two bills of sale before I leave," Portia said. "I'll call you when I'm on my way to get you."

An hour later Portia pulled into Ginger's driveway. She and Celeste got out of the car and walked to the front door. Portia rang the doorbell and looked at Celeste. "What if Ron answers?"

"Who the heck cares if he answers? We just wanna know why Ginger isn't at work and why she may need the whole week off. And if Ron knows what's good for his ugly behind, he won't piss me off."

"Maybe we should've called first, Celeste."

"Why? So she can lie to us and say she has an upset stomach? We both know better than that, Portia."

No one came to the door so Portia rang the bell again. "You think she's in there?"

Celeste walked to the garage door and stood on her tippy toes to look inside the window. She came back to the front door. "Ron's car is gone but Ginger's is in there."

Portia called Ginger's home number from her cellular phone. She and Celeste could hear the telephone in the living room ringing. After the fourth ring, Ginger's answering machine picked up. Portia disconnected the call and dialed Ginger's cellular number. Her call was immediately sent to Ginger's voicemail.

"Her cell phone is not on, Celeste. I'm starting to get nervous because something isn't right."

Celeste took Portia's cellular phone from her hand and dialed Ginger's home number again. After the greeting, Celeste talked to the answering machine. "Ginger, it's me and Portia. We're outside on the porch. Can you please open the door? We're not leaving until you do. We saw your car in the garage, Ginger. We know you're in there." Celeste disconnected the call, gave Portia her phone, and rang Ginger's bell profusely.

Ginger slowly opened the door. Portia and Celeste saw her face and both of their mouths fell open.

Chapter 3

Lying in the Bed I Made

Ginger lay on her living room sofa in excruciating pain. Celeste held a Ziploc bag filled with ice cubes against her black, swollen, and completely closed left eye while, at the same time, Portia pressed ice cubes against Ginger's bruised ribs where Ronald had kicked her. They listened as Ginger told them what happened the night before.

A single tear dripped from Portia's eye as she tended to her best friend. "Ginger, why do you continue to let this happen?"

The pressure they applied to Ginger's broken body was extremely painful. Each time Celeste or Portia touched her, she winced and moaned. Her upper lip was swollen and bloody. "It was my fault, Portia. I should've known better."

Portia looked at Celeste's face because she knew the crap was getting ready to hit the fan.

Celeste snatched the bag of ice from Ginger's face and frowned. She shouted, "What the heck did you just say, Ginger?"

Portia grabbed Celeste's hand. "Celeste, please calm down."

Celeste snatched her hand away and glared at Portia. "You don't tell me to calm down. I wanna know why she feels that this is her fault." Celeste looked at Ginger's swollen eye, the Band-Aid above her right cheek, and the bruise on the side of her stomach that represented possible broken ribs. "How is this your fault, Ginger, and what happened to your jaw?"

"While Ron was rolling my face in the peaches on the counter, the lid from the can sliced my face. But had I made sure the peaches were in heavy syrup, this never would've happened."

Celeste dropped the bag of ice on the floor and sat down on one of the chaise chairs. "I don't believe this."

Ginger painfully sat up. "Celeste, I need you to understand."

Celeste glared at Ginger. "Understand what? How stupid you are?"

Ginger was offended. "So, I'm stupid now?"

Celeste gave a sarcastic chuckle. She shrugged her shoulders. "You must be."

"I'm just trying to get you to understand my situation."

Celeste held up her right hand to silence Ginger. "You know what, Ginger? For the sake of our friendship, I suggest you not say that to me again because I will never understand why you continue to let a man, who ain't even your husband, live in your house and treat you like you're worthless."

Portia knelt in front of Ginger and looked deep into her eyes. "Honey, Ronald has brainwashed you. He's got you making sure that there's no toothpaste left in the sink after you brush your teeth. He makes you iron his drawers. Now, who do you know irons drawers, Ginger? Do you remember the time he knocked your tooth out because you forgot to raise the toilet seat after you used the bathroom? Don't you think that's extreme? Your toilet seat, Ginger. The one that's in your house, in your bathroom, has to stay up at all times."

"And do you remember getting up in the middle of the night to pee and you fell down in the toilet and cracked your funny bone when your elbow hit the wall?" Celeste asked Ginger. "That fool wouldn't even get up to take you to the emergency room. Me and Tony had to get out of our beds at three in the morning."

Tears were running down Ginger's face. "I know Celeste, but—"

"But nothing, let me finish. Ever since you've been with Ron your life has been a living hell. You lost a baby at the hands of that creep. Your nose has been fractured. He dragged you through the house by your hair. He snatched an earring out of your ear. Who took you to the hospital and sat in the waiting room while your ear was sewn together? Me and Portia, that's who.

"Today, you have a black eye, a busted lip, a cut on your face that may leave a permanent scar, and your ribs may be broken. So, I want you to look me in the eye and tell me why you feel the need to stay with this man."

The words were effortless for Ginger to say: "Because I love him."

Celeste jumped to her feet and screamed, "Oh my God. You're so freakin' stupid. You know what? I've heard enough. I'm out of here." Celeste looked around the living room for her purse.

Portia ran to Celeste to keep her from walking out of the front door. "Celeste, please don't go. She needs us."

"No, Portia. What she needs is a freaking psychiatrist."

Ginger slowly stood while holding her side. Her entire body felt as if she had been hit by a bus. "If she wants to leave, Portia, let her leave. I don't need her here."

Celeste rushed to Ginger and stood in her face. She spat her words out. "I came because I was worried about you. You dumb broad."

"You don't need to worry about me!" Ginger screamed. "I'm three times seven plus six. That means I'm grown, fully grown. What you need to do, Celeste, is worry about your own life and concentrate on why you can't get pregnant instead of trying to tell me what to do and how to live my life. I got this. Okay? Stay out of my business and focus on your own problem."

Portia gasped loudly. Her mouth dropped wide open. She and Ginger both knew that was a sensitive subject for Celeste. Portia couldn't believe that Ginger had uttered those words. She came and stood between them. "Okay, you two. Stop it right now."

It was too late. Ginger opened up Pandora's box and Celeste was fired up and ready to go head to head with her. She ignored Portia and looked at Ginger. "I know you didn't go there, Ginger."

Ginger wasn't intimidated at all. "Yes, the heck I did. It doesn't take a specialist to tell you why you can't conceive. You know why." Ginger's neck danced. "We all do." She looked at Portia. "Don't we?"

Portia didn't answer. Her heart beat at an alarming rate. Her eyes darted back and forth between Celeste and Ginger.

Ginger connected eyes with Celeste. "The only one who doesn't know is Tony."

Celeste's eyes were the size of golf balls. It seemed as though all of the air had been vacuumed out of Ginger's living room. Celeste struggled to breathe. She literally had to force air into her lungs. Her nostrils swelled with each breath she took.

"Ginger, don't do this," Portia begged. "You're wrong."

Celeste placed her open palm on Portia's chest and pushed her back. Then she stepped closer to Ginger. As Celeste spoke to Portia, she looked into Ginger's eyes. "Let her say what she's gotta say."

Portia stepped between them again. The three of them were sisters. She refused to allow Ginger and Celeste to fight. "Both of you calm down. Ginger, you need to apologize and shut the heck up."

Ginger became defensive. "Why are you telling me to shut up? And what the heck do I gotta apologize for? I'm sick and tired of her acting like she's Miss High and Mighty. She lives in the biggest glass house and is always the first one to throw a doggone stone."

Ginger focused on Celeste's eyes while speaking to Portia. "We all know that the abortion she got in Bebe's basement with a coat hanger messed her up."

That was the straw that broke the camel's back. Celeste pushed Ginger's chest and she fell backward onto the sofa. Ginger grabbed her side and screamed out in pain.

Celeste advanced toward Ginger. "You dirty heifer."

Portia grabbed Celeste's wrist and pulled her back. "Celeste, stop!"

She snatched her hand from Portia's grip and looked at Ginger with tears in her eyes. "I thought you were my girl. The three of us swore, in high school, that we'd never mention that."

Ginger sat on the sofa moaning from the pain in her side.

"She didn't mean it, Celeste. She's going through a lot right now."

"So is everybody else, Portia!" Celeste snapped. "It's time for you to stop babying and making excuses for her grown behind." Celeste took it a step further with Portia. "And if you weren't so busy screwing everybody's husband, maybe we could get Ginger the help she needs. And why can't you find your own man instead of breaking up happy homes?"

Portia was stunned. Why did Celeste turn on her? Portia felt that since she wasn't sleeping with Anthony then Celeste should have nothing to say about the way Portia lived her life. "Let me tell you something, Celeste. This ain't about me. And what I do is my business, not yours."

"It is my business because I know I can't trust you around my man."

Ginger stood up holding her side. Things were getting out of hand. She, Portia, and Celeste were as close as sisters could be. Even though Portia enjoyed keeping company with married men, Ginger felt that Celeste's comment to Portia was out of order. Portia loved both Celeste and Anthony. Ginger knew that Portia would never betray Celeste that way. "Okay, y'all. That's enough."

Portia snapped her head at Ginger. "You sit your crippled behind back down. All of this is your fault."

"How is this my fault?" Ginger asked. "I didn't call y'all over here. You just showed up, uninvited, like you always do. I have to constantly tell you and Celeste to stay out of my business. Every time I look up, you're running over here trying to break down my door. I can handle my own problems and I suggest the two of you do the same. We all have issues. I ain't the only one. Humph, looks to me like we're all damsels in distress."

Celeste looked at Ginger. "Well, you know what, damsel? You ain't even gotta worry about me coming to your rescue ever again. Both you and Portia can kiss my behind." Celeste found her purse on the cocktail table. She snatched it up and stormed toward the living room door.

Ginger was closely on Celeste's heels. "How about you and Portia get the heck out of my house? And y'all can kiss my behind on the way out." Ginger needed them to leave before Ronald returned home. She didn't know where he had gone that morning. He told Ginger that he was going to make a run. That usually meant that he had gone to purchase drugs. If that was the case, Ginger knew he wouldn't be gone much longer. Portia and Celeste had to leave so that she could straighten the living room to make it look as though no one had entered it.

Portia grabbed her purse and keys from the chaise chair she had sat on. She got to the door and swung it open then turned to look at Ginger. "I guess the next time that I see you will be at your funeral."

"Get out of my house, Portia," Ginger cried out.

Portia looked at Celeste. "I haven't forgotten about your birthday next week. I'll send you a Cabbage Patch doll. That's the closest you'll ever get to having a real baby."

Portia tried to close the door behind her but Celeste caught it, swung it back open and yelled after her, "At least I got my husband to lean on. Whose husband will be in your bed tonight?"

"Could be yours," Portia yelled over her shoulder as she walked down Ginger's driveway. She got in her car and sped away.

Before Celeste left Ginger's house, she turned to look at her. "You are not my sister. You're dead to me. You hear me? You're dead to me." Celeste stormed out and slammed the door behind her.

Ginger's world fell apart. She, Celeste, and Portia had had some major disputes in the past. But Ginger knew that time was so very different. Words were spoken that had never been spoken before. Words that were off-limits, taboo, and forbidden. Their bond had been broken. That day their friendship had been tested and failed. Their sisterhood had become nonexistent. After the showdown that had just happened, Ginger knew that it would take an act of God to bring her, Portia, and Celeste back together again.

She locked the front door and hobbled over to the living room window and pulled the curtain back. Portia was long gone but Ginger saw Celeste walking down the street. Tears flowed down Ginger's cheeks.

She went into the bathroom to wash her face. In the vanity mirror, she looked at her eye and the bandage that covered the cut on her jaw. Her enlarged bloody lips resembled Marge Simpson's. Ginger placed her face in her hands and cried. She was trapped in a situation that she desperately needed to get out of. But how could she do it without the help and support of her girls? Ginger knew that, no matter what, she had Jesus, and that's who she called on. "My Lord, please help me."

Portia drove around the corner and pulled over to the curb. She put the gear in park. She had just fought with her two best friends and she needed a minute to compose herself. Portia felt that fight was one hundred times worse than the fights that she, Celeste, and Ginger had had before. Portia couldn't get over the words the three of them had used to purposely harm each other. Portia knew that Ginger's bruises would eventually heal but the words spoken in hatred, among the three of them, would follow her to her grave. They would be with her forever.

Her cellular phone rang and Portia looked at the caller ID: **Gregory Lawson 555-2174.** *His wife must have a headache.* It was time for Portia to perform her wifely duties without the benefits of being a wife. Portia didn't live in a five-bedroom house surrounded by a white picket fence like Gregory's wife did. Portia didn't have access to Gregory's bank account like his wife did. But he did offer Portia half of her rent and utilities as long as she was available for sex whenever he demanded. The first of May was approaching and rent was due. Portia had no choice but to return Gregory's call and oblige him.

At that moment she realized that she couldn't call on Celeste or Ginger to discuss how her life had turned out that way. Portia couldn't lean on them to talk her out of doing what she knew was the wrong thing to do. Her friends had become her enemies. But Portia knew there was one person who would never turn His back on her.

She placed her face in her hands and cried out to Him. "My Lord, please help me."

Celeste walked three blocks from Ginger's house and sat on a bench to wait for the next bus. Tears ran down her face as she thought about what had just happened back at Ginger's house. She and Portia had gone there to see about Ginger because Celeste had awakened with Ginger's well-being heavy on her heart. When Diane told Celeste that Ronald had called off for Ginger that morning, Celeste knew her friend was in trouble and she had to get to her.

Celeste went over the events in her mind to try to figure out just how the situation had gone so wrong. At what point did a caring visit turn into an all-out brawl between her and her two best friends? The words that were said had cut each other deeply. Celeste knew that fight was worse than any other they'd had. Scabs had been snatched off of sores and old wounds had resurfaced. Too much damage was done and Celeste knew, deep down inside, that there was no turning back.

Suddenly she felt her menstrual cycle begin to flow. It was proof that no baby had been conceived over the weekend, and confirmation of what Celeste already knew but had yet to tell her husband. She was living a lie and her marriage would soon suffer if she didn't confess to Anthony what had happened years ago in a dark, dingy, cold basement.

Celeste couldn't cry on Ginger's or Portia's shoulders anymore. They weren't there to console Celeste and encourage her to keep her head up and to keep the faith that her womb would someday bring forth a child. Celeste placed her face in her hands and cried. She called on her Heavenly Father. "My Lord, please help me."

Chapter 4

The Secret She Kept

It had been three weeks since Portia and Celeste stood in the middle of Ginger's living room and the three of them cursed each other. In church they didn't acknowledge one another whatsoever. For the past twenty-one nights, unbeknownst to them, Ginger, Portia, and Celeste cried themselves to sleep, missing one another.

In the past, comforting and holding Celeste as she sniffled off to dreamland after an argument with her best friends was nothing new to Anthony. When he married Celeste six years ago, he also married the relationship she shared with Portia and Ginger. It had been many a night since he vowed to love, honor, and cherish Celeste that Anthony listened to her side of an argument after a heated fellowship with her best friends.

Celeste once came home angry and upset after spending a day at Oakbrook Mall with Ginger and Portia. They had been shopping in Lord & Taylor when Celeste laid eyes on a white silk dress she just had to have. The dress was so beautiful; Ginger decided that she'd get it in black while Portia opted for the same dress in red. The idea of the three of them buying the same dress didn't sit well with Celeste. Considering the fact that she had seen the dress first, Celeste thought that she should be the only one to get it. She explained to Ginger and Portia that anyone with morals wouldn't buy the same outfit as their friend.

"Well, I guess we don't have any morals," Portia said as she and Ginger carried their dresses to the cash register.

That following Sunday, each wanting to be the first to wear the dress, the three of them came to church dressed alike. Celeste couldn't believe they had the gall to wear the dress to a place the three of them frequented weekly. But what really pushed her over the edge was when a church member approached her and said, "You, Portia, and Ginger look cute today. Portia said your dresses cost one hundred twenty dollars. I think I'll go to Lord & Taylor after service today. Ginger said it comes in navy, too." Celeste didn't talk to her best friends for three days. How dare they tell what the dress cost and where it came from?

It was Anthony who got an earful about how inconsiderate Ginger and Portia had been. But no matter how bad the disagreements were, within seventy-two hours, one of them would make the telephone call that brought the trio back together again.

However, it had been almost a month since Celeste had spoken to her friends and Anthony was fit to be tied at her attitude. For almost a month, Celeste served him overcooked meals and undercooked meals. At least four nights of the week Celeste opted for takeout.

She told Anthony if she never set eyes on her best friends again, it would be too soon. Yet each time the telephone rang and **Portia Dunn** or **Ginger Brown** didn't show on the caller identification, Celeste would pout. Anthony, a motorman for the Chicago Transit Authority, was constantly paged throughout the day with urgent messages from Celeste. In between runs, Anthony would return her calls just to hear her say, "I can't believe neither one of them has called yet," or "Do you think I was wrong, Tony?"

Anthony never took sides when it came to resolving an issue between his wife and her friends. Whenever Celeste asked for his opinion on a matter, Anthony would say, "Celeste, that's between you and your girls," and he would leave it at that. Anthony learned his lesson years ago when he told Celeste that she was wrong in a situation with Portia and Ginger and should be the one to apologize. That bit of advice had cost him two nights of celibacy. Celeste told Anthony that he should always side with his wife no matter what the case may be.

Anthony drove Celeste to work and kissed her cheek before she exited the car. "Have a great day, baby," he encouraged her.

Celeste smiled slightly at him then sighed. "I'll try. Is there anything in particular you want to stop and get for dinner tonight?"

Anthony exhaled loudly. "Takeout again, Celeste? We've been eating fast food every other night for the past month."

Celeste sighed louder. "I just haven't been in the mood to cook."

"Celeste, you haven't been in the mood to cook, clean, do laundry, talk, or make love. Whatever this issue is that you have with your girls, I suggest you do what you gotta do to squash it. For weeks I've watched you slam doors and throw things. Then you cursed at me when you got your period. I let you have your moment because your doctor said that stress from trying to conceive would be overwhelming. But I'm not Ginger or Portia. I'm your husband and I ain't done a darn thing to you.

"Normally the three of you would have made up by now but this is ridiculous. You can be mad, Celeste, but be mad at the right people. Eating fast food four times a week stops today. The slamming of doors stops today. Turning your back to me when we go to bed at night stops today. Having cramps doesn't justify you talking to me anyway you want. And I want you to stop paging me throughout the day whining about Ginger and Portia."

Celeste looked at her husband with tears in her eyes but Anthony didn't regret what he'd just said to her. Celeste needed to understand that she couldn't continue to take out her frustrations on him or their marriage. Her tears didn't move him that morning.

"I've had enough of this crap," Anthony stated. "When I pick you up after work we're gonna go home and cook dinner together. Then we'll finish the evening off with a little one-on-one in the bedroom."

Celeste's tears dripped onto her cheeks. She knew Anthony was right. He'd always been her biggest supporter and he didn't deserve to be treated that way. "Okay."

With his first finger Anthony wiped Celeste's tears then leaned over and softly kissed her lips. "You know I love you, right?"

Celeste smiled. "I do."

They arrived home at six-fifteen in the evening and Celeste immediately walked to the caller identification box that sat on an end table in the living room. She pressed the scan button. Ginger or Portia hadn't called her cellular phone all day but Celeste was hopeful that one of them would have called her home and left a message. There had been two calls but neither call was from Portia or Ginger.

Anthony saw the disappointed expression on Celeste's face. "They didn't call, huh?"

Celeste didn't answer him.

Anthony stepped to her. "Baby, why are you doing this to yourself? Just call your girls. You know you want to."

"After what they said to me, Tony? I don't think so."

"Celeste, you never told me what Ginger and Portia said that's got you so upset with them. What did they say?"

Celeste froze. She and Anthony had been married for six years and she had yet to share with him what happened during her sophomore year in high school. Celeste couldn't tell him that Ginger's recollection of the abortion she had in high school was the reason the three of them weren't speaking.

Early in her marriage, in a private session with her gynecologist, Dr. Bindu, Celeste revealed her secret. After examining Celeste, Dr. Bindu explained to her that the wire coat hanger that was used many years ago had caused irreparable damage. Her right fallopian tube had been punctured and her entire uterine wall was contaminated. Too much scar tissue had developed. In his opinion Dr. Bindu advised Celeste that her chances of conceiving were next to impossible.

Celeste had decided that it was in her best interest if she didn't share the news with Anthony. Instead, for years, she had kept the secret and prayed for a miracle. She would continue to pray that God would bless her womb and Anthony would never have to know about the abortion.

Celeste stood in the middle of her living room wondering how she could answer Anthony's question without revealing the truth. "All of the other times when Ginger, Portia, and I fell out, you didn't wanna know any of the details. So, why are you asking questions now?"

"Because your arguments usually don't last longer than two days," Anthony responded. "In the past the three of you would have made up by now. But you've been walking around here miserable and with your lips poked out for almost a whole month. And every new day that passes when Ginger or Portia don't call, you get even more depressed. That tells me that what happened between y'all had to be something heavy. So, what was it?"

Celeste looked at the mail she'd gotten from the mailbox as she walked toward their bedroom. "It's sista stuff, Tony. You wouldn't understand. By the way, your mother called," she said over her shoulder.

An hour and a half later, Anthony and Celeste were at the kitchen table finishing a meal consisting of broiled tilapia, steamed asparagus, and baked potatoes.

Anthony savored his meal. "Celeste, baby, you put your foot in these potatoes." He inhaled his food and licked his fingers as though he'd gone a whole year without a decent home-cooked meal rather than a month.

Celeste smiled. "I'm glad you are enjoying them. Wait 'til you taste the dessert. I put both my feet in it."

Anthony became excited. "What is it?"

She smiled. "Your favorite."

He returned Celeste's smile. "Strawberry shortcake?"

Celeste nodded her head. Anthony leaned over and kissed Celeste's lips. He then stood from the table and hurried over to the refrigerator. Anthony retrieved the strawberry shortcake from the refrigerator and brought it back to the table. He grabbed two saucers and a knife from the dish rack and sat down. He sliced generous portions for Celeste and himself.

Celeste laughed at the way Anthony hummed as he savored his dessert. "You remind me of a little boy sitting in a high chair swinging his feet while he eats a snack."

Anthony chuckled. "What can I say? It's been awhile."

After dessert Celeste took the dinner dishes to the sink to wash them. She dried the dishes, set them in the dish rack, and turned off the kitchen light. She went into the living room and sat on the sofa. She pressed the scan button on the caller identification again to look for Dr.

Bindu's office number. He was the second person who had called.

When Celeste had found his number she picked up the telephone and dialed. Anthony told Celeste that he was going downstairs to the basement to start a load of laundry.

With Anthony out of earshot, Celeste felt it was safe to make the call. It was late in the evening and Celeste was prepared to just leave a message on the answering service. She was surprised when her call was answered.

"Dr. Bindu's office, may I help you?" the chipper receptionist answered.

"Is this Sharla?" Celeste asked.

"Yes, it is."

"Hi, Sharla. It's Celeste Harper."

"Oh, hi Celeste. How's it going?"

Celeste loved calling Dr. Bindu's office. Sharla was always in a good mood. "Everything is good, Sharla. Thanks for asking."

"Did you get your period this month?" At her first appointment with Dr. Bindu, while Celeste sat and waited for her name to be called, she and Sharla had hit it off. Without going into great detail Celeste confessed to Sharla that she and her husband hadn't been successful in conceiving a baby. Sharla told Celeste that if anyone could help her become pregnant, Dr. Bindu could. She had witnessed many women get treated by Dr. Bindu and overcome their fertility issues. Sharla insisted that Celeste was in good hands.

"Yeah, unfortunately I did. But I'm returning Dr. Bindu's call. Is he in?"

"He's just finishing with a patient. Hold on a moment."

Celeste shifted her position on the sofa and placed her legs beneath her in the shape of a pretzel. She looked over her shoulder to make sure Anthony wasn't in earshot of her telephone call.

A couple of minutes later Dr. Bindu was on the line. "Mrs. Harper, how are you?"

"I'm fine, Dr. Bindu," Celeste whispered. "I'm a bit puzzled why you called."

From the basement, Anthony came upstairs, went to the telephone on the kitchen wall, and picked up the receiver to call his mother.

"Well, I'm concerned about the results of your latest exam," Dr. Bindu explained. "There's more scar tissue than I thought. You said a wire coat hanger was used to abort the fetus years ago and it seems that the hanger may have caused more damage than I originally detected. I'm pretty sure this is the reason why your periods are so heavy. I've detected fibroid cysts and I'm afraid that you and I should discuss whether a partial hysterectomy is necessary."

Anthony's mouth fell open. He poked his head around the doorway to the kitchen and saw Celeste sitting on the living room sofa with her back to him. Anthony placed the telephone on its base.

Celeste heard the click and turned around. She saw Anthony walking her way. Suddenly all the blood drained from her face. She quickly disconnected the call with Dr. Bindu and looked up at him. The expression on Anthony's face told Celeste that he'd heard the entire conversation.

Anthony's eyes were the size of golf balls. "What the heck was he talking about?"

Celeste became nervous, but she wasn't going to confirm or confess anything until Anthony revealed that he knew her secret. "Um, that was Dr. Bindu."

"I know who it was, Celeste. What was he saying about a coat hanger and abortion?"

Celeste's heart beat so fast she felt it was about to explode from her chest. Her entire body shook with nervousness. She felt as though she had pneumonia. She was chilled to the bone yet she was burning up.

The secret she had hidden from her husband for years was now exposed. That was the moment that Celeste prayed she would never have to face. She had been willing to keep living the lie and take it to her grave if it would save her marriage.

"What was Dr. Bindu talking about?" Anthony yelled.

Celeste flinched at Anthony's outburst. She didn't say a word. She just sat and looked at him with pity in her eyes.

"When did you have an abortion, Celeste?"

She knew it was time for her to confess everything. Celeste silently prayed to God that Anthony wouldn't leave her when she revealed how deceptive she'd been. She looked deeply into her husband's eyes. She didn't know she was crying until a single tear had fallen from her lower eyelid and trickled down her face. "Baby, I'm so sorry. I never wanted you to find out this way." Truth be told, Celeste never wanted Anthony to find out at all. She patted the cushion next to her. "Come and sit next to me."

Anthony stood where he was. He glared down at Celeste. "Just tell me when you had an abortion with a wire hanger."

Celeste wiped the tears from her face. "It was my sophomore year in high school. I got pregnant and I was scared to tell my folks. My mother wouldn't have been able to bear it. And I couldn't even fathom the thought of how disappointed in me my father would have been."

Anthony stood looking down at his wife. "Is it the reason you can't have a baby?"

Celeste's mouth went dry. Since she'd met Anthony she prayed that her promiscuous years would never catch up with her and have to be revealed to him. What was she going to do? How could she explain to her loving husband why she kept such a deep, dark secret from him all these years?

Celeste stood from the sofa and grabbed Anthony's arms that were folded across his chest. "Dr. Bindu believes so."

Anthony released his arms and took a step backward. "So you've been lying to me all these years? Crying every month when you got your period, going from doctor to doctor and making me get myself checked out like I could've been the problem. And all along you knew we would never have a baby." Anthony looked at Celeste with disgust in his eyes. She was damaged goods.

Celeste stepped to Anthony. She tried to grab his hands but he wouldn't let her. She started to cry openly. "When we first got together, all you talked about was getting married and having a house full of kids. You told me that it was your dream to become a father. I didn't know then that the abortion I had five years prior would be a problem for us. That's why I never mentioned it. It wasn't until after we got married and started trying to conceive, and couldn't, that I got concerned. I made an appointment with Dr. Bindu and found out that the abortion killed my chances of getting pregnant."

"And you said nothing to me."

"Baby, I'm so sorry that I kept this from you but I didn't wanna disappoint you."

Anthony looked at her tearstained faced and shook his head from side to side. "All this time, Celeste. All this time you had us fasting and praying that God would do a miraculous thing when you knew all along why we couldn't get pregnant. And I don't buy the crap about you not feeling the need to tell me about the abortion. I could understand you hiding something like, 'Honey, when I was in high school I stole lipstick from the convenience store,' or 'Honey, when I was in high school I pulled the fire alarm just to get out of class early.' That's something you shouldn't feel the need to tell your husband. But 'Honey, in my sophomore year of high school I had an illegal abortion. I don't know if it did any damage but it's something you should know.' The abortion part of your history is something you're supposed to share with the man who asked you to become his wife."

Celeste was distraught. She wanted to reach out and hug Anthony but thought better of it. She wiped more tears from her eyes. "Honey, you're right. I should've told you but I was afraid."

Anthony's voice rose. "Afraid of what, telling me the truth?"

"I was afraid that if you knew my secret you'd leave me."

Anthony looked to the ceiling and exhaled loudly then looked at Celeste. "When God told me that you were my wife, He didn't say that you came with children. I'm not the type of man who would leave a woman I love just because she's barren. If you are barren, I would still love you 'til death do us part. But what about the vows we took, Celeste? What about being honest and trustworthy? What about that? Huh?"

Celeste saw three Anthonys through her tears. "I'm so sorry, Tony. Please forgive me."

"What else have you been lying about?" he asked. "What else have you been keeping from me? What else don't I know? How many secrets do you have?"

Celeste took a step toward Anthony. "There's nothing else, Tony. I swear."

He moved backward to keep Celeste from touching him. "You really expect for me to believe you?"

Sniff, sniff. "There's nothing else, Tony. I promise." Sniff, sniff.

Anthony shrugged his shoulders. "How can I trust you? Put yourself in my shoes, Celeste. How would it make you feel if I had failed to tell you I had a vasectomy before I met you? Yet, I marry you and let you believe that everything was in working order. And for six years we're trying to get pregnant but can't and I know I'm the reason. But I didn't tell you because I thought you wouldn't marry me. I'm just hoping and praying the procedure I had done would reverse itself. Wouldn't you feel six years of countless doctors visits were a waste of your time? Wouldn't you be hurt and disappointed that I wasn't open and honest with you from the beginning?"

Again Celeste reached out for him and Anthony stepped backward, this time raising his hands in the air. He yelled at her, "Don't touch me! You are a liar and a manipulator." He grabbed his car keys from the cocktail table and walked to the front door.

Celeste ran after him. "Where are you going, Tony? Please don't leave like this. Don't leave me, Tony, please." Celeste grabbed him by the elbow.

He pushed her into the wall and gritted his teeth. "I said don't touch me." Anthony walked out the front door and slammed it behind him. The force almost shattered every window in the living room.

Celeste fell to her knees crying after him. "Tony, Tony, Tony. Come back. Baby, please come back. I'm so sorry. Oh God. I'm so sorry."

Celeste sat with her back against the front door. She was all alone. Whenever she and Anthony argued, she would call Portia and Ginger and the three of them would gather around Portia's kitchen table and eat chocolate cake, chocolate candy bars, and chocolate ice cream. They would kick up their heels, unbutton their pants, and rotate the chocolate around the table as Celeste vented. Then the next morning like clockwork Portia and Ginger would call Celeste and yell at her for making them gain five pounds in one night.

But for the first time in Celeste's six-year marriage, she didn't have Anthony, Ginger, or Portia. And there wasn't any edible chocolate in her house, not even a single Hershey's Kiss. Celeste bowed her head and cried harder.

Chapter 5

Sleeping with the Enemy

Ginger arose at three o'clock a.m. on a Wednesday morning, choking and coughing uncontrollably. Ronald was asleep with his back to her. Ginger got out of bed and hurried into the kitchen for a glass of water. The lukewarm liquid was soothing to her throat. She set the glass in the sink and went back to bed. No sooner than her head made contact with the pillow Ginger started to cough again.

Ronald sat up, exhaled loudly, and frowned at her. "Take that noise out of here."

While trying to suppress her coughs, Ginger got up and left her bedroom and went into the guest bedroom and lay across the queen-sized bed. Within twenty minutes her coughs subsided and she was able to drift off to sleep.

At approximately 5:05 a.m., Ginger lazily turned from her side and lay on her back. She opened her eyes and was startled to see Ronald's silhouette standing over her. Though it was still dark outside, the light shining from the hallway helped Ginger to see that he was completely naked. She anxiously sat up but Ronald's fist came full force and sent her flying back onto the pillow. Ginger felt her chest cave in and she screamed out in pain.

Ronald placed his palm over her mouth. "Shut up and be still," he ordered.

Tears welled up in Ginger's eyes as she watched Ronald climb on top of her and spread her legs with his own. He removed his hand from her mouth and raised her gown to her waist. He was breathing heavy and Ginger's nostrils inhaled stale alcohol mixed with morning breath. It was nauseating. The smell made her sick to her stomach.

"Ron, please don't do this."

A slap across the left side of her face took Ginger's breath away. Immediately, Ronald kissed where his opened palm made contact. "Did that hurt, baby? Huh? Did I hurt you?"

Ginger closed her eyes and prayed that God would help her out of that situation. Ronald grabbed her chin and turned her face toward his own. Tears were streaming from Ginger's eyes down to her ears.

He licked her tears with his tongue. He ran it from the corner of her right eye to her ear. "Mmm, your tears taste good. You ought to cry more often."

At the smell of his breath Ginger's stomach began to rumble. Telling Ronald that his breath was foul would only guarantee another blow to her face but Ginger had to do something to get his mouth away from her nose. "Ron, you're heavy. Please get up."

"You wanna know what I found in the kitchen sink when I got up this morning, Ginger?"

Ginger knew she was in trouble. He was talking about the glass she drank water from two hours ago.

"Do you remember what I said the last time I told you about leaving dirty dishes in the sink overnight?"

"Ron, I was sick this morning. Didn't you hear me coughing? I just had a glass of water."

"You left a dirty glass in the sink overnight," he reminded her.

Ginger sobbed. "No, it was this morning."

He grabbed Ginger's chin and turned her face toward the window. "Look outside. Is the sun up?"

She moaned. "No."

"Is the sky light blue?"

She squeezed her eyes shut. *Lord, where are you?* There was no way out of a butt whipping that was surely coming her way. Ronald kissed her lips softly and asked the last question again. "Is the sky light blue, Ginger?"

She cried out again. "No."

"Well, if the sun is not up and if the sky is not light blue then it must be nighttime, right?"

The stench coming from Ronald's mouth caused Ginger's dinner, from the night before, to move around in her stomach. *Lord, please help me.*

Ronald kissed her lips softly again. "Answer me, baby. Is it nighttime or daytime?"

"It's nighttime."

"So, you left a dirty glass in the sink overnight?"

"Yes, I'm sorry."

"Do you know what the penalty is for leaving dirty dishes in the sink overnight?"

Ginger's dinner had made its way up to the bottom of her throat. She swallowed repeatedly trying to keep it down.

Ronald used his thighs to spread her legs wider.

More tears ran from Ginger's eyes to her ears. "Ron, please. I'm sorry."

He rose up and plunged himself into her. Ginger hollered out when he tore into her flesh.

Again, Ronald slapped the right side of her face. "Shut up!"

He withdrew himself and plunged into Ginger again and again. She tried her best to keep quiet but couldn't do it. Each time he entered her, she yelled.

Ronald placed his hand over mouth and spoke directly into her nostrils. "I like this early morning lovin'."

Within one minute Ginger felt Ronald's body stiffen; then he relaxed and fell down on top of her. "Was it as good for you as it was for me, baby?"

He didn't wait for a response. Ronald got up and left the bedroom. On his way out, he spoke to her. "I want that glass washed before you go to work."

Ginger leaned over the side of the bed and vomited on the hardwood floor.

The water in the shower was scalding hot. Ginger stood under the sprinkler trying to get Ronald's scent off of her. She lathered her soap sponge and scrubbed her face, arms, and legs as hard as she could. When she rotated her private area with the soapy sponge, she felt intense burning. Ginger removed the sponge and saw blood then noticed streams of blood going down the drain. She rinsed her left hand free of soap and felt between her inner thighs. The slightest touch caused a shriek to escape Ginger's throat. She removed her hand and saw it completely covered in red. More and more blood ran down the shower drain. Ginger stared at it in disbelief. She began to experience what felt like lightning bolts piercing her abdomen. The pain was so severe that it sent Ginger to her knees. "Jesus, help me," was all she could say.

Suddenly clots of blood flowed down her legs to her ankles on their way to the drain. "Not again, Jesus," she moaned. "Please don't take another baby from me."

Ginger stayed on her knees in the running shower crying until her uterus emptied itself and the pains subsided. When she felt strong enough, Ginger stood and washed her body.

After the shower Ginger got a maxi pad from beneath the vanity in her bathroom, pressed the adhesive to the center of her panties and pulled them up to her waist. She dressed in a quilted nightgown covering her from head to toe then went into the kitchen to wash the glass.

Ginger's private area was so swollen and sore she had to walk back to her bedroom gap-legged. She started to apply cocoa butter lotion to her legs when her eyes were drawn to a photograph of her and Ronald smiling into each other's eyes in the early weeks of their relationship.

Ronald came into the bedroom carrying his jacket and keys. He walked to Ginger and kissed her cheek. "I got to make a run. Hit me on my cell if you need me."

Ginger closed her eyes and exhaled. Just the thought of Ronald touching any part of her body was repulsive to her. In her twenty-seven years on earth Ginger has been pregnant twice and not one child was evident to show for it.

She sat on the side of the bed and thought about calling her doctor. After her first miscarriage at the mercy of Ronald's hands, Ginger had begged her doctor to tie her tubes. Her doctor explained to her that a procedure that extreme couldn't be done on a woman who didn't have any children or on a married woman without her husband's consent.

It took Ginger eight years to shed the weight birth control pills put on her petite frame since she started swallowing them in her early twenties. She'd been birth control pill free for two years and she refused to travel down that road again. Condoms were out of the question according to Ronald. He told Ginger that taking the time to put on a condom puts a damper on lovemaking.

"Birth control is the woman's responsibility," Ronald said to Ginger. "Since men can't get pregnant, why should we be held accountable for what could happen?"

That question to Ginger was asked after her first miscarriage. From then on, Ginger relied on an ovulation predictor to tell her when she and Ronald could have sex. Considering the fact that Ginger had gotten pregnant again after she started using the ovulation predictor told her it wasn't predictable at all.

Ginger picked up the photograph of her and Ronald from the nightstand, and carefully sat down on the bed wincing at the pain in between her legs. She reminisced about the time she told Celeste and Portia that she'd met someone with potential. It was back in the days when if one of them had a date, all three of them had a date.

Four years ago on a Friday night in February, Ginger rang Portia's telephone with excitement in her voice. "Girl, I've got something to tell you."

"I already know. You're pregnant," Portia stated.

Ginger's heart leapt in her chest. She was twenty-three years old and single but she wasn't celibate. Every month Ginger looked forward to getting her period. To every other woman, what seemed like the worst days of her life were days of joy for Ginger.

It was normal for her to count the days of the week on a calendar to make sure her menstrual cycle was right on time. If Ginger's period didn't flow on the first day it was supposed to, she would sit on the toilet and push like she was constipated or trying to deliver a baby. There were times when Ginger had pushed so hard, she'd made herself dizzy. One episode of pushing resulted in a case of flaming hemorrhoids. When the pushing didn't work, Ginger would get on her knees and cry out loud, "I ain't gonna do it no more, Lord. I promise, I promise, I promise. Please bring my period, Jesus. No more sex, Lord. I'm begging you, Jesus. Please have mercy on me."

And when God showed a little mercy on Ginger, she would double her tithes the following Sunday morning. Ginger would walk to the front of the church and drop her envelope in the basket while displaying the biggest grin on her face. And if cramps were making their presence known, Ginger would pat her lower abdomen, smile, look up toward heaven and say, "Thank you, Lord."

There was a time when Ginger's period was three days late. But on the fourth day her prayers were answered. Ginger felt so good; she bought her favorite foods and invited Portia and Celeste over for a Period Party.

Celeste gave her a gift-wrapped box of tampons. Ginger opened a card that read:

Congratulations on getting your period. I hope you get many more.

Portia's gift was a box of Midol. Ginger gave the box back to Portia. "You can keep those. I love my cramps. They let me know that my friend Flo ain't too far behind."

Portia looked at Ginger. "You know you're stupid, right? If you didn't know, now you know."

That night was the first of many Period Parties yet to come.

"Don't play like that, Portia. Ain't nobody pregnant," Ginger said. Portia was taking the telephone conversation a different way. Ginger was calling to share the news that she had met a guy.

"Somebody is because I dreamed of fish last night."

"Well, it ain't me. So it must be either you or Celeste."

"It's gotta be Celeste then because it sure isn't me. You know she and Tony have been trying to get pregnant since forever."

"Hold on a minute, Portia. I'm gonna get her on the three-way." Ginger clicked over and dialed Celeste's number then reconnected Portia to the line.

The telephone rang four times; then Portia and Ginger heard Celeste say, "Harper residence."

Portia was the first to speak. "Are you pregnant?"

Celeste frowned at no one in particular. "What?"

Ginger joined their conversation. "She asked if you were pregnant."

"And before you answer you should know that I dreamed of fish last night," Portia said.

"Nope, I'm not pregnant. As a matter of fact, I'm bleeding right this moment."

Ginger frowned. "That's TMIH, Celeste."

"And what does TMIH mean?"

Ginger and Portia chanted in unison, "Too much information, honey."

"Well, if y'all don't wanna know the details, don't ask the question. And why are you two on my line tonight anyway?"

Ginger spoke. "I'm calling to let my soul sisters know that I met this guy today and I think I'm gonna go out with him."

"What does he look like?" Celeste asked.

"I don't know. I haven't seen him yet."

Portia didn't get that. "What do you mean you don't know? You said you met him today."

"I did meet him today," Ginger confirmed.

"That doesn't make any sense, Ginger. I wanna know how you can meet a guy and not know what he looks like."

"Okay, Celeste, I'll say where I met him but I don't want y'all to trip. Especially you, Portia."

Since Ginger made that comment to her, Portia knew Ginger was getting into something that she shouldn't. "Ginger, I will reach through this telephone line and choke you if you don't tell us where you met this guy. And I can tell by the way you're stalling that something ain't right with him."

"That's not true, Portia. You see how you're already jumping to conclusions?"

"If you don't want me jumping to conclusions, come on out with it."

"I will in my own time, stop rushing me."

Portia was fed up. "Ginger, stop beating around the bush and tell us when he's getting out of jail."

Celeste and Portia laughed but Ginger didn't think it was funny at all. "Okay, just for that, I ain't telling y'all nothing."

Portia could hear in Ginger's voice that she was hurt. "I'm sorry, honey. I didn't mean it. Go ahead and tell us where you met him."

Ginger took a deep breath and held it for three seconds, exhaled, and spoke extremely fast. "I met him online in the chat room this afternoon. His name is Ronald Bailey and he lives in New Orleans. He mentioned that he grew up in the Ninth Ward."

Celeste yelled into the telephone. "The Ninth Ward? Do you know what the Ninth Ward is, Ginger?"

"I guess it's a specific neighborhood."

"Okay. Why don't you do the honors, Portia? Because if I tell her, she'll think I'm blocking."

Portia cleared her throat. "Ginger, honey, baby, sugar bear, cutie pie, you are so precious. Gangbangers and thugs make up the Ninth Ward in New Orleans."

The man Ginger had met online gave her the impression that he was an upstanding citizen. "What are y'all talking about and how do you know?"

"We just do," Celeste answered.

"Well, be that as it may, Ronald is flying here on Friday afternoon and we're meeting at the Shark Bar at eight o'clock. Can you two be at your posts?"

"Of course. We would never break our pact, Ginger," Celeste said.

"Celeste is right," Portia added. "This is your first date with Mr. New Orleans. And whenever one of us has a first date with someone, we all go."

"Portia and I will try to get a table close by. Relax, everything will be cool."

That conversation among the three best friends was four years ago. And as Ginger stared into Ronald's eyes in the photograph, she wished she had listened to Celeste and Portia when they warned her about men from the Ninth Ward because Ronald Bailey was a thug in every sense of the word. Ginger didn't know anything about him being a gangbanger but she could surely testify about him being a Ginger banger because he banged her head against the wall every chance he got. Ginger should have known Ronald was a few ribs short of a full slab when, only after ten minutes of meeting her, he said, "Girl, you're so fine I would put hot sauce on my ears and fight Mike Tyson for you."

Ginger set the photograph on the nightstand and dressed for work. She let out a loud sigh as she thought about what the forthcoming hours would bring. It was parent-teacher conference day and after the morning she had, Ginger wasn't looking forward to "You must be mistaken, my child would never behave in that way," or "I raised my son better than that, he isn't capable of saying that," or "My daughter's grades didn't start to slip until she got to your class."

Ginger drove into the school parking lot and put the gear in park. At eight-fifty a.m. parents were lined up outside of the door waiting for the school to open. Ginger lowered her head and closed her eyes. "Father, in the name of Jesus, I don't wanna have to cuss anyone out today. So, I'm asking you to write on my tongue as I deal with these ghetto parents."

The first mother to approach Ginger introduced herself as twenty-year-old Tequila Tangeray-Cristal Daniels. Ginger couldn't help but to wonder if Tequila's father's first name was Jack. Somehow it went with the flow. Ginger taught third grade, which meant the young mother was only twelve when she conceived.

Miss Daniels's complaint threw Ginger for a loop. She wasn't there to find out why her son was failing social studies, mathematics, and English, though she should have been. She had a more pressing issue with her son's teacher. "My son says you make all of the kids pray, one by one, before class starts and I don't think that's fair."

It may or may not have been fair but Ginger knew she was breaking the law by bringing religion into her classroom but she didn't care. It was prayer that had stopped Ginger from strangling the eight-year-olds when they got in her face and challenged her.

Oh Lord, here we go. "And why is that, Courvoisier?"

Ginger watched as this barely legal female placed her right hand on an underdeveloped, almost nonexistent hip, and rotate her neck. "First of all, it's Tequila. T-e-q-u-i-l-a. Tequila. And my parents didn't force me to pray and go to church."

I can tell, Ginger thought.

"They let me make up my own mind. So, I don't force my son to go to church either. It's up to him whether he wants to pray or not."

Of course Ginger could've easily "gone there" with the unwed mother but she remembered the talk she had with God. Having an eight-year-old child at the age of twenty was the result of being brought up in a churchless and prayer-free home.

Ginger felt pity for Tequila. She was only a baby when she had a baby. Ginger would be willing to bet her paycheck that Tequila's mother was no more than fifteen years her senior. *Probably a generational curse.*

"Look, Miss Daniels. This school sits in the heart of the west side of Chicago. There are dope dealers on every corner. Don't you read the *Sun-Times* or watch the news? Every week a young girl in this neighborhood is raped or assaulted. A young black boy is murdered every month and that's the norm. It's rare that a teenager in this neighborhood graduates high school without some type of criminal record under his or her belt. Our young black men are becoming extinct. The only things we have to hold on to are our prayers. I don't have control over what goes on in your household and I can't dictate how to raise your son but from nine to three-thirty, Monday through Friday, these are my kids. And as for me and my classroom, we will pray. Now, if you have a problem with that, I suggest you talk with the principal. But you should know that she's saved too."

The way Ginger's day at school started was pretty much how it ended. She had to defend the power of prayer nine times. One father had the nerve to flirt with Ginger in the presence of his wife. Ginger never liked parent-teacher conferences. She'd rather have a normal day of yelling at unruly, hardheaded kids than counseling their ignorant parents.

That evening she pulled into the garage and parked next to Ronald's car. He was lying on the sofa watching television. Ginger said her hellos and went straight to her bedroom. She changed into her quilted nightgown covering her from head to toe, then paid a visit to the bathroom and she made sure to raise the toilet seat.

In the kitchen, Ginger searched the refrigerator for something to prepare for dinner. *I bet that fool has been lying on the couch all day. The least he could do is have dinner ready when I get home but I guess that's too much work, right?*

She saw a pound of ground beef and thought she better use it before it spoiled. It had been sitting in the refrigerator for two days. Spaghetti would be quick and easy. Ginger set a pot of water on top of the stove and heated a cast iron skillet. She put the ground beef in the skillet. From the spice cabinet, Ginger withdrew bottles of seasoned salt, oregano, lemon pepper seasoning, ground pepper, garlic powder, and olive oil, then set them all on the counter next to the skillet.

She opened the utensil drawer and was astonished. Everything was missing. Gone were the spatulas, can opener, and measuring spoons. Only one fork, one spoon, one butter knife, and a wooden rolling pin remained in the drawer. Ginger opened the cabinet over the stove and saw one plate, one cereal bowl, and one glass.

What the heck?

The ground beef was beginning to brown and, not having anything to stir it with, Ginger removed the skillet from the heat and placed it on another burner. She went and stood at the archway to the living room. She dared not enter it. "Where are all of the dishes?"

Ronald kept his eyes on the television as he answered her. "I threw them away."

Ginger knew there was no way she could've heard him right. "What?"

"Since you insist on leaving dirty dishes in the sink overnight, this is what it comes down to."

Is he crazy? "My grandmother left me those dishes, Ronald. They were antiques and can't be replaced."

He met Ginger's eyes. "Is that supposed to mean something to me?"

Ginger couldn't believe him. She saw two empty forty-ounce bottles of beer on the cocktail table. "Why bother saving one plate, one glass, a knife, fork and spoon?"

"Those are for me," Ronald said. "I want them cleaned at all times and you better not use them."

Ginger's blood began to boil. "So, the heck with me, huh?"

Ronald looked at Ginger. "I guess so."

"What am I supposed to eat with?" she asked.

"There are paper plates, cups, and forks in the pantry."

"Ron, you can't be serious."

He looked at her again. "Ginger, I'm through with it."

When Ronald said that he was done with a conversation, he meant it. If Ginger said anything else to him on the matter, it would be an invitation for a technical knockout.

With tears in her eyes, Ginger went into the bathroom and locked the door. She ran the water in the sink so Ronald wouldn't hear what she was doing. She sat on the ledge of the tub and cried. It was time to get Ronald out of her house and out of her life.

But how? Portia and Celeste would know what to do but where were they? "I need my girls. Where y'all at?"

Chapter 6

Is Your Husband Married?

On Friday morning, as Portia drove south on Pulaski Avenue toward the car dealership where she worked, her cellular phone rang. She recognized Richard's work number. Portia wasn't especially happy to speak with him. Because of Richard's lack of funds, Portia hadn't been able to keep up with her hair and nail appointments. She answered the phone with an attitude. "Richard, if you don't have any money for me, I don't wanna talk to you."

"And a good morning to you too. I see you're in a great mood."

Portia wasn't in the mood for small talk. "Whatever. I need my hair and nails done, Richard. You and I had an agreement that you would keep an allowance coming my way. And considering how much time you spend in my bed, you should add the cost of a full-body massage to the amount of money you give me."

Richard sighed. "Look, Portia, I think Tamara is starting to suspect something. We have joint checking and savings accounts and she's asking questions about large sums of money being withdrawn. Twice I've been able to convince her that I lent it to my brother but I don't know how many more times she'll buy that."

Portia couldn't care less what Richard was talking about. His wife asking questions was not her concern. "So, what are you saying, Richard?"

He exhaled into the telephone. "I'm saying as of last week what was usually my job of balancing the books is now my wife's. There's no way I can keep giving you money without her finding out about it. And the five hundred bucks I was gonna give you, I gave to her."

Portia almost slammed into the car ahead of her. *What? No money?* Without knowing it Richard had slapped Portia in the face. She glanced at her cuticles. The acrylic on Portia's nails was no longer near them. She was in desperate need of a fill-in. "What the heck you mean you gave it to her? What did you give her my money for?"

"This is Tamara's birthday weekend. She and her sisters are leaving tonight to spend the weekend at a spa in Lake Geneva. So I—"

Portia cut him off. "So, you decided to take my diva money and give it to your wife so she can lay up all weekend."

"Well, she is my wife, Portia. What was I supposed to do? I told you she was getting suspicious about money missing from our accounts."

"Then come up with another freakin' way to get me my money!" she yelled. "Why can't you cash your check and give me my cut before you deposit the rest?"

Richard shook his head from side to side. "That won't work."

Portia shrugged her shoulders. "Why not?"

"My paychecks are automatically deposited into our joint checking account."

"Richard, you need to figure something out then. Like I said, you and I had an agreement. As long as I'm squatting, twirling around, and dropping it like it's hot, you are to keep me looking good. I mean unless something has changed. Has your wife all of a sudden got a li'l freak in her? Ain't that the reason you came to me in the first place?"

"Look, Portia. Now that Tamara has taken over the books, there's no way I can give you money like I use to but I got a hundred for you. I'll bring it by tonight after Tamara and her sisters leave."

Portia couldn't believe her ears. "Zz . . . wha . . . di . . ." she stuttered. She couldn't get the correct words out of her mouth fast enough. She calmed herself down. "A hundred dollars? One hundred dollars, Richard? What the heck am I supposed to do with a hundred dollars? That will barely cover my fingernails and toenails. What about my hair?"

"I'm sorry, baby, but that's the best I can do. I don't wanna do anything to upset Tamara; she comes first."

"Yeah, until she claims another headache and doesn't wanna be submissive. Then as usual you'll be rubbing in between my thighs at two in the morning."

Richard was getting frustrated. "Why are you trippin', Portia? You knew I was married when we met. From the very beginning you knew what you were getting into. My wife's needs come first and they always will. And I don't appreciate you questioning me on what I do for her because it ain't none of your business. One hundred dollars is the best I can do right now. Do you want the money or not?"

Oh. Okay. I see how this is gonna go down. It was obvious that Richard didn't know who he was messing with. Portia could be a professional home wrecker when she wanted to. And right then she felt the urge to drive a bulldozer straight through Richard's front door. "Yeah, I want it. But instead of you bringing it to me, I'll come by your house and get it."

"Uh-uh. You know you can't do that."

"Why not? Didn't you say Tamara was leaving town tonight? Just call me when she leaves."

"Why can't I bring the money to you like I've been doing?" he asked.

"Because my grandmother is visiting," she lied effort-lessly.

"Okay, baby. Listen, I'm sorry things had to turn out this way. I really wish I could do more for you but I just can't risk Tamara finding out about us. I need to chill on giving you money."

"It's okay, honey. I understand. Like you said, wifey comes first." Portia disconnected the line and spoke to herself. "You can't pay my rent, huh, Richard? Oh, you're gonna pay all right. You're gonna pay dearly." Portia was on an emotional high. Taking her money away was like taking away the air she breathed. Portia would see to it that Richard realized that he had messed with the wrong woman.

They didn't leave Richard's house all weekend. Like she had done many times before, Portia sacrificed another Sunday morning worship service to lie in a married man's bed.

After the twelfth sexual encounter in three days, she announced to Richard she was leaving.

"Can you take a shower with me before you go?" Richard asked while snuggling her neck.

Portia couldn't deny him that. "Of course, honey. Why don't you go ahead and get the water nice and warm for me. I'll join you in a minute."

As soon as she heard the water running in the shower, Portia set her plan in motion. She removed the diamond stud from her left ear and placed it in between the mattress and box spring at the edge of the bed. She went into the kitchen and withdrew a used condom, one of many, from the bottom of the garbage can. *He didn't even flush the evidence down the toilet.* "Men are so stupid." She brought the condom back to the bedroom and placed it beneath the bed close to the edge. Portia withdrew her date planner and an ink pen from her purse. She tore out the page of the present date and wrote Richard's wife a message. Portia placed the note next to the condom.

Richard stood six foot two so Portia figured he'd never see the condom and note beneath the bed, but it wouldn't take his wife long to spot it. With her plan in motion Portia showered with Richard for what she knew would be the last time ever.

On Monday afternoon Tamara arrived home from Lake Geneva. She took her luggage into the bedroom and set it by the dresser. As usual Richard didn't bother to make the bed, which was one of Tamara's pet peeves. Instead of making the bed, she decided to strip it and put clean sheets on the bed.

As she was tucking the corner of the fitted sheet on her side of the bed, Tamara saw something sparkle. She pulled the edge of the mattress up and saw the diamond stud. When she picked it up to examine it, it slipped from her fingers and fell to the floor. Tamara stooped to retrieve it and saw something else that caused her already-weak heart to skip a beat. She picked up the earring and the condom and studied them. It was not her earring and she and Richard didn't use condoms. Before the thought of her husband being unfaithful could manifest in her brain, Tamara picked up the note and read the words:

Is your husband married?

Tamara felt as though she were in the Twilight Zone. Suddenly her heart started to race and she gasped for air. Tamara fell forward on her knees. She released the condom, earring, and note before collapsing onto the floor.

***

An hour later Richard arrived home excited to see his wife. Knowing Tamara would arrive home from Lake Geneva early that afternoon, Richard had cut his workday short.

"Tam, baby, I'm home," he announced when he entered the foyer.

She didn't answer and Richard went to search for her in the kitchen. When he didn't find Tamara there he went toward their bedroom. "Tam. Where you at?"

Richard saw Tamara lying on her stomach next to the bed. He rushed to her. "Baby. Baby, you okay?"

Next to Tamara's head Richard saw the note, condom, and earring. He couldn't comprehend why the earring and condom were there but when he read the words on the note, he put two and two together. *What the heck?* Richard broke out into a sweat.

Tamara stirred and began to moan. Richard turned her over and laid her on her back. "Tam, baby, can you hear me?"

"Who is she?" Tamara's words were just above a whisper.

Richard knew that wasn't the time to talk about his mistress that had set him up. He needed to call an ambulance.

Richard sat at Tamara's side at Rush-Presbyterian-St. Luke's Medical Center. He looked at the IV dripping into her arm and the three patches pasted on the center of her chest.

Her cardiologist stood by her bed. "It was a mild heart attack, extremely mild. I told you four months ago to avoid anything strenuous or anything that would get your heart rate up. You're lucky, Tamara. This could have been a full-blown heart attack. You've got to learn to take it easy."

Tamara didn't respond to the doctor. She looked at Richard.

"And your blood pressure is way too high," the doctor stated. "But I can prescribe something to help with that." The doctor wrote something on his chart. "I'll send the nurse in with your medication and I'll be back to check your vitals later."

"How long?" Tamara asked Richard when they were alone.

Richard saw tears running from the corners of her eyes down to her ears. His own heart ached. He was the reason Tamara was in the hospital. "A little over a year."

Tamara turned her face toward the window. He reached for her hand and held it tight. "Tam, baby, I am so sorry."

Tamara kept her hand in Richards hand and continued looking out of the window. "Why wasn't I enough for you?"

"You are enough. She means nothing to me, I don't love her."

"Of all the places, Richard, why my bed? My sheets? My house? Did you do with her all the things you do with me?"

"Tam, please don't do this. I don't wanna talk about that."

"I know how you perform, Richard. I know what you like to do. It makes me sick to my stomach to know that you shared yourself with another woman. What is it about her, Richard? You're always telling me how beautiful I am. Is she prettier than me? Do you see her face when you make love to me?"

Richard caressed Tamara's hand. "No, baby. It's nothing like that."

Tamara looked at him and saw filth and disgust. "I've always known you to be a man with morals, Richard. What I don't understand is how you can fall for a woman who has no shame in sleeping with another woman's husband. Furthermore, in his wife's bed. But you know what, Richard? Whomever the whore is, I can't fault her. She doesn't owe me a darn thing. You are the one who made vows to me. It's you who is in covenant with me, not her."

Richard hung his head in shame. "Tam, I made a mistake. I'm sorry."

Tamara's voice rose along with her blood pressure. "You keep saying that but what does it mean? What are you sorry about, Richard? For getting involved with that whore or for getting caught? You said you've been screwing this chick for a year and you ain't been sorry all this time, so why are you sorry now?"

"I'm sorry about everything, especially for hurting you. I never meant for this to happen."

"You never meant for me to find out, you mean."

"No, Tam. Stop putting words in my mouth. I never meant for any of this to happen. The whole affair."

"Who is she?" Tamara asked.

"Just somebody I met awhile ago."

"Who is she?" Tamara asked him again. "Do I know her?"

"No, you don't know her." Richard didn't want to confess to Tamara that she had met Portia when they bought their car a year ago.

It was Portia who greeted Richard and Tamara when they arrived at the car dealership. She saw the couple come in and directed them to a car salesman. Richard returned to the dealership and sought Portia out. He reminded her that he was there the day before and he couldn't get her off of his mind.

"You were here with your wife, right?" Portia had asked.

Richard had chuckled shamefully. "Yeah, well, uh . . ."

"It's okay," Portia had said. "I don't have a problem with that."

Tamara continued to interrogate Richard. "Are her boobs bigger than mine? Is her butt bigger than mine?"

"Tam, please don't do this."

"I wanna know what made you turn to her. I do everything for you, Richard. I cook for you, keep the house clean, and I give you sex when you want it."

Tamara's last statement was a true statement. During her menstrual cycle was the only time when Tamara wasn't submissive. But she couldn't hold a candle to Portia when it came to the kind of sex Richard enjoyed having. Tamara was too conservative, too proper, and didn't like to explore the marriage bed and see all that it had to offer. There was never any foreplay with Tamara. For the right price Portia fulfilled Richard's every fantasy. If he told her to jump, she would climb on top of the dresser and dive on top of him. If he told Portia to squat, she would make her butt cheeks touch the floor. And foreplay was mandatory and exciting. Portia danced for Richard. She teased him with feathers and handcuffs. She rocked his world.

"I was at your every beck and call. How could you do . . ." Tamara choked on her tears.

Richard scooted closer to her bed. "Baby, I can't say I'm sorry enough. I'll do whatever it takes to make this up to you, I promise."

Tamara didn't want Richard in her presence. "Get out of here."

Richard looked at his wife pleadingly. "Baby, please."

Tamara gathered what little strength she had and yelled as loud as she could, "Get out!"

Richard stood and walked toward the door with his head hanging low. Before he left his wife's hospital room he turned around. "I love you, Tam."

Tamara connected her eyes with Richard's. He had just confessed to her that he'd been unfaithful for an entire year. Tamara wondered if Richard even knew what the word "love" meant. Looking at Richard standing and pleading for her forgiveness disgusted her. "You can take that lie to your whore. She just might believe you."

Richard left Tamara's hospital room hastily. He knew her parents and sisters were on their way to see about Tamara and he didn't want to be hassled by their questions. Besides he had a more pressing issue. Richard had somewhere else to be, someone else to see, and something else to do.

Richard had been sitting in his car and waiting for Portia to come home for over four hours. He had a lot to think about during that time. Like the countless times that he had come through for Portia when she needed her car note paid. The numerous times she called and cried that her rent was due, Richard was there with cash in his hand. And the biweekly hair appointments and monthly nail appointments that Richard afforded Portia should have been enough. But when Richard thought about it, the money he sacrificed behind his wife's back was never enough for Portia. She always wanted more. Of course Richard knew that withdrawing money from the bank account he shared with Tamara was risky, but the sexcapades that he and Portia shared were worth it.

As he sat in his car outside of Portia's apartment building and waited for her, Richard made a vow to himself that he would never cheat on Tamara again. He realized that not even Portia was worth losing his marriage for.

Portia didn't see him parked across the street from her apartment complex as she drove into her assigned parking spot. Richard sat patiently gripping the steering wheel tightly as he watched Portia exit her car and enter the building. Through the glass doors Richard saw her retrieve her mail from the mailbox in the vestibule. He watched Portia insert her key in the lock of the glass door and proceed to the elevator. Portia disappeared from Richard's view. He waited five more minutes before exiting his car.

In her apartment Portia was just about to make herself some dinner when her doorbell rang. She walked to the intercom next to the front door. "Who is it?" she asked after she pressed the talk button then released it to listen.

"It's me."

She frowned. "Who is me?"

"It's me, Richard. Buzz me in," he said as calmly as he could.

Richard never visited Portia unannounced. And even though he tried to sound normal Portia knew exactly why he was down in the lobby of her building. Richard had told Portia that his wife would be home from her weekend trip that afternoon. And since Richard was ringing her doorbell, Portia figured the missus must have found the gifts she had left behind.

"What do you want, Richard?"

In the lobby Richard paced back and forth in front of the small, round speaker mounted on the wall. "I wanna talk to you."

Portia knew exactly what Richard wanted to talk about but she asked the question anyway. "About what?"

Richard was so hot and bothered, he began to sweat. "I just wanna talk."

Portia wasn't absolutely sure that Richard's wife had found the gifts she left behind but since Richard was at her apartment and sounding a little too calm, wanting to talk about nothing, Portia wasn't about to take any chances. "This is not a good time, Richard. I'm busy."

Richard's breathing got heavy. He made two tight fists then released his hands. It took every ounce of self control he had to stay calm. "Please, baby. I had a rough day. Let me in." He was willing to say whatever was necessary to get Portia to allow him access.

Portia contemplated but her gut instinct overruled. "I said this is not a good time, Richard. And you know better than to come to my apartment without calling first."

Richard slammed his fist against the speaker. He could no longer restrain himself. "I'm through playing with you, Portia. Buzz this door open. Now!"

His outburst was the confirmation that Portia needed. At that moment Portia knew that Richard was in trouble with his wife and Portia also knew that she was the reason. "You must be crazy if you think I'm gonna let you in here when you're acting a fool. What is wrong with you?"

"What the heck do you think is wro . . ." Richard took a deep breath and calmed down. "You're right, I'm sorry. I just got something on my mind that I gotta talk to you about. Will you please buzz me in?"

"No, Richard. Go home and talk to Tamara." Portia released the talk button and walked away.

Richard's inner core exploded. His wife's name coming out of Portia's mouth was the match that ignited him. For ten minutes he paced the foyer. But lucky be a man that evening when an elderly woman strolled into the building struggling with three grocery bags. Richard was quickly at her side. "Let me help you with those, ma'am."

The gray-haired old woman stood no more than four feet tall. She was more than happy to release the load. "Thank you." She allowed Richard to take her bags and inserted her key into a lock that would give him entry. The old woman escorted Richard to her third-floor apartment. "Just leave the bags right here by the door, sugar. I can get them from here."

Richard set the bags on the floor outside her door.

The woman opened her purse to give Richard some money. "Here ya go, sugar. I sho 'preciate it."

"That's okay, ma'am. I don't want your money," Richard said. He wasn't the least bit interested in the old woman's money. He had to get to Portia.

The woman pressed the money into Richard's hand. "Go on and take this and buy yourself something nice."

In his hand was a shiny nickel. Richard put it in the right front pocket of the jeans he was wearing. "Thank you, ma'am," he said and scurried back to the elevator. He got back on and pressed the button for the sixth floor. Moments later he stood outside of Portia's unit and knocked.

Portia had just slipped on her nightgown when she looked through the peephole. "How did you get up here?"

"Don't worry about that. Open the door."

Portia slid the safety chain into its lock then opened the door. Through a one-inch crack she saw a distraught Richard. There was sweat on his brow and Richard's jaw line was tight. "What do you want?" she asked irritably.

"Take the chain off the door."

"If you wanna talk then talk from the hallway."

In a split second the chain on the door snapped and Richard had Portia pinned against the wall, in the foyer, by her neck. Her feet left contact with the floor as he slid her up the wall.

"What is wrong with you? Huh? What the heck is wrong with you, Portia? Why are you playing games with my wife?" As he spoke showers of Richard's saliva landed on Portia's face.

Very little air was getting to her lungs. Portia gasped and coughed. She tried to remove Richard's hand from around her throat. Her legs swung from Richard's knees to the wall behind her as she kicked. The acrylic on Portia's fingernails slashed Richard across his face. Richard yelled out and released her. Portia fell to her knees and tried to crawl away but wasn't fast enough. Richard grabbed Portia by her hair and threw her across her living room. The back of her head met violently with the porcelain end of the cocktail table and she screamed. Portia saw stars. Richard rushed to Portia and kicked the right side of her neck. Again she screamed.

He stooped and punched her in the middle of her chest. "Do you know what you did to my wife? Huh, do you?"

The blow Richard applied to her chest took Portia's breath away but she managed to bellow out another scream. He dragged Portia by her arms, to her bedroom, as she kicked and hollered. Richard possessed the strength of Hercules. He picked Portia up and threw her on the bed. She tried to get up but another blow to her chest sent her flying backward. Richard dove on top of Portia and lifted her gown to her waist. Portia used all of her might to wiggle from under him but couldn't do it. Richard covered Portia's mouth with his left hand to silence her screams. With his right hand he unzipped his pants and forced himself into her. "You screwed with my wife so now I'm screwing you."

Though Richard had been on top of Portia many times, that time it felt like he'd gained fifty pounds. She could do nothing but lie there and moan.

When Richard had finished doing what he came to do he stood and looked at her. Portia rolled onto her side and cried loudly. Her tears didn't move Richard at all. He wiped sweat from his forehead. He panted as he spoke to Portia. "I'm gonna tell you this one time and one time only. Stay away from Tamara. Don't call her, don't e-mail her, and don't even come within one hundred feet of her. If I even hear of you contacting her . . ." He paused. "I swear I'll kill you." He zipped his pants and turned to walk away.

"You won't even have a wife when she finds out that I'm pregnant!" Portia spat the words out of her mouth. She wasn't pregnant but she wanted to make Richard angrier than he already was.

That was the straw that broke the camel's back. She was just beaten and raped but Portia didn't care. She was determined to have the last say so even it cost her life.

Richard stopped in his tracks, turned back around, and gave Portia a glare that let her know she had just made a mistake, a grave mistake. The glare she saw in Richard's eyes put the fear of God in Portia. It wasn't like all the other times when he had ogled her with lust and pleasure. It was a different look. A look that Portia had seen on victims' faces in Stephen King's horror movies when the music started to play. The kind of music that warned viewers that something tragic was about to happen. Someone was going to die.

Richard rushed toward Portia and leapt on top of her and punched her face over and over and over again. He didn't let up until she stopped moving and lay still.

Chapter 7

Dead or Alive

It was approximately 2:00 a.m. when the loud shrill of the telephone startled Celeste. Whenever the telephone rang in the wee hours of the morning it usually meant that something was wrong.

She nervously answered it on the second ring. "Hello?"

Ginger was hysterical. Screaming and talking fast at the same time. Celeste couldn't make out anything she was saying. "Ginger, calm down. What happened?"

The only words Celeste comprehended were, "Portia," "hospital," and "dead." It was Ginger's last word that made Celeste sit up on the bed and scream to the top of her lungs.

Anthony was sleeping on the living room sofa when he heard Celeste. The sofa had become his place of rest since the evening he overheard Dr. Bindu accidentally reveal Celeste's secret. He jumped up and ran into their bedroom. In the dark Anthony accidentally stubbed his baby toe on the edge of the cocktail table. He cursed out loud. He grabbed his toe and hobbled into the bedroom.

Celeste had dropped the telephone on the floor and was rocking back and forth on the bed crying loudly. "No, Jesus, no. Not Portia. Please, God. Don't take my sister from me."

Anthony turned on the light in the bedroom and saw Celeste sitting up on the bed. He saw her rocking and moaning. "What happened? Who was that on the phone?"

Celeste threw the covers from her body and hurried to the closet. "That was Ginger. She's at the hospital. She said Portia is dead."

Anthony's eyes grew wide. "What?"

"Portia is dead!" Celeste yelled. "I gotta get to the hospital." Crying, she raised her nightgown over her head and slipped into a pair of jeans and a T-shirt.

Anthony couldn't believe what Celeste had just said to him. Her words overruled the pain in his toe. "What do you mean she's dead? What did Ginger say?"

Celeste slipped into a pair of flat mules and ran past Anthony and out of the bedroom. "Come on, Tony. Let's go. Let's go!"

Anthony was dressed in pajama bottoms and a T-shirt. His attire would have to do because he didn't have time to change. He slipped into his house slippers and chased Celeste out of the bedroom. He grabbed his keys from the cocktail table. They both hurried out of the front door.

Anthony started the engine. "Put your seat belt on," he said to Celeste. He fastened his own seat belt and sped away from the curb.

"Oh, my God. Tony, please get there quick."

"Which hospital?"

"Rush-Presbyterian."

Anthony sped toward the Eisenhower Expressway. "What did Ginger say?"

Celeste reached into the glove box for a Kleenex tissue and blew her runny nose. "The only thing I heard was that Portia was at the hospital and she was dead. I dropped the phone and started screaming."

"Ginger didn't say how or why or what happened to Portia?"

Celeste became irritated. Anthony was asking way too many questions. Questions that Celeste didn't have any answers to. "No, Tony. Ginger was hollering on the phone. I could barely understand her at all. The only words I could comprehend were Portia is dead." Celeste placed her face in her hands and cried openly. "Oh, my God. How could this happen?"

Ginger was already in the waiting area of the emergency room at Rush-Presbyterian hospital, on the west side of Chicago, when she saw Anthony and Celeste rush in and head straight to the nurses' station.

"Celeste," Ginger called out and stood from her chair.

Celeste saw Ginger and ran into her arms. They held on to each other and cried. Anthony walked over and put his arms around both of them. "Why don't you two come and sit down?"

Celeste didn't want to sit. She let go of Ginger and looked at her. "What happened?"

Ginger's eyes were puffy and red. Her hands were shaking as she tried her best to answer Celeste. "I got a call from the woman who lives in the unit next to Portia. She said she heard yelling and screaming coming from Portia's apartment and called the police. When the police got there, Portia's front door was ajar and the security chain had been broken. They found her lying unconscious on her bed. She had been beaten."

Celeste's eyes grew wide. She let out a shrill sound and placed her hand on her heart. "Oh, my God. Who would do such a thing to Portia? Could it have been a robbery gone wrong?"

Ginger shrugged her shoulders. "I don't know. Her neighbor said she didn't see anyone arrive at or leave Portia's apartment."

"Who is the neighbor and how did she know to contact you?" Anthony asked Ginger.

"Her name is Josephine something. I can't remember what she said her last name was. Anyway, she said since she and Portia were two women living alone, they should give each other the phone numbers of their next of kin just in case something happened to either one of them." Ginger looked at Celeste. "Portia had given Josephine your telephone number, too. When Josephine contacted me she said that she was going to call you next but I told her that I would call you myself."

Celeste's mind went back to Ginger's telephone call. "You said that Portia was dead."

"I said she might be dead. Josephine told me that Portia wasn't breathing when the paramedics carried her out of the apartment. I've asked the nurse at the desk what was going on with Portia and she told me the doctor will come out and speak with me as soon as he can."

"Ginger, why isn't Ron here with you?" Anthony asked. At a time like that Anthony felt that a man should be with his woman. Ronald knew that Ginger, Celeste, and Portia were best friends. Celeste and Anthony were going through a rough patch but there was no way on God's green earth that he would let Celeste deal with Portia's trauma alone. And furthermore it was the middle of the night. Anthony felt that Ronald should have been by Ginger's side for her safety. Anthony couldn't fathom Celeste leaving the house alone at that hour.

Ginger shrugged her shoulders. "I don't know where that fool is. He wasn't home when I left. I've called his cell phone three times."

Anthony shook his head from side to side. He and Ronald were not friends. He tolerated Ronald for Ginger's sake. But when Celeste had shared that Ronald had beat Ginger because she let the gas hand fall below the half-full line without filling the tank up, Anthony decided that it would be in Ronald's best interest that they stay as far apart as possible. Anthony did wonder, though, where Ronald could be at that hour. "He should be right here with you, Ginger. What man doesn't return his woman's calls? For all Ron knows, it could be you laying up in the emergency room."

Ginger was embarrassed that Ronald wasn't there to comfort her the way Anthony was supporting Celeste. She was even more embarrassed that her best friend's husband had noticed and commented on her missing so-called boyfriend.

Celeste was taken aback by Anthony's forwardness about Ronald. She knew that Anthony didn't care for Ronald but Anthony had always encouraged Celeste to stay out of Ginger's relationship. It threw Celeste for a loop when Anthony spoke to Ginger that way. "Okay, Tony, let's all calm down. Now is not the time for this."

Anthony had said his piece. He was done with the Ronald situation. He just hoped that Ginger would finally see that Ronald was a loser. Anthony wanted Ginger to understand that if her boyfriend couldn't be by her side while her best friend fought for her life, she didn't need him. Anthony went and sat down in a chair.

Ginger looked into Celeste's eyes. She had been missing her and Portia for a month. "I'm sorry for what I said to you and Portia in my living room last month."

Celeste pulled Ginger into her arms and squeezed tight. "I'm sorry too. We all said things that we shouldn't have."

"I missed y'all so much," Ginger wiped the tears that were falling down her face.

"We're together now and that's all that matters. We need to pray for our sister."

Ginger and Celeste were sitting and holding hands when the doctor came into the waiting room and approached them. "Are you the family of Portia Dunn?"

Anthony, Celeste, and Ginger all stood. "Yes," Ginger answered nervously.

"Let's sit down," the doctor said, already making his way toward a chair.

When a doctor tells family members to sit down, it means bad news is coming. "We don't wanna sit down," Celeste stated. "Just tell us. How is Portia?"

Anthony saw the expression on the doctor's face. He looked as though he didn't have good news. Anthony came and stood in between Ginger and Celeste. He wrapped his arms around their waists for support.

The doctor looked at all of them. "She's alive."

The loudest sigh came from Ginger. "Thank God. Oh, thank God."

Celeste fell into Anthony. "Thank you, Jesus."

"Ms. Dunn was barely conscious when she arrived," the doctor said. "But we brought her around."

"Can you tell us what happened to her?" Anthony asked.

The doctor folded his arms across his chest and exhaled. "Well, she was severely beaten. Her right jawbone is fractured. Ms. Dunn's entire face looks as though she was mauled. She was hemorrhaging behind her left eye duct but we managed to get that under control. By the looks of her, whoever did this wanted her dead."

"Oh, my God," Celeste cried out.

"I don't understand it," Ginger said. "Why did this happen to her?"

"Anything else, Doctor?" Anthony asked.

"Yes, there is one more thing I need to make all of you aware of."

Ginger and Celeste braced themselves.

Celeste wiped her eyes. "What is it?"

"Ms. Dunn was sexually assaulted as well."

"My Lord," Anthony said out loud.

Celeste and Ginger grabbed each other and held on for dear life. They sobbed on each other's shoulders.

"Can we see her?" Anthony asked.

"A police officer is interviewing Ms. Dunn now. She's very weak but I'll allow you to spend five minutes with her. She's been sedated but, yes, you can see her."

Anthony, Celeste, and Ginger thanked the doctor for his report. As soon as the doctor exited the waiting room a Chicago police officer walked in and stood in front of them. "Excuse me, I was told that you were the family of Portia Dunn."

"Yes, we are," Celeste said matter-of-factly.

"I'm Officer Dale Caridine. Do you mind if I ask you a few questions?"

Ginger put her purse strap on her shoulder. "We were just on our way to see Portia." She attempted to walk pass the officer.

Officer Caridine stepped in Ginger's path. "It will only take a moment." He retrieved a small notepad from his uniform shirt front pocket. "I tried speaking with Ms. Dunn but she's still in shock and wasn't very helpful." He looked at Ginger. "What's your name?"

Ginger rolled her eyes and exhaled loudly. She wasn't in the mood to be interrogated. Her best friend needed her. "Ginger Brown."

He jotted down Ginger's name then looked up at her. "And how are you related to Ms. Dunn?"

"Celeste and I are Portia's best friends."

Officer Caridine looked from Ginger to Celeste then from Celeste to Ginger. "Best friends? So, you're not related to her?"

"Not by blood, no," Celeste offered. "Portia, Ginger, and I have been best friends since high school."

"I see," Officer Caridine commented then wrote in his notepad. He then looked back up at Celeste. "Are you Celeste?"

She nodded. "Yes. Celeste Harper."

"What about Ms. Dunn's family?"

"She has no family," Ginger offered. "We're her only family. Her parents are deceased and she has no siblings."

"No grandparents, uncles, aunts, or cousins?"

"None that we're aware of," Celeste stated.

Officer Caridine looked at Anthony standing close to Celeste. "And your name is?"

"Anthony Harper. Celeste is my wife."

Officer Caridine wrote Anthony's name on his notepad then looked at all three of them. "Do any of you know of any enemies that Ms. Dunn may have? Anyone who may have a reason to want to hurt her?"

Try every married woman in Chicago, Ginger thought. "No."

"I can't think of anyone," Celeste answered.

Officer Caridine looked at Anthony. "How about you?"

"I have absolutely no idea who would want to hurt Portia." Anthony said.

Officer Caridine jotted down what each of them said. "Please, think hard. Have any of you witnessed her argue with anyone lately? Can you recall a conversation in which Ms. Dunn may have mentioned that someone was out to get her?"

The three of them answered together. "No."

Officer Caridine didn't have anything else to write into his logbook. He placed it in his coat pocket and gave each of them a business card. "If anything comes to mind that can help me find out who did this to your friend, please call the precinct and ask for me."

When Officer Caridine left them alone Celeste said, "Let's go see Portia."

Anthony had to catch Celeste as her knees buckled when they walked into Portia's hospital room. Somewhere behind the black and blue bruises, the swollen eye, blistered lip, and overall disfigured face was the pretty Portia they all knew.

The doctor had told Anthony, Celeste, and Ginger that Portia was sedated but her eyes were open. Tears ran from the creases of her eyes down to her ears. Ginger and Celeste stood on opposite sides of her bed and each of them held Portia's hand.

"Oh, my God," Ginger cried out. "I don't even recognize her."

Anthony stood at the foot of Portia's hospital bed and wondered how a man could beat a woman that badly. Anthony couldn't think of any reason, any excuse. There couldn't be a logical explanation. He was angry.

A tear dripped from Ginger's chin. She squeezed Portia's hand. "How are you doing, honey?"

"I'm sorry for what I said to you," Portia mumbled through swollen lips.

More tears dripped from Ginger's chin. She, Portia, and Celeste hadn't spoken a word to each other in weeks. Ginger felt bad that it took a situation like Portia's attack to bring them back together. "That's in the past."

Portia turned her head in Celeste's direction. "I said something that hurt you and I'm sorry. I love you so much."

Through her tears, Celeste saw two Portias. "I'm sorry too. I love you back." It took all the strength that Celeste had for her to get those words out of her mouth.

"Who did this to you?" Anthony asked Portia.

Portia closed her eyes as tears ran down the sides of her face. She didn't answer Anthony's question.

As far as Ginger knew, all of the men Portia dealt with were married but harmless. She'd never known Portia to have any drama with any of them. Ginger assumed that Portia's attacker was a stranger. "Do you know the person?"

Portia sniffed and exhaled.

Celeste wiped Portia's tears with the back of her hand. And since Portia hadn't answered either Anthony's or Ginger's question, Celeste knew that Portia knew exactly who had beaten and raped her. "You do. Don't you?"

Anthony came and stood next to Celeste. "Tell me." His jaws were tight. Anthony thought of Ginger and Portia as his sisters. It was Anthony who they called whenever they had a flat tire. It was Anthony who Ginger called, before she met Ronald, when she thought an intruder was in her home. And it was Anthony's threat that had sent an ex-stalker of Portia's running for his life.

Portia slowly shook her head from side to side. "I can't, Tony," she cried out.

Ginger frowned at Portia. "Why not?"

"Because he'll kill me," Portia whispered then turned her head away from Anthony and Celeste.

Ginger understood Portia's dilemma perfectly. She was in that exact situation before. She too had been trapped in the anger of a man that threatened to kill her if she spoke of his abuse toward her.

Anthony gently placed his hand on Portia's chin and turned her face back toward him. "Tell me who did this to you."

Portia tried to turn her face away but Anthony firmly kept his hand and her face in place. Portia saw a tear run down his face. When Portia thought about it, since she had met Anthony, he'd always been the big brother she never had. Over the years, it was Anthony who Portia had called when she needed someone to hang a ceiling fan or to assist with furniture delivery. And it was Anthony who Portia called when she couldn't get her car started in the dead of winter. And now it was Anthony who stood by her hospital bed, late in the midnight hour, with tears in his eyes.

Portia looked at him and knew he deserved an answer. "Richard."

"Richard?" Celeste and Ginger shrieked. They knew Richard very well. The times they'd been in his presence, Richard had treated Portia with kindness and respect. He showered her with flowers, candy, gifts, and plenty of money.

In a split second Celeste was calling after Anthony as he abruptly left her side. He went back to the waiting room and dialed a number on his cellular phone.

Craig Hatch, a deacon at their church and a Chicago police officer, was cruising the south side of the city with his partner when he answered Anthony's call. Anthony knew that Deacon Hatch worked the graveyard shift.

"What are you doing up at this hour?" he asked Anthony when he saw his name displayed on his caller ID.

Anthony told Officer Hatch why he was awake and where he was. Not only were Anthony and Craig brothers in Christ who served on the finance committee at their church, they often shot a game of pool together. And they were also teammates in a bowling league.

Before Portia had acquired a taste for married men she and Craig had dated. It was after their third date that Craig realized that Portia's taste was too rich for his blood. Not only did she demand that Craig dress her from head to toe for each date, Portia required that he foot the bill even when she invited him out to eat. Craig's common sense told him that if he didn't want to become bankrupt before the age of thirty-five he needed to cut Portia loose.

"I'm all tapped out, beautiful," Craig told Portia at dinner.

Portia just finished the last of her lobster platter. "You can't hang, huh?"

Craig chuckled. "Nah. I can't even front no more. I can't afford you but I'll tell you what. If you ever need me to shoot someone, call me. I'm your man."

After making the call to Officer Hatch, Anthony went back to Portia's hospital room and convinced her to tell him where Richard lived. No one, not even Celeste, could hold Anthony back once he had the information that he needed from Portia. He left quickly.

As soon as Anthony disappeared from their presence, Ginger looked at Celeste and said, "Richard is in trouble."

Thirty minutes later Officer Hatch and his partner, with Anthony in the back seat of their cruiser, were headed toward Richard's house. When they arrived, Officer Hatch instructed Anthony to stay seated in the police car.

He and his partner got out and rang Richard's doorbell. A sleepy teenage boy answered.

Officer Hatch pointed the high beam of his flashlight in the boy's face. "Does Richard Clark live here?"

"Yeah, but he ain't here."

"Who are you?" Officer Hatch asked.

"I'm Damion, his nephew."

"Where's Richard?" Officer Hatch's partner asked.

"At the hospital with my auntie."

"Which hospital?" Officer Hatch asked.

"Rush-Presbyterian."

Officer Hatch and his partner looked at each other. That was the same hospital where Portia was and where they had picked Anthony up from. "Let's go," Officer Hatch said to his partner. They both hurried back to the cruiser.

Officer Hatch got behind the wheel and started the engine. He turned the red and blue warning lights on and sped away from the curb.

**

Back at Rush-Presbyterian hospital, Officer Hatch, his partner, and Anthony approached the nurses' station on the eighth floor. Officer Hatch flashed his badge to a nurse sitting behind the information desk. "We're here to interview a patient by the name of Tamara Clark."

The nurse looked at the badge and then pointed to her left. "She's in room 824."

The three men walked to room 824 and stood outside the door. Officer Hatch looked at Anthony. "You're gonna be cool, right?"

Anthony knew what his answer had better be. "Yeah, Deac, I'm cool." Later Anthony would repent for the lie he'd just told.

Richard and Tamara were asleep when Officer Hatch, his partner, and Anthony walked into Tamara's hospital room. Richard lay next to Tamara on a rollaway bed when he felt a tap on his leg. He stirred, opened his eyes, and saw two police officers and another man standing next to the rollaway bed. Richard noticed that the officer standing the closest to him had tapped his leg with a nightstick.

"Are you Richard Clark?" Officer Hatch's partner asked.

His question stirred Tamara. She opened her eyes and saw what was taking place.

Richard sat up on the bed. "Yeah. Why?"

As soon as Richard confirmed who he was, Anthony rushed from behind the officers and slammed his fist into Richard's nose.

Tamara's eyes grew wide. She saw the officers pull Richard up from the bed with blood dripping from his nose. "What's happening?" she asked. Her voice was just above a whisper.

Richard knew why the police were there. As for who Anthony was and why he hit him, Richard had assumed that Anthony was somehow related to Portia.

Officer Hatch's partner read Richard his rights. When Tamara heard him tell Richard that he was being arrested for the rape and attempted murder of Portia Dunn, her already-weak heart started to skip beats. She became short of breath and she lay in bed panting for air that wasn't forthcoming.

Officer Hatch handcuffed Richard and turned to lead him out of the hospital room. As they passed Anthony, he took the opportunity to punch Richard in his face again.

"You like to hit women? Huh? Is that what you're into, punk?"

Blood spewed from Richard's nose to Tamara's bed sheets.

Officer Hatch pushed Anthony back. "Tony, man, I told you to be cool."

Anthony looked at his friend. "This is cool, Deac, I ain't got warmed up yet." He slammed his fist into Richard's face again. More blood spewed onto Tamara's sheets.

Richard was helpless with his wrists in handcuffs behind his back.

"Tony, that's enough," Officer Hatch insisted. "How am I gonna explain this to my sergeant?"

"The suspect resisted arrest," Officer Hatch's partner answered. "He gave us a hard time."

When they dragged Richard out of the hospital room, nurses were rushing in to see why Tamara's heart monitor was singing. She was having a full-blown heart attack. At the same time Richard was being placed in the back seat of the police car, Tamara's eyes rolled to the back of her head. Her heartbeat became slower until there were no beats at all. Tamara was dead.

Chapter 8

When Enough Is Enough

It was almost five-thirty a.m. when Ginger returned home from the hospital. She pressed the button on the garage door opener. She saw that Ronald had parked his car in the middle of the two-and-a-half-car garage leaving no room for Ginger to squeeze her car in.

"He's so darn ignorant." She sighed.

Ginger was not in the mood to attempt to ask Ronald to move his car over. The request would only escalate into an argument. Ginger had been up all night. She was tired, irritable, and sleepy. Ginger put the gear in reverse and backed down the driveway. She parked on the street and went inside.

It was almost daybreak and Ginger knew that if she lay down, not even the loudest alarm clock would be able to wake her up in time for work. In the bedroom, she saw Ronald in bed snoring loudly. On the nightstand was an empty forty-ounce bottle of beer. On a plate next to it was a sandwich-size Ziploc plastic bag containing a small amount of white powder. Ginger knew it was cocaine.

Lord Jesus, give me strength. I'm so tired of this crap.

Ginger showered, slipped into a nightgown then sat at the kitchen table to grade papers. Fifteen minutes had elapsed when she heard the toilet flush. Ginger froze. *Oh, God.* She closed her eyes and exhaled deeply. She remembered that she didn't raise the toilet seat after she used it. There was going to be trouble.

Ronald came and stood in the kitchen doorway. "Where you been?" His eyes were bloodshot and his speech was slurred. He was intoxicated and high.

"I was at the hospital with Portia."

"You're a lying whore," he spat. "You were out screwing around."

Ginger had enough of the abuse. Verbal abuse, mental abuse, and physical abuse. Seeing Portia lie in a hospital bed with a battered face and broken body, clinging to dear life, made Ginger's own situation a reality. She realized that if she continued to allow Ronald to use her as his personal punching bag, she herself would have to be admitted to a hospital. While driving home Ginger thought about how it could have easily been her, instead of Portia, lying in a hospital bed, beaten and broken, at the hands of a lunatic. Ginger also recalled what Officer Phyore Montgomery had told her:

"You are a beautiful black woman. Learn to love yourself. It hurts me deeply to get called to a house and find one of my black sisters unresponsive from domestic abuse. And I'm gonna tell you something, Miss Brown. Eventually he will kill you. It happens like that all the time."

Ginger boldly stood and walked to Ronald. "Well, heck, where were you at two this morning when I got the call about Portia? Huh? I called your cell but you didn't wanna answer. So, if anyone is allowed to point the screwing-around finger, it's me." Ginger took it a step further with Ronald. "And what if I was out screwing around? What are you gonna do about it?"

Ronald was lethargic but not incoherent. It took him a long moment to realize what Ginger had just said. He wondered if she had really just challenged him. "What?"

Ginger stood her ground and folded her arms across her chest. She spoke very slowly so that her words would penetrate through the cocaine Ronald snorted. "If I was with a man, there ain't a darn thing you can do about it."

A sober Ronald would have had his hands around Ginger's throat in less than a second. But right then the alcohol and drugs weren't on his side. He lunged toward Ginger but lost his balance and landed on the kitchen table instead. The table legs gave in to his weight and Ronald crashed to the floor.

Ginger knew that in the state Ronald was in, she could take him. After almost losing Portia at the hands of a man, Ginger vowed to never let Ronald put his hands on her again. It was a brand new day for Ginger and if Ronald touched her, he was in for a new awakening.

Ginger saw Ronald trying to get to his knees and knew that the time to take back her life was right then. The moment had come for her to defend herself. With all of her might Ginger kicked Ronald in his side. He yelled out and fell back onto the floor.

Ginger rushed to the telephone on the kitchen wall and dialed 911.

"911. What's your emergency?" the dispatcher asked.

The two years of dramatic acting classes Ginger took in college were getting ready to pay off. She screamed into the telephone, "Help me, please! He's tryin' to kill me!"

Ginger sounded hysterical. The dispatcher tried to calm her down. "Ma'am, please take your time and tell me what's going on."

Ronald was trying to get up. Ginger set the cordless phone on the counter, picked up a chair, and broke it across Ronald's back. He hollered and fell back to the floor. Ginger got back to the telephone and pretended like she was auditioning for a role in a thriller.

"He's going crazy! Please, please help me!" Ginger let out a shriek that almost busted the dispatcher's eardrums.

"Okay, ma'am. The police are on their way. Stay on the line."

Ginger placed the telephone in front of her mouth and screamed, "No, Ron, no. I'm sorry. Please don't hit me again," before disconnecting the line. She looked at Ronald lying on the floor mumbling and moaning. She heard him call her the B word. Ginger looked around the kitchen for something to beat the crap out of him with. She remembered the wooden rolling pin in the utensil drawer. Ronald had thrown everything away except the rolling pin. That had to be God working in her favor, Ginger thought.

She got the large wooden rolling pin out of the utensil drawer and hit Ronald across the back of his head as hard as she could. Either he was too drunk to feel it or he was dead because he didn't move. But that didn't matter to Ginger. She had seen too many movies when the woman thought her attacker was dead but wasn't. Ginger was going to make sure Ronald wasn't getting up. She raised the rolling pin over her head and swung it at thirty miles an hour. She hit Ronald so hard across his back, the rolling pin cracked.

She raised it again and with all of her might, she slammed it onto the left side of his brain. Ginger heard something break. She hoped it was Ronald's skull. He wasn't moving. Blood ran out from under Ronald's head.

Outside on the front porch police officers were knocking on Ginger's front door. "Police, open up."

When the police broke down Ginger's living room door, they found her in the kitchen straddling Ronald. She was still bashing his head.

An officer pulled his gun from his holster and pointed it at Ginger. He saw what looked like a very small bat in her hand. "Put the bat down!" he ordered.

She looked like a madwoman. Ginger was sweating profusely and her hair was pasted to her face. She was breathing heavy.

The officer walked farther into the kitchen with his gun aimed at Ginger's head. "I said put the bat down."

Ginger refused to drop the rolling pin. She wanted to kill Ronald before he got the chance to kill her.

A female officer appeared in the archway to the kitchen. "It's okay," she said to her fellow officer. "Lower your weapon. This is a domestic situation."

When Ginger saw Sergeant Phyore Montgomery she dropped the rolling pin and started crying uncontrollably. Sergeant Montgomery went to Ginger and pulled her off of Ronald. She led Ginger out of the kitchen. "Call an ambulance," she said to the other officer.

Sergeant Montgomery took Ginger into the dining room, pulled out a chair, and sat Ginger down. She knelt before Ginger. "What happened?"

Ginger was a basket case. Her body shivered. She was covered in Ronald's blood. "I wasn't gonna take it anymore. One of us was gonna die." Ginger stared into Sergeant Montgomery's eyes. "And it wasn't gonna be me."

"Didn't I tell you this was gonna happen?"

Two paramedics rushed in and tended to Ronald. "We have a pulse," Ginger heard one of them say.

Ginger was disappointed. "I didn't do it right," she mumbled. "I should've killed him. Ron deserved to die."

"Don't ever say that again," Sergeant Montgomery scolded Ginger.

The paramedics loaded Ronald on a stretcher and proceeded to carry him through the living room and out the front door.

Ginger jumped up from her chair and blocked them. "Take him out the back door."

Both paramedics frowned.

Ronald demanded that Ginger not enter the house through the white, immaculate living room. And she didn't want him to travel though it either. Ginger didn't care that he was on a stretcher. "Take his dirty behind out the back way," she demanded.

Sergeant Montgomery pulled Ginger out of the paramedics' way. "Let them through."

The first officer who had arrived on the scene approached Ginger and Sergeant Montgomery. "I need a statement."

Sergeant Montgomery spoke. "She did what she had to do to get him off of her."

Ginger looked at her with a surprised expression. She had expected Sergeant Montgomery to arrest her.

"I'll write the report myself," Sergeant Montgomery said. She gave Ginger a reassuring smile. "We're done here."

When the police had left, Ginger went into the kitchen. The amount of blood that was on the floor and the splatter on the walls made up the perfect crime scene.

Ginger thought about the miscarriages she suffered at Ronald's hands. The rapes and beatings flashed before her eyes. But she had taken her life back. No more beatings. No more verbal abuse. And no more miscarriages.

Ginger opened the pantry door and got a pail and mop. After she cleaned Ronald's blood she showered, then called Celeste's house.

Anthony stood at the kitchen counter with his right fist submerged in a bowl of ice cubes. Celeste came into the kitchen from the bathroom with a small box of gauze wrap.

"Tony, I can't believe you and Deacon Hatch did that to Richard. Have you ever heard the term 'crooked cop'?"

Anthony didn't feel the least bit guilty for what he'd done. "Celeste, please. Deacon Hatch and Portia worship at the same church. She's his sister in Christ."

Celeste looked at Anthony. "Tell me something, Tony. How did God get the glory out of Deacon Hatch handcuffing a man's hands behind his back and you beating the crap out of him?"

"Why you gotta bring God into everything? Some things He lets us handle on our own."

Celeste looked at Anthony as though he were insane. Before she could comment the telephone rang. "Who in the heck is calling at seven in the morning?" Celeste asked.

Anthony answered the phone with an irritated greeting. It was Ginger. She told Anthony that she and Ronald had gotten into a fight and she had beaten him with a rolling pin.

"What the heck is going on? It must've been a full moon last night." Anthony glanced at the knuckles on his left hand. "I got one good fist left. Is he still there?"

Celeste heard Anthony's question. "Is who still where?" she asked.

"No. He was taken away in an ambulance," Ginger told Anthony.

"Are you all right? You want us to come over there?"

"Come over where?" Celeste asked.

"No. I'm okay," Ginger answered.

"Well, call us if you need anything. Anything at all." Anthony hung up the telephone and told Celeste Ginger's story.

Celeste couldn't believe the events that had taken place over the past five hours. "My Lord. Has this been a wild morning or what? Is Ginger okay?"

"Yeah, she killed Ronald."

Celeste's eyes grew wide and she shrieked, "What?"

"My bad," Anthony said. "She should've killed him."

Later that day Richard was charged for the attempted murder and sexual assault against Portia.

Chapter 9

New Beginnings

Four months later, after morning service, Celeste kissed Anthony good-bye then walked over to where Portia and Ginger were standing in the vestibule of the church.

"Tony has a meeting with Pastor Ricky Harris. Let's go and hang out at Leona's. A sista can really go for chicken fettuccini right about now."

Portia looked at Celeste. She stood rubbing her very small protruding belly at sixteen weeks pregnant. "Look, we ain't trying to hear what you and Celeste number two have a craving for. Ginger's got another pressing issue."

Celeste looked at Ginger. "Like what?"

"Like that *foine* brotha behind you," Portia answered. "The tall one in the navy suit. He's pretending to be in a deep conversation while at the same time he's keeping one of his eyeballs on our girl here."

Celeste turned around and saw who Portia was talking about. She saw the man in the navy suit and sure enough his eyes were glued to Ginger while talking with another man. "Hey, isn't that Joseph Banks? The new guy who reports the news on WGN channel nine every morning?"

For the past month, every morning at six o'clock sharp, Celeste and the citizens of Chicago and the surrounding suburbs, awakened to Joseph's handsome face dressed in tailor-made suits.

Portia's mouth dropped open. "OMG, it is him. He looks even better in person."

Celeste turned back around. She nudged Ginger's arm. "All right, Ginger, girl. You got a famous man sopping you up in the church. But how can he look at you and hold a conversation with someone else at the same time? You think he's a li'l cockeyed?"

Portia laughed at Celeste.

"He ain't cockeyed," Ginger said, eyeing the copper-colored specimen standing about fifteen feet away from her. "A skilled man can do that."

Portia nudged Ginger's shoulder. "So, uh, what's up with him? You've been holding out on us or what?"

"Do you know him personally?" Celeste asked Ginger.

Ginger shook her head from side to side. "Nope. I don't know him nor am I interested." The latter portion of Ginger's statement was untrue. She was very much interested in who Joseph Banks was. No other man had looked at her that way before.

Ginger couldn't remember the last time she was admired by a member of the opposite sex. For the past four years, she'd been beaten, spat on, kicked around, and ridiculed. Ginger probably wouldn't recognize a compliment if it slapped her in the face. But she did like the way Joseph got her attention. Between the words he exchanged with the man he was chatting with, he managed to smile at Ginger.

"Good Lord," Ginger mumbled out loud. Joseph had a nice set of teeth. White teeth. Even teeth. Teeth that belonged on the boxes of Aquafresh toothpaste. She returned his smile.

"I saw that," Celeste said to Ginger. "Nor are you interested, huh? Weren't those your exact words?"

"Humph, well, we can't tell," Portia commented. "I do believe I see a little flirt in you, Miss Schoolteacher."

Celeste saw Joseph size Ginger up from her metallic stilettos, to her twenty-six-inch waist, up to her new interlock hairdo. "He hasn't taken his eyes off of you for a second, Ginger. I mean seriously."

Just then Joseph excused himself from the company he was in and made his way toward Portia, Celeste, and Ginger. He came and stood in front of Ginger and spoke directly to her. "Hi."

Ginger was sandwiched between Celeste and Portia. She was glad about that because at that moment, as she gazed at his smile up close, she teetered like a seesaw. Ginger didn't know if it was the smell of his cologne, his broad shoulders, or his sensual, deep voice but she was drunk in Joseph's presence. *Lord, please have mercy on me.*

With her girls at her side, Ginger felt confident that Portia and Celeste would catch her if her knees betrayed her. Yes, he was that fine. She looked at Joseph's lips. Smooth, not chapped. His mustache and goatee were trimmed perfectly. For the first time in her life, Ginger was mesmerized. Portia was right. Joseph looked better in person. "Hi."

He looked deep into Ginger's eyes and repeated himself. "Hi." His voice was even more sensual than when he uttered that same word moments ago.

Joseph put the F in the word "flirt." But since Ginger was feeling good and since he put the ball in her court, she went for it. "Hi," she said in her sexiest voice.

Celeste leaned back and spoke to Portia behind Ginger's head. "Did they just greet each other twice?"

"Yep, but did you take note of her sultriness?"

"I think somebody is coming out of her shell," Celeste said.

Ginger broke the stare from the man in front of her and looked at her friends. "Okay, y'all do know I can hear what you're saying, right?"

"Really?" Celeste asked. "You seem to be in a world of your own."

Ginger rolled her eyes at Celeste then looked at Joseph standing in front of her. "Please forgive my friends' rudeness. Sometimes she really do have manners."

"All is forgiven," he said, smiling. "My name is Joseph Banks. How are you lovely ladies on this fine Sunday afternoon?" His eyes were fixed on Ginger's as he addressed all three of them.

"We know who you are," Celeste said.

"You did say ladies, didn't you?" Portia asked Joseph. "Meaning plural?"

Joseph looked at Portia. "Yes, I did."

"I just wanted to know because you seem to be only talking to Ginger."

Joseph arched his eyebrows and looked at the woman who stood directly in front of him. "Ginger." He said her name dreamily. "What a beautiful name. Perfectly fitted for a beautiful woman."

Celeste was impressed. "Wow."

Although Ginger tried with all of her might not to, she couldn't help but to smile at his comment. "Thank you."

"What I'm about to ask you may seem a bit forward but are you married?"

"Well, actually, I—"

Portia cut Ginger's words off. "Nope. She's not married, engaged, or in a committed relationship. She's not dating or seeing anyone at the moment. You're right on time."

Ginger's mouth dropped open at Portia's boldness.

Joseph grabbed Ginger's left hand, brought it to his mouth, and kissed the back of it. "Ginger, is it?"

Ginger looked at the Adonis and slowly nodded her head. She was in a trance.

"I was just on my way out to get some dinner. And since I haven't been in Chicago for very long, I haven't met a lot of folks. I'd hate to dine alone. So, would the three of you care to join me?" Joseph was a stranger. He hoped that by inviting her friends along, Ginger would accept his invitation.

Ginger couldn't move. *Lord, are you for real? I need to know. You've brought me through too much stuff to be playin' with me.*

Again, as Joseph spoke to the three of them, his eyes were only focused on Ginger's.

Portia being Portia lightly tapped his right shoulder. "Um, excuse me. You did say the three of us, right? Because again your eyes are focused only on Ginger's."

"Absolutely. I'm speaking to the three of you," Joseph answered Portia while staring at Ginger.

He's doing it again, Celeste thought, remembering how Joseph was speaking with someone else while ogling Ginger.

Portia extended her hand to Joseph. "Well, in that case, I'm Portia and the lady standing on the other side of Ginger is Celeste. And it's a good thing you invited all three of us to dinner because we travel in a group."

Joseph chuckled and shook Portia's hand. His first impression of her was that she was very straightforward and outspoken. It was a turn-off for him but since she was a friend of Ginger's, Joseph was willing to tolerate her. "It's a pleasure to meet you. But I'm curious about why you travel in a group."

Celeste, being the eldest of the three, had always been a bit overprotective. "Because that's how we roll. We always have and always will. We are a package deal." Their ritual wouldn't be broken. All three of them went on each other's first dates. Joseph looked good, smelled good, smiled good, and talked good. But for all Celeste knew he could be another Ronald. He could be a wolf in sheep's clothing.

Ginger was vulnerable, open, and on the rebound. It had been four months since she beat Ronald to a pulp and gotten him out of her home. The day after the paramedics carried Ronald out on a stretcher, Ginger had gone to the courthouse and filed a restraining order against him. The damage Ginger did to Ronald's skull caused him to endure three months of physical therapy to learn how to speak properly again. The restraining order would keep Ronald one hundred feet away from Ginger for the next two years.

Ginger craved the attention that she'd never gotten from Ronald. Celeste was very protective of Ginger. Momma bear needed to watch her cub closely.

"How about dinner, Ginger?" Joseph asked her again.

Joseph was a fine specimen. But Ginger had been single for four months and it felt good to be stress free. She no longer had to worry about dirty dishes or strands of hair left in the sinks. She didn't need to worry about racing home to beat a curfew. In four months Ginger hasn't had to ask a man for permission to go to church on Sundays. She was living a celibate lifestyle. No more rapes that led to miscarriages. Ginger didn't know Joseph from a can of paint. He could very well be her knight in shining armor. But four months of freedom wasn't enough time for Ginger to have healed from the four years of abuse. She needed more time. "Joseph, your invitation to dinner is lovely and very much appreciated. But Celeste, Portia, and I have already made dinner plans." That was Ginger's way of turning Joseph down politely.

Celeste and Portia looked at Ginger like she was insane but kept quiet.

Ginger crushed Joseph's heart and the disappointed look on his face told it all. "Oh well, maybe next time then." He wasn't giving up on Ginger. He had read her body language. Joseph wasn't mistaken that she was interested. Ginger's eyes and smile told him she was. But something had kept her from connecting with him. She wasn't smiling anymore. Joseph didn't know what it was but he had all the time in the world to figure it out. Ginger had built barriers all around her. But one by one, Joseph decided that he'd knock them all down. He kissed the back of her Ginger's hand again then turned and walked away.

He had only stepped three feet away when Portia called after him. "Joseph?"

He paused then turned around to face the ladies.

"We're dining at Leona's Italian Restaurant on Madison Street. If you're ever in the mood for delicious Italian food, that's a good place."

Ginger's chin hit the floor. She couldn't believe what Portia had just done.

"Is that right?" Joseph asked Portia.

"Yep. Great food," Portia answered, not caring that she had just crossed a line with Ginger.

"Thanks. I'll keep that in mind," Joseph said. He looked at Ginger and smiled one last time before turning and exiting the church.

"Girl, are you a fool?" Portia asked Ginger when Joseph was out of earshot. "What's wrong with having dinner with the man? Celeste and I would have been there with you."

Ginger was hot. "First of all why did you tell Joseph where we're going to eat? What if he comes to the restaurant?"

"Humph, the way you just shot him down, you ain't even gotta worry about that. You could have at least accepted the man's dinner invitation, Ginger."

Ginger adjusted her purse strap on her shoulder. "I'm not ready yet."

"To do what? Eat some food?" Portia couldn't understand Ginger's hesitation.

"You can't force her to do something she's not ready for, Portia," Celeste said. "She's gonna mess around and miss her husband."

"Oh, Portia, please," Ginger said, waving her hand at Portia to dismiss her words. "Joseph is not my husband."

"How do you know?" Portia asked. "You won't even break bread with the man."

Ginger exhaled loudly. Her personal life and what she did with it was her business. "Look, I don't wanna talk about this. Can we please go and eat?"

Portia noticed Ginger's fed-up expression. "Don't get an attitude with me. I'm trying to help you out. I don't want you to miss out on a blessing, Ginger. We all know you're due for one."

"Trust me, when God sends my husband, I'll know it. I will hear God clearly when He speaks."

"Well, you need to clean the wax out of your ears because He just spoke," Portia stated and walked away.

At Leona's Italian Restaurant, Ginger, Celeste, and Portia were enjoying the all-you-can-eat salad and breadsticks while they waited for their main courses. Celeste was the first to reach for the second helping of the warm breadsticks as soon as their waitress set the basket on the table. Ginger and Portia watched in awe as Celeste swirled the breadstick on her salad plate to soak up the Italian dressing before inserting it into her salivating mouth.

"Celeste, you're really milking this all-you-can-eat thing, aren't you?" Portia teased.

Celeste took another bite of the breadstick. "All you can eat means eat all you can. And besides, I'm eating for two." She was ecstatic about her pregnancy. Celeste had given up all hope of conceiving. She and Anthony had come to terms that they would never become parents. After seeing Portia in the hospital room and after hearing what Ginger had done to Ronald, Celeste and Anthony had become close again. Anthony returned to the marriage bed and within a week Celeste was pregnant.

When Celeste had skipped her menstrual cycle, she didn't pay it any attention because that was normal for her. Her cycle was always all over the place and unpredictable. When she didn't get it the second month, Celeste had taken a home pregnancy test. When the color blue appeared on the white plastic stick, Celeste's heart skipped a beat but she didn't tell Anthony just yet. She made an appointment with Dr. Bindu and he confirmed to Celeste that she indeed was carrying a bun in her oven. Celeste was so happy that she hopped off of the examining table and hugged Dr. Bindu tight and kissed him on his cheek. Dr. Bindu congratulated Celeste, wrote her a prescription for prenatal vitamins, and sent her on her merry way.

On the way home from Dr. Bindu's office, Celeste stopped at a grocery store and purchased a small sheet cake with butter cream icing. She had the words "Congratulations, Daddy" put on it. She brought the cake home and set it on the kitchen table. When Anthony came home, Celeste was sitting at the kitchen table waiting for him. He walked into the kitchen and saw the cake.

He had a curious expression on his face. "Daddy?"

Celeste opened her hand and showed Anthony the stick with the blue line. She sang the words, "We're having a baby."

Anthony's eyes grew wide. He yelled and pulled Celeste from her chair. He picked her up and swung her around. "For real? For real?"

"Yes. I went to see Dr. Bindu today and he confirmed it."

Anthony was ecstatic. "We're really gonna have a baby in nine months?"

"Well, in about six months."

Anthony pulled Celeste into his arms. "This is the best news ever."

"Won't God do it?"

Portia looked at Celeste's mouth chewing at rapid speed. "Well, you look like you're eating for two hundred. You've already gained ten pounds in three months."

"So what?" Celeste said after swallowing a piece of the delicious seasoned breadstick. "I got my man already."

"Don't you wanna keep him?" Ginger asked.

Celeste rolled her eyes. "Girl, please. Tony ain't going anywhere. You should see all of the doughnuts, cookies, and candy he brings home for me to eat."

"Only because you beg for it," Portia reminded Celeste. "That baby weight will stay on after you drop the load."

"And how many babies have you had, Portia?" Celeste snapped. "Why are you so worried about what I eat and how much weight I gain?"

"Because I'll be the one who'll have to listen to you moan and cry about how wide your behind has gotten."

"As my sister, ain't that what you're supposed to do?"

"Absolutely not," Ginger chimed in. She reached across the table and removed the basket of breadsticks from Celeste's reach. "No more bread, Celeste."

If looks could kill, Ginger would be six feet under at that moment. But Celeste had already eaten four breadsticks so she didn't put up a fuss when Ginger took the basket away. Celeste made a mental note in her head to ask the waitress for breadsticks to take home with her. They would be her midnight snack.

The waitress came and set their entrees in front of them. The ladies lowered their heads and closed their eyes as Portia prayed. "Lord, we thank you for this fellowship. We're grateful for another opportunity for us to get together and feast because you know we like to eat. We ask that you bless the food and the hands that prepared it. Now, Lord, I ask that you touch Celeste. She thinks that just because she's pregnant she can inhale everything that crosses her nose."

Celeste and Ginger opened their eyes and looked at Portia.

"Help her to understand, Lord, that gluttony is a sin. Then, Lord, I ask that you touch Ginger right now. Open her eyes so that she can see a good man when he comes into her life. We ask these blessings in Jesus' name. Amen."

When Portia opened her eyes she saw that Ginger and Celeste were scowling at her. Ginger didn't appreciate Portia's prayer. "What the heck was that, Portia?"

She looked at Ginger and shrugged her shoulders.

"What did you mean by *we* ask these blessings? Celeste and I don't have a problem with the way our lives are going. If anyone needs prayer, it's you."

"Me?"

"Yes, you," Celeste answered.

"How do you figure I need prayer?"

"Well, for one, you talk too much. You knew Ginger didn't want to be bothered with that man from the church but you just had to tell him where we would be eating. If Ginger wanted him to know, she should have been the one to tell him, not you."

"I was just looking out for her, Celeste. What's wrong with that?"

Ginger inserted a forkful of lasagna into her mouth and spoke. "Will y'all quit talking about me like I'm not sitting at this table? First of all, Portia, you know what my motto is, and in case you've forgotten, I'll tell you again. I'm three times seven plus six. If you do the math you'll realize that that means I'm grown, fully grown at that. I can look out for myself."

"I can't tell. Joseph was practically begging you to have dinner with him. It's not like he was asking for your hand in marriage."

Ginger gently laid her fork down on the table then turned her whole upper body toward Portia.

"Uh-oh," Celeste mumbled. Ginger's body language told her that it was about to get heated in the restaurant. And whatever Ginger was getting ready to say to Portia, Celeste felt Portia had it coming. She was out of line and Ginger was right to put her in her place.

"You know what, Portia? Whomever I decide to dine with will be my decision, not yours. If you're so worried about somebody having dinner with Joseph then, darn it, you do it. Oops, my bad. You only deal with married men, don't you?"

"Uh-oh," Celeste mumbled again. She would've interceded and asked Ginger to lower her voice and calm down but Portia was way out of line. Ginger was telling her exactly what she needed to hear. While Ginger had the absolute right to let Portia know that she was crossing a boundary, Celeste wondered why Ginger would bring up Portia's past sin. It wasn't that long ago when the three of them had turned on each other when Ginger brought up Celeste's abortion that she had in high school. Now that Celeste was pregnant, she needed her best friends more than anything. She couldn't go through another separation from Ginger and Portia.

"Well, excuse the heck out of me for trying to be a friend," Portia responded to Ginger. "Maybe I should just shut my darn mouth."

"You definitely should," Ginger commented sarcastically.

Their waitress approached the table and asked if they needed anything else. Celeste told her that everything was wonderful and to quickly bring the check. She was thankful for the interruption and wanted to leave the restaurant before Ginger and Portia started up again.

"Your bill has already been paid, ma'am."

Portia, Ginger, and Celeste all looked at one another. "By whom?" Celeste asked the waitress.

"A gentleman came into the restaurant and asked for the waitress that was assigned to your table. When I approached him, he demanded that I bring him the bill." She looked at Ginger and extended a folded piece of paper to her. "This note is for you. The gentleman asked me to give it to the lady wearing the black dress."

Among the three of them, there would be no mistake who the waitress gave the note to. Portia was wearing a burgundy dress and Celeste wore a teal-green dress. Ginger took the note from the waitress's hand and read it out loud. "'Ginger, I pray that your lasagna was as satisfying to your taste buds as paying for it was to my heart. Joseph Banks.' OMG," Ginger said.

"Wow," Celeste commented on Joseph's note. "So what happens now?"

"Watch it, Celeste," Portia warned. "You know you can't get in her business."

Ginger glared at Portia and rolled her eyes. Clearly Portia was trying to get under her skin but she had a more important issue. Arguing with Portia would have to wait.

Ginger looked all around the restaurant but didn't see Joseph. She motioned for the waitress, who had walked away, to come back to their table. "The man that gave you this note, where is he sitting?"

"He didn't dine in," the waitress answered. "The gentleman requested the bill for this table and paid it. He wrote this note and asked me to give it to the lady in black when you were finished eating. Then he placed an order for takeout. He sat at the bar and waited for his order. When his order was brought to him, the gentleman left."

Ginger was impressed with what Joseph had done. She had shot him down when she rejected his dinner invitation at church. But he still thought enough of Ginger to come to the restaurant where he knew she would be dining and pay for her dinner, as well as Portia's and Celeste's dinners. Joseph was chasing her and Ginger liked that. But he had placed his order to go. Ginger felt bad that Joseph was home eating alone. She decided that if Joseph approached her again, she would engage him. She opened her purse and searched for her wallet. "Well, I can at least leave a tip."

"That won't be necessary, ma'am. The gentleman left a very generous tip."

"Aw, sookie, sookie, now," Celeste said. Her upper torso danced.

Ginger folded Joseph's note and put it in her purse and pouted. "I feel horrible."

"Well, you should feel horrible," Portia stated. It was too good to be true that her silence and non-meddling would last. "Got the poor man stalking you and paying for your meal while he has to dine home alone."

"I thought you were gonna mind your business," Ginger said. "Is that too much to ask for?"

Portia shrugged her shoulders. "I'm just saying."

"Please don't start up again," Celeste begged. "Let's all go home happy, okay? Morning service was good. Our dinner was good and free. And our little Gin-Gin here has an admirer. I say we order the biggest, most chocolatest dessert and splurge."

"Oh sure," Portia said. "It's always about food with you, ain't it, Celeste?"

Celeste picked up the dessert menu and scanned it. She exhaled. "Chocolate does wonders for the soul."

Chapter 10

A Blast from the Past

After Bible Study on Tuesday evening, Ginger excused herself from the sanctuary. Five minutes later she exited the ladies' room and was startled to see Joseph standing outside of the door, off to the side, waiting for her.

He looked in her eyes and smiled. "Hello, beautiful."

Ginger was surprised yet happy to see Joseph. Since he had paid for her, Celeste, and Portia's meal on Sunday, Ginger had not been able to dismiss Joseph from her mind. "Hi there," she said smiling. "I didn't know you were here in Bible class this evening."

"I got here a little late so I decided to sit in the back of the church. I didn't want to cause a scene. I didn't know you were here either until you stood up and left the sanctuary. I thought you were leaving the church. That's why I followed you. I wanted to talk to you." Joseph scanned Ginger's attire. The black slacks and cropped pumpkin-colored V-neck wrapped top she wore fit her nicely. He also took notice of the five-inch black patent leather stilettos Ginger wore. "You look beautiful tonight, Ginger."

Ginger was a dainty girl, extremely feminine, and took pride in her attire. She would try on four or five outfits before she made a decision. That evening the pumpkin-colored blouse, black slacks, and stilettos was the fifth outfit she had tried on. Ginger knew she had made the right decision because Joseph loved it.

"Thank you." Ginger scanned Joseph from head to toe. His navy blue slacks and pink button-down polo shirt looked good on him. Ginger admired a man who was secure enough in his manhood to wear the color pink. It was Ginger's favorite color. "You look nice yourself."

He smiled. "It's good to see you again. How have you been?"

"I've been well, thank you. And you?"

"Things are going well. My stove was finally delivered today. Now I can leave that fast food stuff alone and cook a meal and eat properly."

Ginger chuckled. "I know what you mean. Lords knows I've had more than my share of fast food lately. But I'm sure my hips can speak for themselves."

"Your hips are lovely, Ginger. Don't ever think differently."

Ginger's dark skin turned crimson red. She smiled in embarrassment. "Excuse me?"

"I didn't stutter, did I? I said your hips are lovely." Joseph paused. "And so are you."

Ginger stood looking at Joseph in amazement. She had no words.

By the expression on her face, Joseph knew he'd embarrassed Ginger so he opted to change the subject. "Did you enjoy your lasagna on Sunday?"

Ginger's thoughts were still on what Joseph said about her hips. Ronald had never said anything like that to her. He complained that her baby toe was shaped like a thumbtack. She recalled Ronald telling her that she was too short. Ginger remembered a time when she came home with a new short, tapered hairdo and Ronald told her that she looked like a man. Thinking back on Ronald's verbal abuse, Ginger had only heard part of Joseph's question. She shook her head vigorously from side to side and brought her attention back to the man standing in front of her. "I'm sorry, what did you say?"

"I asked if you enjoyed your lasagna on Sunday."

"Yes, I did. And I got your note. Portia, Celeste, and I thank you so much. But you didn't have to pay our bill, Joseph."

"Of course I had to pay. I was being obedient. My steps are ordered, Ginger."

Ginger laughed and mocked him. "God told you to pay for my dinner? Is that what you're saying?"

"When He speaks, I move." Joseph took a step closer to Ginger and looked into her eyes. "You wanna know what else He told me?"

She swallowed hard. Then she swallowed again. Ginger was afraid to ask Joseph what else God had told him. She didn't want to know. But she wondered who Joseph was and what was he doing in her life. Why was he there at that particular time?

Joseph noticed her hesitation and he asked the question again. "Do you wanna know what else God told me, Ginger?"

He stood so close to Ginger that she could smell his breath when he spoke. *Wintergreen Tic Tacs.* She knew exactly what it was. Ginger always carried a box of the small, white after-dinner mints in her purse. The warm but cool scent flowed through Gingers nostrils like a summer breeze. Ginger was intoxicated in his presence. Her equilibrium was off. She felt herself sway. She slowly opened her mouth and said, "Yes." The sound of her own voice brought Ginger out of the trance. "I mean no. I mean maybe, but not right now."

Joseph leaned in. Ginger's heart had started to race. His face was getting closer and closer to her face. *Oh, my God. He's gonna kiss me.*

Within an inch from Ginger's lips, Joseph moved to her left jawbone and whispered in her ear, "He told me that you were my wife, my Eve."

Ginger shifted her weight from her right leg to her left. Joseph was mesmerizing her. But she had only met him two days ago and he was already talking about marriage. He couldn't be serious. "You don't know anything about me."

"I know that you are an angel. And God doesn't send too many of those down here. He told me to get you while the getting was good."

At that moment Ginger knew that everything Ronald wasn't, Joseph was and more.

Joseph reached for Ginger's left hand and kissed the back of it softly. "Ginger, I know you're gonna run from me. I expect you to. But there will come a time when your legs are going to get tired and give out. That's when I'll be there to catch you. You are a prize and I'm pressing toward the mark for the prize of the high calling." He kissed the back of Ginger's hand again and walked out of the church doors.

Ginger stood still for a few moments taking everything that Joseph had just said in. She followed Joseph outside and saw him getting in his car. Ginger stood on the church steps and watched his car pull away from the curb. Though she didn't want to, Ginger liked Joseph. She liked the way he was wooing her. But it was foreign to Ginger. She didn't know how to receive it. And it had only been two days since she met Joseph. How in the world could he possibly know that she was his wife?

"But two days, Lord? Really?" she said out loud.

Ginger walked to her car, got in, and started the engine. She reached in her purse for her cellular telephone. She buckled her seat belt then pressed Celeste's home number on speed dial. A woman, a church member, walked by Ginger's car, tapped the driver's side window, and waved. Ginger waved and smiled at the woman just when Celeste answered her call.

"Hi, Gin-Gin," Celeste greeted her when she saw Ginger's cellular number on the caller ID.

"Hi, Momma Bear. I missed you and Portia at Bible class this evening. Where are you guys?"

"I haven't a clue where Portia might be. I was a little tired after work today. I've been on my feet all day and my ankles are swollen. I've been in bed since I got home."

Celeste was only four months pregnant but she behaved as though she were in her third trimester with twins. She complained that her breasts were sore. She complained that her back ached. She was already wearing maternity blouses that made her look as though she were wearing a tent. And now she complained that her ankles were swollen.

Ginger knew that having a baby had been Celeste's obsession since she and Anthony had gotten married. And Ginger was ecstatic when Celeste had shown her the blue mark on the home pregnancy test stick. And Ginger even screamed louder than Celeste when she had called Ginger with the good news when she had left Dr. Bindu's office with confirmation. But Ginger thought that Celeste was exaggerating her symptoms.

"If your ankles are swollen, you should soak your feet in Epsom salt. Do you have any? I could stop at Walmart and get it then bring it by."

"I sent Tony already. He should be back soon. So, how was Bible class?"

That was another thing that irritated Ginger. The way Celeste ran Anthony was absolutely ridiculous. Lately it seemed that every time Ginger talked with Celeste, Anthony was out chasing one of her cravings. From all the running he'd been doing, the poor man would be burnt out by the time the baby arrived.

"Well, that's what I called to talk with you about. Bible class was good but it's what happened afterward that's got me jacked up."

"Uh-oh," Celeste said. "Hold on, and I'll dial up Portia and get her on the line."

"No. Please don't." The last thing Ginger needed was Portia telling her what she should and shouldn't do about Joseph. It was one thing to give advice but Portia was bossy, opinionated, and thought she knew what was best for everyone. Ginger didn't want to argue, she just wanted to share with Celeste what happened with Joseph after Bible class. Had Portia been added to their conversation she would tell Ginger to run off and elope with Joseph that evening.

"Wow, that was a first," Celeste said when Ginger stopped her from calling Portia. The three of them often ended their days with a three-way chat.

"You know, Celeste, I just wanna talk and get some emotions out without being judged or made to feel inadequate. Portia isn't capable of controlling herself."

Celeste chuckled. She knew Ginger was speaking the truth about their friend. "Okay, so tell me what happened after Bible class."

Ginger settled in her driver's seat and exhaled. "I think I like Joseph, Celeste."

"You *think* you like him?"

She exhaled again. "I guess I really don't know how I feel but I definitely feel something for him. I stepped out of the ladies' room at church this evening and found Joseph standing off to the side waiting for me."

"Really?"

"He's so different from Ronald, Celeste."

"Uh, yeeeaaahhh. You think? Ronald had never stared you down with dreamy eyes, followed you to a restaurant, and paid for your meal."

"You got that right. And he never indicated that he wanted to marry me either."

Celeste was sitting up in bed. Her back came away from the pillows she was leaning against. "Joseph asked you to marry him?"

Ginger laughed at Celeste's high-pitched tone. "Of course not. But he told me that God told him that I was his wife. Joseph said that I was running from him but eventually he'll catch me. He called me his Eve."

"As in Adam and Eve?"

"That's the only Eve I know," Ginger said. "But it was the way Joseph said the words, Celeste. I mean he's so charming, and handsome, and . . . and . . ."

"And charming and handsome," Celeste said then laughed.

Ginger returned the laughter but had started to tear up. "I don't know what to do."

"You gotta get to know Joseph. Spend time with the man and learn who he is. Obviously he's convinced that he's found his soul mate. He likes what he sees and he's determined to make you his one and only. I love it."

Ginger wiped a tear away that had fallen on her right cheek. "But, Celeste, it's only been two days since I met the guy."

"Well, let me tell you something about God. When He does something, it doesn't take Him long."

On Wednesday morning Celeste sat at her station behind the counter, bowed her head for a quick word of prayer then removed the NEXT WINDOW sign. Immediately a lady approached. "Good morning, Celeste."

Celeste looked up and recognized an old friend she hadn't seen in years. "Hey, Latricia. It's been a long time. How are you doing, girl?"

"I'm fine." Latricia noticed the maternity blouse Celeste was wearing. "And I can see that you're doing fine too. How far along are you?"

Celeste rubbed her small round belly, something she loved to do. "I just started my my second trimester."

Latricia looked at the size of Celeste's stomach. It was the size of a large cantaloupe. "Really? I think either you or your doctor may have miscounted. Are you sure you're not having twins?"

"Girl, bite your tongue." Celeste chuckled. "God won't put no more on me than I can bear. He only gave me enough patience for one. I don't think Tony and I could handle two babies." Truth be told, because of Celeste's fertility issues, she would be over the moon if she gave birth to twins.

"It's good to know that you and Tony are still together," Latricia said. "So, how is Mr. Anthony Harper?"

Celeste looked at Latricia with a weird expression. "You know Tony?"

"Of course," Latricia said matter-of-factly. "Remember a couple of years ago? Down on Taylor Street? You and I were standing in line chatting while waiting to buy Italian ice. He walked up to you and kissed your neck. You introduced us then. You don't remember that?"

Celeste recalled that moment. "Oh, you're right. I remember now. Tony is fine. Thanks for asking. What brings you in here today?"

"I need to cash a check." Latricia opened her purse and pulled out her checkbook. She filled it out, turned it over, and endorsed the back. Then she gave the check to Celeste.

Celeste accepted the check and saw that Latricia had written the check for $3,500. She looked at Latricia.

"Oh, you need my ID?" Latricia asked when she saw how Celeste looked at her.

"Girl, no. I know who you are." Celeste keyed Latricia's bank account number into her desktop computer. Her eyes grew wide when she saw Latricia's balance.

$387,979.23 jumped out at Celeste in big, bold black numbers. She couldn't pull her eyes away from the computer screen.

Latricia noticed Celeste's hesitation. "Something wrong, Celeste?"

"Uh, no. From the balance on your account, I say that everything is right. Girl, what do you do for a living?"

"I don't work."

Celeste glanced at the computer screen again to make sure that she had indeed seen at least six digits. "You don't?"

"My husband is a motorman for the Chicago Transit Authority," Latricia offered.

Celeste smiled. "Really? So is Tony but our bank account don't look like yours."

"And we own four chicken shacks. David and I."

Celeste looked at the check Latricia had given her and saw two names on the top left corner. She was so intrigued by the amount of money in the bank account, Celeste hadn't noticed there was a second name. "David and Latricia Hall?" She looked up from the check at Latricia. "When did you get married?"

"A year ago," Latricia answered, smiling.

"Well, congratulations. How's married life?" Celeste asked.

"It has its ups and downs but, overall, we're happy."

Heck, with that kind of money you better be happy. "And that's all that matters, Latricia." Celeste stamped the check on the reverse side and opened the cash drawer. "How would you like your cash?"

"All hundreds would be good."

Humph, humph, humph. Must be nice. Celeste saw that she had only a few hundred-dollar bills in her drawer. She closed it. "You're the type of customer who requires a visit to the vault. I'll be back in a few." Celeste closed her cash drawer and stepped away.

She returned with a stack of one-hundred-dollar bills in her hand. "Here we are," she said. Celeste stood on the opposite side of the counter and started to count the money. She laid the bills on the counter one by one. "One hundred, two hundred, three hundred, four hundred, five hundred, six . . ." Celeste stopped counting. Something dawned on her.

She looked at the man's name on the computer screen: **David Hall**. Celeste could have sworn Portia said she was dealing with a guy with that same name who lived in the Chatham area. Celeste read the address on the account. Latricia and her husband resided in the 8800 block of South State Street, right in the heart of Chatham.

Celeste froze. *Oh, my God.*

Latricia noticed Celeste's hesitation in counting the money. "What's wrong, Celeste?"

Celeste quickly composed herself. "I thought I felt my baby move," she lied.

"Wow. That must feel so good."

"Yeah, it does." *Lord, please forgive me for lying.* Celeste continued counting the money, placed it in an envelope, and gave it to Latricia. "There you go. Will there be anything else for you today?"

Latricia placed the envelope in her purse. "Nope, this should hold me for a while."

Suddenly Celeste recalled that Portia also said that David drove trains. Celeste tried to breathe but couldn't. In shock she stood staring at Latricia with an open mouth.

"Celeste, are you okay? You look like you just seen a ghost."

Get it together, Celeste, she told herself. "Um, yeah, I'm all right. The baby is doing gymnastics. I haven't gotten use to it." Celeste was angry at Portia for putting her in that position.

On the back of a savings withdrawal slip, Latricia wrote down her home and cellular numbers. "Let's stay in touch, Celeste. And be sure to send me an invitation to your baby shower."

Celeste didn't quite smile at Latricia but she did the best she could. "Okay, Latricia. I sure will. You take care."

Latricia said her good-byes and walked away from Celeste's station. Before the next customer could approach her, Celeste set the NEXT WINDOW sign on the counter and went to the lounge to lie on a chaise chair. She put one hand on her belly and the other on her forehead then sighed. "Oh, my God," was all she could say.

"Attention, all teachers. Miss Brown, please come to the principal's office. Miss Brown, please come to the principal's office."

Ginger was in the middle of giving a spelling test when she heard the page. "Jamia, I want you to be in charge and take names," she said to the student who sat closest to her.

Jamia got excited. For once she got to rule the class. She got up from her own desk and sat in Ginger's seat behind the big desk. "Don't worry, Miss Brown. I got this."

"I'm sure you do, Jamia." Ginger looked at all the students and made an announcement. "I'll only be gone for a few minutes. I don't wanna see any names on Jamia's list when I get back. Is that clear?"

"Yes, Miss Brown," the class mumbled.

"I can't hear you," Ginger stated.

They yelled, "Yes, Miss Brown!"

Ginger left her classroom and walked down the corridor to the administration office and approached the twenty-year-old secretary. "Renita, did you page me?"

Renita had been filing folders into a cabinet when she looked at Ginger standing on the opposite side of her desk. "Yes, I did. Diane wants to see you in her office."

"Do you have any idea what she wants?"

Renita displayed a huge grin on her face. "Nope."

Ginger cocked her head to the side and looked at Renita curiously. "Yes, you do."

"No, I don't," Renita insisted and kept her smile.

"Then why are you smiling?"

"I can't smile?"

Ginger gave Renita a long stare then looked toward Diane's door and saw it closed. "Who's in there with her?"

"No one. She's waiting for you."

Ginger slowly walked to Diane's door and knocked. "It's open," Ginger heard Diane say. She turned the knob and walked in. She saw Diane sitting behind her desk.

"Why am I being paged in the middle of a spelling test?"

Diane looked up from a memo she was writing. "You had a delivery today, a special delivery, might I add."

Ginger frowned at her. "What kind of delivery?"

Diane nodded her head toward the sitting area in her office. Ginger looked to her right and saw roses on top of roses on top of roses. "What in the world?"

Diane stood up and walked around her desk. She grabbed Ginger's hand and practically skipped over to the sitting area. "Girl, you're looking at five dozen roses. Count them. Five. Dozen. For Ginger Brown. All five of them, girl." Diane walked around the table where the roses were sitting in glass vases and counted them. "One, two, three, four, five. See, I told ya. Five dozen roses, girl." Next to the first dozen was a small envelope with Ginger's name on it. Diane picked it up and gave it to her. "Open it."

Ginger tore the envelope open, pulled out a small white card, and read it silently.

Diane exploded with anticipation. "Who are they from?"

"If you'd let me finish the card, you'll know," Ginger fussed.

Diane pulled a chair out from under the table and sat down on the edge of the seat. "Read it out loud."

Ginger looked at Diane. "Diane, you act like you're sitting on the front row at a male strip club. Haven't you ever received flowers before?"

"Nope. I have to live vicariously through other people. Will you please read the card?"

Ginger knew Diane was anxious to find out who had sent her the roses to the school. "What are you willing to do to get me to read it?" Ginger teased.

"I might just give you a beat down if you *don't* read it."

Ginger chuckled. "It's written in calligraphy and it reads as follows." She looked at Diane. "Can a sista get a drum roll, please?"

Diane was more than happy to oblige. She turned toward the table and started tapping it quickly with both hands. Before Ginger could get the first word out, Diane's telephone rang. Ginger saw that she wasn't paying it any attention.

"Aren't you gonna answer your phone?"

"Nope. Read the card."

If Ginger didn't know any better she would've thought Diane was a dope addict waiting for her next fix. "It could be important. What if it's a call you don't wanna miss?"

Diane exhaled and balled up her lips. "Ginger, in about one minute you're gonna be missing two front teeth. Read the darn card."

"Okay, okay," Ginger said. "Let's not get hostile." She looked at Diane's hands then at her eyes.

"What?" Diane asked hastily.

"I told you that I need a drum roll."

Diane impatiently began tapping the table again. "I'm two seconds off of you, Ginger."

Ginger brought the card to her face and read it. "'Roses are red, violets are blue. Buying you dinner and flowers can't compare to what I'm prepared to bestow upon you. Ginger, these roses are beautiful but they don't measure up to the beauty I see in you. Joseph Banks.'"

Diane leaned back in the chair and crossed her left leg over her right knee. "Who is Joseph Banks and where can I get me one just like him?"

Ginger was smiling wide as she place the card back in its envelope. "Joseph is a man I met in church on Sunday. He asked me to dinner and invited Portia and Celeste to come along. I turned him down and told him the three of us already had dinner plans but big mouth Portia just had to tell him where we would be eating. He came to the restaurant and requested the bill for our table, paid it, and left. And last night at church I bumped into Joseph when I was coming out of the bathroom. He was standing there waiting to tell me that I was an angel sent from above and God told him to get me while the getting was good. He also said that God revealed to him that I was his Eve."

Diane was impressed. "Wow. So, what are you gonna do?"

Ginger sat down in a chair next to Diane. "Diane, Joseph seems nice but I don't know him. After all the mess Ronald put me through, how do I know that I can trust Joseph?"

"Ginger, are you sure that you've crossed that bridge with Ronald?" Diane asked. It seemed that Ginger was holding on to feelings she may still have for Ronald.

"Not only did I cross it, Diane; I burned every step behind me so I wouldn't cross back, even if I wanted to."

"Well, if there's no turning back, the only thing to do is move forward, honey. And if you ask me, dinner and five dozen roses was the right kind of inspiration that you needed to put your feet in gear."

Ginger looked at all the roses Joseph had sent. "I hear you, Diane. One thing puzzles me though. How did Joseph know where to find me?"

They both said at the same time, "Big mouth Portia."

At the end of the day, Ginger went back to Diane's office to retrieve her roses and saw that Diane had left already. Ginger set one of the vases on her desk. She wrote "Now someone can live vicariously through you" on a Post-it note and pasted it to one of the roses. Ginger looked at the four remaining vases filled with beautiful red roses.

Speaking with Diane helped Ginger realize that she couldn't run from love. If Joseph was heaven-sent, then Ginger would accept her blessing with open arms. "Okay, Lord, I don't know where this is going to lead, but I trust you."

Chapter 11

A Dam Situation

Ginger walked in her front door and set two vases of roses she was carrying on the cocktail table. Since the day she beat Ronald with the rolling pin, Ginger entered her home through the front door. She went back to her car and retrieved the other two vases and brought them inside. After fluffing and sniffing the roses for what seemed like the hundredth time, Ginger pressed the play button on her answering machine. The first message was from Celeste.

"Ginger, gurrrrlllll, call me as soooooon as you get in. You won't believe what I found out today." Beep.

"Hmm, sounds like you have some good, hot gossip, Celeste," Ginger murmured.

"Ginger, I did something I hope you'll forgive me for. That guy, Joseph, begged me for your work location. Please don't be mad." Beep.

"I know you can't help yourself, Portia. You're just a busybody," Ginger said to the answering machine. She erased both messages and went to her bedroom and changed from her work clothes into a pair of palazzo pajamas. She was walking into the kitchen to see what she would make herself for dinner when the loud shrill of the telephone startled her. Ginger grabbed the receiver from the wall next to the refrigerator. "Hello?"

"Did you get my message?" Celeste rushed the words from her lips.

"Yes, Celeste, I got your message about ten seconds ago. I was gonna call you back but can a sista get in the door, sit down, and kick her heels up first?"

"Are you in the door yet?"

"Yes."

"Are you sitting down?"

Ginger pulled a chair out from beneath the new marble kitchen table and sat down. "Yes."

"Did you kick your heels up?"

"Yes, Celeste!" Ginger yelled into the receiver. "What is so urgent?"

"Do you remember Latricia Jenkins from high school?"

Ginger tried to imagine a face to go with the name. "Uh-uh."

"Yes, you do. She's the girl who used to pull the fire alarm just so that we could get out of class. Remember?"

"Oh, yeah," Ginger said when her memory cooperated. "The chubby girl with the thick glasses. We were juniors then. Man, those were some good times."

"Well, she ain't chubby anymore and she lost those bifocals. Anyway, Latricia came into the bank today to cash a check."

"How is she doing?" Ginger asked.

"She's fine. She said she got married a year ago."

"Good for her."

"I don't know how good it really is, Ginger," Celeste said remembering the information she had found out earlier that day.

"What do you mean?"

"Latricia is married to a guy named David Hall and they live in the Chatham community."

Ginger didn't see how Celeste concluded that Latricia and her husband living in the Chatham area of the city couldn't be good. Chatham was an excellent community. "Uh-huh. And?"

"Ginger, what did Portia say her current beau's name was? And where did she say he lived?"

Ginger's mouth fell open. She sat straight up in her chair. "Oh, my God. You think it's the same David Hall?"

"I hope it's not the same guy, Ginger. Do you remember where Portia said David worked?"

"She was bragging that he made a lot of money working for the Chicago Transit Authority. She was all excited that she found another sugar daddy to pay her rent."

"That's what I remembered too. And Latricia said her husband drove the trains for the Chicago Transit Authority," Celeste confirmed.

Ginger's mouth fell open again. "Celeste, no."

"I'm telling you, Ginger, I was too outdone. You see how small this world is?"

"You really think it's him?" Ginger asked.

"How many David Hall's can there be living in the Chatham community and working for the Chicago Transit Authority?"

Ginger shook her head from side to side. "Humph, humph, humph," she moaned. "Portia should be ashamed of herself. How did Latricia seem? Did she appear to be happy when she mentioned her husband?"

"She said she and David had their ups and downs. That's no different from any other marriage. God knows Anthony and I certainly have taken our ride on the rollercoaster of love. Latricia looked healthy and pretty though. And she doesn't have to work."

"Humph, if I had a husband pulling a choo-choo, I wouldn't be working either," Ginger stated.

"Not only is Mr. David Hall supporting a wife who cashes thirty-five-hundred-dollar checks for play money, he's also taking good care of Portia." Celeste recalled the balance in Latricia and David's bank account. "And judging from the amount of money they have in the bank, heck, David could support Latricia, Portia, and about four or five other women, if he wanted to. And, Ginger, you and I both know that our sista is a high-maintenance chick."

Ginger was intrigued. "Well, how much money do they have?"

"You know I can't tell you that but I will say this. David and Latricia ain't hurtin' at all, honey. They ain't hurtin' at allllllll."

Ginger chuckled. "If I'm not mistaken, isn't David the cosigner of Portia's brand-new Escalade?"

"Cosigner and note payer."

"You'd think after the beating Richard put on Portia for giving his wife a heart attack, she would be done with married men."

"Humph, Portia didn't even flinch when she found out that Richard's wife had died."

"You're right," Ginger stated. "She didn't even accept any fault in it at all. No remorse or regret. Portia moved on to the next married man."

Celeste exhaled. "It's like she has no conscience. I don't know why she can't find her own man."

"Because it's a game to her, Celeste. Portia doesn't wanna be in a committed relationship. She claims she doesn't want to be smothered. She knows that a married man will go home to his wife at night and that's just fine with her. Portia's motto has always been, 'You don't have to love and live with a man for him to take care of you'."

"Well, you know what, Ginger? One of these wives will eventually catch up with Portia and beat the crap out of her much worse than the hurtin' Richard put on her. These women aren't playing when it comes to their husbands. David has a great job and the CTA has excellent benefits. Latricia doesn't have to work. You think she's just gonna let Portia take her husband from her? And did I mention that Latricia and David own four chicken shacks? She ain't letting that man go."

"But that's the thing, Celeste. Portia doesn't want David like that. She's not trying to take these men away from their wives. She's in these relationships for the security the men give her."

"That doesn't make it right, Ginger."

"Oh no, don't get me wrong. I'm not making excuses for her trifling behind. What Portia is doing is totally wrong as two left feet and I'll be the first to say that. I'm just telling you how she thinks. She doesn't want a ring from these men, only money."

That bit of information didn't settle well with Celeste. She didn't care what Ginger was talking about. Celeste loved her husband and she took her marriage seriously. And, yes, Portia was her very best friend but Celeste meant what she said in Ginger's living room, months ago, when the three of them had argued. Celeste told Portia that she couldn't trust her around Anthony. The words were said in anger but Celeste meant them wholeheartedly. It was all about the money as far as Portia was concerned and she didn't care whose husband was supplying it. Celeste couldn't say that even though she and Portia were as close as sisters, Portia would never make a play for Anthony. "Be that as it may, these wives won't understand that. If they see a woman trespassing on their territory, all heck will break loose."

Ginger sensed hostility in Celeste's voice. "Why are you so upset? This is Latricia's problem."

"A chick like Portia is every married woman's problem. In the bank earlier today, Latricia was happy and she seemed fulfilled. She gave me the impression that she was content in her marriage but I know the real deal." Celeste placed herself in Latricia's shoes. What if Anthony was paying for another woman's rent, car note, hair, and nails on the down low? It would destroy Celeste if she found out that Anthony was rolling in between bed sheets with someone else. "I'm upset because I'm a wife and I don't know what I'd do if I found out Tony was knocking boots with a Jezebel and paying for it."

"Darn, Celeste, you may as well come on out and call Portia a whore."

"Ginger, will I be lying if I did? I love Portia just as much as you do but we both know these married men pay her top dollar for booty. They're not giving her twenty bucks here and there. Portia gets her rent paid, car note paid, jewelry, and furs for sex. Now you tell me, if she's not a whore, what is she? I know Tony loves me. He tells me every day. And I'm positive David Hall is telling Latricia that he loves her, too."

Ginger heard Celeste loud and clear. But Portia wasn't cheating by herself. The married men she dealt with were more than willing to commit adultery. "Well, Celeste, you can't fault only Portia. It takes two to tango."

"I'm aware of that, Ginger. But women need to know that we cheapen ourselves when we sleep with married men. We accept the fact that we will always be second and never number one. Who wants to sneak, creep, and hide all the time? Only women with low self-esteem and no morals who don't think they're worth anything or that they deserve better. It's rare that a man leaves his wife for a trick and if he does, he'll do the same thing to the trick that he did to his wife. Yeah, it takes two to tango but a man could only dance around a chick if she allows him to."

"What can I say, Celeste? You are right. Portia doesn't care what the outcome will do to the wife. Finding out about a cheating spouse, man or woman, can be devastating and tragic. Look what happened to Richard's wife. She died of a heart attack. I fault Portia for that. Our sister or not, she's a woman and she should know better."

For years Ginger and Celeste had driven down that road with Portia. Trying to get her to realize that she was wrong for carrying on with another woman's husband was like talking to a brick wall.

"Portia is grown, Celeste. How many times have we confronted her about the way she's living? If she wants to sleep with married men, she'll do it. There's nothing we can do about it no matter how much we preach."

Celeste agreed. "You're right. The only thing we can do is be at the hospital when they call us 'cause married women don't play when chicks like Portia threaten their marriages. "

"Well, since there's nothing we can do about Portia, let's change the subject." Ginger was more than happy to change the subject to a happier one. "Guess what I got today."

"What?" Celeste asked.

"Mr. Joseph Banks sent five dozen red roses to the school."

"Well, I am not at all surprised. The man is serious and he's coming correct. So, what are you gonna do about it?" Celeste hoped Ginger would let her guard down and stop running.

"Diane asked me that same question. The truth is I don't know what I'm going to do. I don't know the man, where he's from or anything."

"Ginger, you're the one preventing that information from coming forth. Obviously, Joseph wants to share it with you but you won't give him the time of day. Don't block the blessing, girl."

"But after all I've been through—"

"Stop it right there, Ginger. Do you hear yourself talking? You said, 'after all I've been through.' Understand what you're saying. You've been through some mess but you survived it. You are no longer in that mess. You should've been at church when Associate Minister Gordon preached a sermon titled 'Your Blessing Is on the Other Side of Through.' You're in a dam situation, Ginger."

Ginger frowned. "A what situation?"

"A dam situation. You know what a dam is, don't you? A dam is a body of water confined by a barrier. Ronald represented the barrier in your life. He blocked everything God wanted you to have. But Ronald is gone now. You've got to knock the barrier down and you do that by seeing yourself blessed, seeing yourself prosper, and seeing yourself taking back everything the devil stole from you. You know what happens when a hole is punched in a barrier? Water oozes through the hole. But when the barrier is knocked completely down, the dam gushes forth and saturates everything in its path. Going back to what Minister Gordon preached about. Your blessing, which is the dam, is on the other side of through, which is the barrier. Joseph Banks is in the dam. And so far, by getting rid of Ronald you've only punched a small hole in the barrier. According to Joseph's card, only dinner and five dozen roses were able to ooze through that small hole. He said that couldn't compare to what he's prepared to bestow upon you. If Joseph is able to squeeze dinner and flowers through a small hole, can you imagine what he has on the other side of the barrier?"

Tears had begun to flow from Ginger's eyes. Celeste was preaching. "But I don't know who Joseph is, Celeste. My instincts tell me he is a wonderful man but I feel like God brought him into my life at the wrong time. I'm not prepared for Joseph."

"That's how God works, honey. And just so you know, He never does anything at the wrong time. When you least expect it, He will drop a bomb on you. And from what I can see Joseph Banks is *da bomb*. You claim you don't know Joseph but you don't know what else is in the dam either. And since when are the saints of God allowed the privilege to tell Him how and when to bless us or who to bless us with? My advice to you is to trust God and knock down that barrier and let Joseph and everything else come gushing at you. It's time for you to live, Ginger. Don't make the mistake of allowing *fear* to *interfere* with your future." Celeste hoped Ginger picked up on the dynamic of the words she just spoke to her. "In Malachi, chapter three, God says that He'll open a window and pour you out a blessing that you won't have room enough to receive it. So, my sista, I'll ask the question again. What are you gonna do?"

Sniff, sniff. Ginger wiped the tears from her eyes. "I'm gonna break through the barrier."

Celeste smiled. She was pleased. "That's what I'm talkin' about. Get out of that dam situation and go get your stuff, girl. Walk toward the light, Carol Ann. Walk toward the light."

Ginger burst out laughing at Celeste's chosen line from the movie *Poltergeist*.

On Saturday evening Portia and Celeste watched Ginger pace Celeste's living room as they all waited for Joseph to ring the doorbell.

"Ginger, you have on six-inch stilettos," Portia said. "They're made for sitting pretty, not walking."

Ginger couldn't stop pacing. "I know, I know. I'm so nervous. Celeste, I really thank you for allowing Joseph to pick me up here. I don't want him to know where I live yet."

Celeste waved her hand at Ginger. "Girl, please. You act like we haven't done this before. Remember when I met Tony? For the first four months of our relationship, he thought I lived with Portia." Celeste looked across the living room at Portia sitting on a divan. "Remember that, Portia?"

"I sure do. Tony called my apartment so many times looking for you he got on my nerves. Every twenty minutes, it was ring, ring, ring. 'Is Celeste home?' Tony kept calling like he thought I was lying about your whereabouts. I don't care how much you deny it, Celeste. I think you were breaking Tony off a piece for him to sweat you like that."

"What? Girl, please, Tony had to marry me before he got this candy."

Ginger laughed at her. "Celeste, why do you always refer to your vajayjay as candy?"

"Because it's sweet," Celeste boasted. "Whenever you hear Tony say to me, 'Give me some sugar,' he ain't always talking about a kiss."

The three ladies were laughing at Celeste's comment when Anthony walked in from the kitchen. In his hands was a glass of water and two tiny pink pills. Immediately the laughter stopped.

He looked at them. "Don't get quiet now. I know you're in here male bashing."

Celeste, Ginger, and Portia were silent with mischievous grins on their faces.

Anthony approached Celeste. "It's time for your prenatal medicine, baby."

Celeste took the glass and pills from Anthony's hand. She popped the pills in her mouth and chased them with three gulps of water. She gave Anthony the glass. "Thank you, babe."

Anthony was about to leave the ladies alone when the doorbell rang. "I got it." He set the glass on the cocktail table and went toward the door. He opened the door and welcomed Joseph into his home. "Hey, man, how are you doing? I'm Tony, Celeste's husband."

Joseph stepped into the living room and shook Anthony's hand firmly. He recognized Anthony's face from church. "I'm Joseph Banks. It's nice to meet you."

Anthony escorted Joseph farther into the living room and they both saw Ginger sitting on the sofa sandwiched in between Portia and Celeste. Anthony wondered when they had taken that position. Before Joseph rang the doorbell Portia was sitting on the divan near the window, Celeste was seated in a chair next to the fireplace, and Ginger was doing her best to wear a hole in the carpet in the middle of the living room. Now they look like sardines in a can.

"Good evening, ladies," Joseph greeted them.

They all presented the same silly grin. "Good evening, Joseph," they answered in unison.

Anthony chuckled. "Are y'all Charlie's Angels now?"

Joseph walked to Ginger and reached for her hand. She gently placed her hand in his and stood. He saw the mauve-colored knee-length fitted ribbed wrap dress she was wearing. "You're breathtaking. I've been waiting all day for the chance to see your face again."

Ginger blushed. "My goodness. Thank you, Joseph." Never in all of her life had a man told Ginger that he had been waiting to see her.

"Thank *you* for accepting my invitation to dinner. My heart is pleased. I am in awe just standing here in your presence. You excite my soul."

Portia and Celeste were in awe of Ginger's beau. Anthony's eyebrows rose from Joseph's statement to Ginger and he had to admit that Joseph was smooth. Anthony would have to use that line on Celeste. *You excite my soul, Celeste,* Anthony imagined himself saying.

"Joseph, Ginger, why don't you sit for a while?" Celeste offered.

"Yeah, let's all sit and chat," Portia added.

Joseph glanced at his wristwatch. "I'm sorry but we can't. Our reservations are in a half hour." He turned to walk toward the front door with Ginger's hand in his. Joseph extended his free hand to Anthony. "Tony, it was a pleasure."

Anthony accepted Joseph's handshake and said, "Likewise. Be careful with my girl. She means a lot to me."

Joseph turned around and looked at Ginger's best friends. "Celeste, Portia, it was good seeing you again."

When Ginger and Joseph exited the living room, Anthony shut the door behind them, then leaned his right shoulder against it and looked at Portia and Celeste still seated on the sofa. "That guy is all right with me. Did y'all hear the line he dropped on Ginger?"

Portia stood up. "Yeah, we heard it." She looked at Celeste. "You ready?"

"Yep," Celeste said, rising from the sofa. She started toward her bedroom. "Just let me get my purse."

"Where are y'all going?" Anthony asked.

Celeste stopped walking and looked at him. "On Ginger's date."

Anthony shook his head from side to side. He couldn't believe they still chaperoned each other's first dates. Celeste had told Anthony years ago they'd been doing it since high school. "When are y'all gonna let each other grow up?"

Portia grabbed her purse and cellular telephone from the cocktail table. "It won't be tonight. And you do know that Ginger and I weren't seated far from you and Celeste on your first date."

Anthony jogged his memory. "I took Celeste on a horse and carriage ride downtown."

"I know. Ginger and I were two carriages behind you."

Celeste returned to the living room with her purse and keys. "We'll be at Bocce's," she said to Anthony. "Call my cell phone if you need me."

"Bocce's? Is that where Joseph is taking Ginger?"

"Yep," Portia answered.

"But you need reservations," he said.

Celeste placed the strap of her purse on her shoulder. "We have them."

Anthony was on board. "Okay, well I'm going too. A brother can go for a nice, juicy steak."

Chapter 12

Oh, Taste and See

Five months later, on a Saturday morning, Ginger walked into A Million Starr's Beauty Salon. Starr, the owner of the salon, greeted Ginger. "Well, if it isn't Miss Ginger Brown." She patted the back of the chair she was standing behind. "Come on and sit down. I'm ready for you."

"Hey, Starr," Ginger said as she made her way to the chair and sat down. "I've got a date tonight and you know I like to be sexy. So, hook me up."

Starr covered Ginger's blouse with a vinyl cape. "Girl, I've been doing your hair every two weeks for the past three years. Can you name a time you left my chair when you weren't sexy?"

Ginger had to admit that each and every time she left Starr's chair she looked like a million dollars. Whether it took Starr four hours to braid Ginger's hair for a sew in, or a two-hour straw set, or if Ginger opted for a relaxer, press, and curl, Starr had special skills. "No, I can't say that I can but tonight I gotta be exceptionally sexy."

Starr stood behind Ginger's chair and looked at her reflection in the vanity mirror. "Look at that glow. Joseph must be something special."

A huge grin appeared on Ginger's face. Every time she sat in Starr's chair, she couldn't help herself from sharing how happy she was with Joseph. "He's a keeper."

Beauticians, barbers, and bartenders often served as a listening ear for when their clients needed to vent and Starr was no different.

In the past years it wasn't unusual for Starr to style Ginger's hair to hide bruises on the sides of her face and neck area. The first time Ginger arrived at the salon with a busted lip at the violent hands of Ronald, Starr was quick to pick up the telephone and call the police. Ginger had begged and pleaded with Starr to not involve the police. Two weeks later when Ginger sat in Starr's chair she couldn't hide the dark purple marks on the nape of her neck.

When Ginger confessed to Starr that she had finally taken her life back and had gotten Ronald out of it, Starr told Ginger that she was proud of her. She had given Ginger a complimentary wash and roller set.

"Good for you, Ginger. Just the mention of Joseph's name and you automatically show all thirty-two teeth. I love it. You got that pregnant woman's type of glow."

Ginger chuckled. "Well, I can assure you that it ain't that. Joseph doesn't even come at me like that. We've been seeing each other for five months and he's been the perfect gentleman. We've talked about sex and he knows how I feel on the subject. Since Ronald has been gone, I've been keeping myself. I asked God to clean me up and I promised Him that I would go to my husband pure. And since Joseph insists that he's my husband he's willing to wait for me."

"Wow. You don't find that kind of love often, Ginger. I hope you're cherishing it."

Ginger smiled. "I definitely am."

"Well, bring that glow on over to the sink."

Ginger stood and followed Starr to the row of sinks and sat in a chair then leaned back. Starr turned on the water and waited for it to become the perfect lukewarm temperature. "So, how are Portia and Celeste?"

"Portia is Portia. She ain't ever gonna change. Still chasing other women's husbands."

That bit of information stunned Starr. "No. Really?" She knew all about Portia's ex-boyfriend almost beating her to death for the cause of his wife's heart attack. "Is she still behaving badly?"

"You heard what I said," Ginger answered.

When the water had gotten to the temperature comfortable enough for Ginger's head, Starr used the sprayer to wet it. "How's Celeste's baby coming along? Isn't she due to deliver soon?"

"She's got a couple more weeks to go. That baby can't come fast enough for me. I wish Celeste would drop that load today because she is evil as heck. Her hormones are all over the place."

Starr lathered Ginger's hair with shampoo. "Really?"

"Celeste is driving everyone around her totally nuts. And poor Tony. I don't see how he maintains his own sanity. She yells at him for breathing, screams at him if he uses a certain brand of soap that upsets her stomach, and hollers at the top of her lungs if he makes the least bit of noise while she's napping. The poor man has to think that Celeste's pregnancy is more of a curse than a blessing."

"Are you serious, Ginger? Is she that bad?" The times Celeste had come to the salon to get her hair done, Starr found her to be as pleasant as she had always been.

"Humph," Ginger commented. "Bad ain't even the word, Starr. Celeste has lost her ever-loving mind. She's rude to the customers at the bank, and it has come to the point that Portia and I don't even want to be around her at all."

Starr rinsed the shampoo from Ginger's hair then saturated it with conditioner. "Hopefully when Celeste delivers the baby she'll be her old self again."

"I guess time will tell. Portia and I are hosting her baby shower next Saturday, Starr. Portia and I are late planning it but we hope the baby will hold off making its debut until after the shower. You should come."

"Saturdays are my busiest days and you know I gotta make my money. But I'll be sure to send Miss Mean Girl a gift." Starr combed the conditioner through Ginger's hair. "So, what are we doing to your hair today?"

"Whatever you want, Starr. I'm easy. Just make me look good for my man tonight."

"Oh yeah, you're definitely smitten." Starr chuckled.

It was near closing time when Joseph reached across the table and caressed Ginger's hand. "You look absolutely stunning tonight." Joseph was always full of compliments and Ginger loved it.

They were seated in a booth at the Rainforest Café in downtown Chicago. The lights in the dining room were dim and candles were lit on all of the tables in the restaurant.

Starr had cut Ginger's hair in a short feather style. It was tapered at the neck. It gave Ginger a more seductive yet sleek look. She smiled. "Thank you. And you are exceptionally handsome."

He looked at Ginger's half-eaten meal. "Did you enjoy your dinner?" On Ginger's plate was the remainder of chicken Alfredo with tomatoes and broccoli.

"It was delicious. Any type of pasta with Alfredo sauce is my favorite." She saw that Joseph's plate was bare of any morsels. "I see you really liked your barbecue ribs."

Joseph leaned back against the seat. "You're making me fat. You know I sit behind a camera every day. Some folks say the camera adds ten pounds."

Ginger laughed out loud. "*I'm* making you fat? Who is the one always wanting to go out to eat?"

"You never turn down my invitations. I have yet to hear you say, 'Joseph, instead of us going out to dinner, how about we stay in. I could make you a bologna sandwich.'"

Ginger laughed out loud. "First of all bologna is for suckas. And second, I ain't nobody's fool. If a man is willing to woo me, you best believe that I'm gonna take full advantage." Being with Joseph was the closest Ginger had ever come to feeling as though she was in a meaningful relationship.

Ginger rubbed her hand across the back of her new haircut. "Besides this girl is getting used to being treated like a queen."

For months Joseph had charmed Ginger. Because she had shared with him the troubled relationship she had with Ronald, Joseph was determined to make Ginger feel special, safe, and secure.

He cocked his head to the side and looked across the table at her. "Is that how I treat you, Ginger? Like a queen?"

"Yes." Ginger paused for a moment. "Can I tell you something, Joseph?"

"You can always tell me anything. What's on your mind?"

"I just wanna say that—"

Ginger's words were interrupted when a gang of waiters and waitresses started to sing the happy birthday song to a man seated in a booth behind her. Ginger looked over her shoulder and smiled when the man had blown out candles on a small cake the gang had brought to his table.

"Aw, that's so nice," Ginger mumbled.

"What were you going to say?" Joseph was very interested in what Ginger had started to say to him. He didn't want her to forget her thoughts.

Ginger connected her eyes with Joseph's. "I just wanted to say that these past five months have been wonderful for me."

"For me as well," Joseph admitted. "I love every moment that we spend together. You are a breath of fresh air."

As usual Joseph was blowing Ginger's mind with his compliments. His words were the complete opposite of "You're pathetic," or "You disgust me," or "I'm sick of you," which had been spoken in her ears for years.

"You talk so good," she said dreamily.

"I mean what I say and I say what I mean. You're easy to love, Ginger. And I do love you. Very much."

Ginger was stunned at what Joseph had just said. No man had ever uttered those three words to her. There were a few times in the past five months when Ginger felt that Joseph was on the verge of saying them but he never did. It never crossed Ginger's mind that she was worthy of receiving a man's love. For so long the enemy had convinced Ginger that she was useless and incapable of being treated the way a woman should. The three words were overwhelming and Ginger's emotions crept up on her. She placed her face in her hands and cried.

Ginger's reaction wasn't what Joseph had expected. He imagined Ginger shouting out and throwing her arms around his neck when he revealed his true feelings for her. He rose from his seat and joined Ginger on her side of the booth. He put his arms around her shoulder. "Hey, hey, hey. Why the tears? Was it something I said?" he asked half jokingly.

Ginger wiped her eyes and looked at him. The way she behaved must have proved to Joseph that she was the biggest nutcase on the earth. "I'm so sorry, Joseph. I'm behaving like a total idiot."

"The last thing I want to do is see you cry."

"It's just that what you and I have is foreign to me. And I love you too, Joseph. I really do. But coming from an abusive relationship causes me to always doubt your feelings. I feel like my life is a maze of emotions and I can't seem to find my way out. Do you understand what I'm saying to you?"

"Of course I do. I understand that you've never been loved by a man. Is that a fair statement?"

More tears fell onto Ginger's cheeks. "It's an absolutely fair statement. And it's sad because, having not been loved before, I don't know how to receive it from you."

It wasn't until that moment, when Joseph sat next to Ginger, and heard those words, that he fully understood how deeply she was scorned. "What did that creep do to you?"

He understood why Ginger never wanted him to walk directly behind her. Often times Ronald would strike Ginger from behind when she wasn't expecting it. Ginger made sure that Joseph was ahead of her at all times.

"Ronald was the devil. He was evil," she said. "I'm so glad that I had the courage to press charges against him for what he did to me. He won't be getting out of prison anytime soon."

Joseph was angry at Ronald for placing Ginger in that state of mind. He wanted to pay Ronald a visit and show him what it felt like to be punched, kicked, and battered. He took Ginger's hand inside his. "I have a mother and three sisters. And I wouldn't think twice about killing a man if he put his hands on any of them. My father raised me the old-school way. He taught me to be a man. A man who protects his woman, his family. It's my duty, Ginger, to love you like you deserved to be loved."

Ginger looked into Joseph's eyes. "I wish I could've met your father. It sounds like he was a great man."

"He was. May God rest his soul. My mother and sisters were the apples of his eye. And that's what you are to me, Ginger. My apple."

Ginger smiled so much that evening her cheekbones were becoming sore. It felt so wonderful to be in the presence of a man who truly cherished her. At that moment Ginger knew that Joseph had been sent from God. And she was no longer going to allow the enemy to keep her from accepting her blessing. Ronald was in her past and Ginger was going to leave him there. From that moment on Ginger would embrace her future. She was open and ready to receive Joseph and all of the love he had to offer her. She wrapped her arms around Joseph's neck and kissed him.

The manager of the restaurant approached their table. "Evening, folks."

Joseph struggled with himself to pull his lips away from Ginger's. "Evening."

"The restaurant is closing in fifteen minutes." He saw Ginger's plate was half full and pointed to it. "Would you like a takeout container for that?"

"Yes. And a slice of your key lime pie to go, please." Ginger was in a good mood. She felt dessert was in order.

The manager smiled. "You got it." He walked away.

Ginger yawned then laid her head on Joseph's shoulder.

"You're not tired, are you?"

Ginger looked at her wristwatch. "It's nearly midnight. I had an early start this morning."

"But the night is still young." He wasn't ready to part from Ginger's company.

The waiter was back at their table with Ginger's dessert and a small Styrofoam container. He set them both on the table along with the bill. "Thanks for choosing the

Rainforest Café to dine this evening. Please don't make this visit your last."

"Everything was wonderful," Ginger said.

Thirty minutes after Joseph had paid their dinner bill he and Ginger were walking, arm in arm, along the Magnificent Mile in downtown Chicago. They window-shopped and looked at all of the latest fashions in the showcase windows of Macy's, Saks Fifth Avenue, Lord & Taylor, and the many other stores that donned overdressed mannequins.

Ginger exhaled then said, "This is the best night of my life." *So this is what being in love feels like,* she thought. It was wonderful and finally she was happy. Ginger closed her eyes and silently thanked God for sending Joseph to her. And she was especially thankful that Joseph's late model Mercedes-Benz coupe wouldn't turn into a pumpkin at midnight. Her fairy tale was real.

Joseph drove his car into Ginger's driveway, then got out and walked around to the passenger side and opened the door for her. He grabbed her hand to help her stand. Immediately Joseph pulled Ginger into his arms, held her tight, and spoke the words, "I love you, Ginger. For better or worse, for richer or poorer, to love and to cherish, in sickness and in health, 'til death do us part."

Ginger's knees buckled. She pulled away from Joseph and looked into his eyes. "Joseph, I—"

He silenced Ginger by placing a finger on her lips. "Shhh, don't say anything. Just go inside."

Ginger obediently walked to her front door and inserted her key into the lock. Before she turned the knob, she looked around and saw Joseph still standing by the passenger door looking at her. She started to say something to him but he stopped her.

"Just go inside, Ginger."

Ginger turned the knob and went inside. She closed the door behind her and leaned against it. "Oh, my God," she said. "What just happened?" She hurried to the telephone on the cocktail table and dialed Portia's number. When Portia answered Ginger told her to hold on and then dialed Celeste's number.

Anthony answered on the first ring. "Celeste is asleep, Ginger."

"I don't care, wake her up. Trust me, Tony, she doesn't wanna miss this."

In the next ten seconds Ginger and Portia heard Celeste's groggy voice. "Hello?"

"Y'all ain't gonna believe what just happened," Ginger said excitedly.

"What?" Portia asked.

Ginger screamed into the telephone. "He married me in my driveway!"

"What color are we wearing?" Celeste and Portia asked at the same time.

Chapter 13

In the Home Stretch

Friday, Celeste's last day at work before she took her maternity leave, was an emotional one. When she arrived at her assigned teller station, she was surprised to see pink and blue paper-cut booties decorating the counter top. The word CONGRATULATIONS in mint green and yellow letters was spelled out across the wall behind her desktop computer.

For most of the morning, Celeste's fellow coworkers rubbed and patted her large belly every chance they got. Everyone wished her, her husband, and her new baby well. Early on in Celeste's pregnancy the senior mother of her church had instilled a belly-rubbing phobia in her. She told Celeste to be careful of whom she allowed to touch her pregnant belly. That not everyone would be happy for her. She convinced Celeste that some folks could possibly rub her belly and whisper horrible things under their breath to try to put a root on her unborn child.

Ever since Celeste heard that advice she flinched each time someone, especially a stranger, touched her belly. Anthony told Celeste that roots were mythical and the mothers of the church needed to get saved.

It was almost 2:00 p.m. Friday and not only were Celeste's ankles swollen to the size of tree stumps, the top portion of her back was aching due to the heaviness of her enlarged breasts. She had just come from a fifteen-minute break when an elderly Caucasian man approached her window.

"Can I have change for two hundred dollars?"

"Absolutely," Celeste responded with a forced smile. She looked forward to the next three hours passing by; then she could go home and wait for her baby's arrival. Celeste made sure the two hundred-dollar bills the man had given her weren't counterfeit before giving the man six twenty dollar bills, four ten dollar bills, six five dollar bills, and ten one dollar bills.

After the man patiently waited for Celeste to count the money and lay it on the counter in front of him, he spoke. "I want it all in coins."

Although it wasn't likely, Celeste thought she hadn't heard him correctly. She looked the man directly in his eyes. "Excuse me?"

"I need fifty-six dollars in quarters, sixty-four dollars in nickels, thirty-one dollars in dimes, and the rest I want in pennies."

The pain in Celeste's back kicked in overdrive. She shifted her weight from one tree stump to the other. "Sir, I don't have that much change in my drawer. Can I give you all singles?"

"No, I gotta have coins," he stated firmly.

Celeste massaged the back of her neck and exhaled. *Lord, you better check me right now 'cause I'm getting ready to snap.* She forced herself to stay calm. Up to that moment Celeste was proud of herself that she had gotten through the day without incident. "Sir, as I've stated before, I don't have that much change in my drawer." Celeste could have gone to the vault and gotten the change to fulfill the man's request but she was being lazy. She just didn't want to.

"Isn't this a bank?" the man asked loudly.

The teller on the left side of Celeste stopped what she was doing and looked at them. She watched as Celeste stretched her arm across the counter to point her finger in the man's face. The teller pressed the alarm button to alert the manager.

"Yes, it is a bank. But who do you think got the time that it takes to count out two hundred dollars in coins?" Celeste asked the man.

The man raised his voice an octave higher. "Get your finger out of my face. It's your job to give me what I ask for. I pay your salary."

Apparently the man thought by raising his voice, he could intimidate Celeste. But she wasn't the least bit fazed. Celeste sang first soprano and could hang with the big dogs.

Just as she was ready to go beyond the highest key the most expensive piano had, her immediate supervisor was at her side. "Is there a problem here?" he asked Celeste.

"Look, Maurice, *you* serve this ignorant, illiterate fool because I'm not doing it." Celeste slammed her cash drawer shut and walked away. She went into the employees' lounge and lay on a chaise chair. Ten minutes later, Maurice came and sat at her feet.

"How many times do I have to tell you that the customers are always right?"

Celeste exhaled. "Maurice, I was not about to stand there and count out two hundred dollars in change. The man was ignorant and illiterate."

"Do you know who that ignorant, illiterate man was?"

"Nope, and I don't wanna know."

"Well, I'll tell you anyway. He's the rabbi at our CEO's synagogue ."

Was that supposed to mean something to Celeste? "I don't care if he was the pope. He was ignorant and I didn't want to deal with him."

Maurice massaged his temples. He didn't feel like dealing with Celeste and her constant mood swings. Ever since she announced her pregnancy Celeste had become unbearable to work with. In the past eight months not a week had gone by without a customer complaint to Maurice about Celeste's attitude. If she wasn't yelling at the customers, she was behaving in a hostile manner to her fellow coworkers.

A customer had filed a complaint one morning that, only twenty minutes after the bank had opened for business, Celeste placed the NEXT WINDOW placard on her work station as soon as the customer stepped to up to Celeste. Celeste had spoken extremely nasty toward the customer and stated that she was taking a break.

And Maurice would never forget the day when, at five months pregnant, Celeste had threatened to do bodily harm to a customer. The customer had asked for two cashier's checks in the amount of one hundred dollars each. To save herself some time Celeste presented the woman with a single cashier's check for $200. After going back and forth with the woman on why it was unnecessary to waste a cashier's check, Maurice came to Celeste's station and ordered her to void the checks and give the customer exactly what she wanted. Fit to be tied that her lunch hour would be delayed, Celeste looked at the woman and said, "Don't let me catch you on the street." Maurice sent Celeste home, without pay, for the remainder of the day and she was forced to endure a five-day suspension.

Maurice knew that Celeste's pregnancy was nothing short of a miracle. Over the years she had shared with her fellow coworkers that she longed to become a mother, and how she prayed daily that God would bless her womb. Maurice had authorized Celeste's days off so that she could attend countless doctors visits. According to the bank's rules and regulations, Celeste should have been terminated from her duties long ago for poor work performance and for conduct unbecoming of an employee. Maurice had shown pity on Celeste and gave her chance after chance to correct her attitude.

But pointing her finger and disrespecting a rabbi, Maurice couldn't overlook. And because it was the chief executive officer's rabbi, Maurice knew he had no choice but do what needed to be done. "This is your last day before you take your maternity leave, right?"

"Yep, and I can't wait 'til five o'clock."

"Why don't you go ahead and call it a day? We'll see you in eight weeks."

Maurice didn't have to tell Celeste twice. She immediately called a taxicab. Forty-five minutes later she was at home lying across her bed in a comatose-like sleep.

The next morning Anthony woke Celeste at seven o'clock with a soft kiss on her cheek. "Good morning, sleepyhead."

Celeste lazily turned from her side to lie on her back. She yawned and stretched. "Morning."

"What's on your agenda today?" Anthony asked.

"Portia and Ginger are finally taking me to register at Baby World for the shower. What are you doing today?"

"Pastor Ricky Harris is speaking at a men's prayer breakfast this morning. I'm going to pick him up and head over to Alpha Omega Baptist Church on the west side. Can I trust you to take your pills at one o'clock?"

Celeste watched Anthony slip into a shirt and tie. "If I remember," she said nonchalantly.

"Babe, you gotta do better when it comes to taking the prenatal pills. We want a happy and healthy baby." Anthony was the responsible one. Every day, at 1:00 p.m., he would text Celeste to remind her to take her medication. "I'll just text you again. How's that?"

"Thank you, Tony. You know my mind ain't worth two cents these days." Celeste rubbed her gigantic belly irritably. The joy of being an expectant mother had worn off months ago.

She didn't care for the morning sickness so late in her pregnancy. Her swollen ankles and constant sleepiness were symptoms that Celeste couldn't get used to. At eight months pregnant it irritated Celeste that she had to empty her bladder nearly thirty times daily.

Truth be told, Celeste had become angry that another human being had taken over her body and stolen her strength and energy. "I want you to know that I really don't like being pregnant, Tony. The only reason I'm going through this is because I'm in love with you and I want to see you happy but don't ask me to do this again."

Anthony chose to ignore Celeste's mood swing. During her pregnancy, Celeste had constantly blamed Anthony for her fingers becoming swollen. She had taken her wedding band off months ago. "You did this to me," she told him.

When she was six months along and Celeste could no longer see her feet when she stood and looked down, she had blamed Anthony for that as well. "Why do I have to be the one who's inconvenienced? I don't think it's fair that men don't have to suffer as much as women do."

Oh, I'm suffering all right, Anthony thought. "Well, you can take that up with God," Anthony retorted.

"I'm taking it up with you!" she snapped.

Out of frustration Anthony had thrown his hands in the air. "What do you want me to do, Celeste? Huh? Tell me what you want me to do? I massage your back when it's hurting, I rub your feet and ankles every night, and I get out of bed at three in the morning to go look for cottage cheese and crushed pineapples. I'm doing all that I can to keep you happy and uplifted because I know you're uncomfortable at times but you're gonna have to chill with treating me like a stepchild. I'm your husband. I ain't the enemy."

Anthony walked to Celeste and kissed her forehead. The sooner he left her presence, the better off the both of them would be. Clearly Celeste wanted to argue about nothing, anything, and everything. Anthony wasn't going to feed into her temper tantrums. "I gotta go because I'm running late. Pastor Harris is waiting on me." He looked at Celeste lying in bed. "You need help getting up?"

"You know I do, Tony," Celeste answered sarcastically. "When have I not needed your help getting out of bed or getting out of the tub? Why would you ask such a stupid question?"

Celeste sat up, placed her feet flat on the floor, and stretched her arms toward Anthony. He grabbed her wrists and planted his feet eight inches apart and pulled Celeste forward. Veins on Anthony's face and neck bulged as he strained and made a grunting noise as though he was using every ounce of energy he had.

Celeste knew he was teasing. "Ha-ha. You ain't funny, Negro."

Anthony playfully wiped his forehead with the back of his hand. "Whew, now that was a workout."

Chapter 14

Krispy Kreme

It was late January and two inches of snow had fallen in Chicago the night before. Portia avoided the expressway and chose to take the scenic route south on Cicero Avenue. She and Ginger were in the front seats grooving to WGOD, the FM gospel station. Edward Primer and the Voices of Joy Community Choir was blasting the speakers in Portia's Escalade.

Ginger was impressed with the interior gadgets and fixtures that decorated the dashboard of the late-model SUV. The wood grain shined so bright it could almost pass for granite. "I never thought I would see the day come to pass when jump-offs live better than most wives do."

"I ain't nobody's jump-off," Portia stated.

Celeste stretched her legs across and took up the entire back seat. She admired the moon roof and the two high-definition flat-screen televisions embedded in the headrests of the front seats. The black leather interior was as soft as silk. "So, what is your title then, Portia? Sidepiece, booty call answerer, unwed gold-digger, chickenhead, clean-up woman, what?"

"It's all the same," Ginger added.

It hadn't fazed Portia one bit how Celeste and Ginger ridiculed her. She was content with the way she lived her life. What she did was between her and God. "I offered to drive today because I wanted to make sure that Celeste was comfortable. But if you prefer, Ginger, I can drive back to your house and the three of us can hop in your broken-down, beat-up, rusted hooptie. And hopefully we won't get shot at when it backfires when we roll down the street."

Ginger looked at Portia. "You don't have to be nasty."

"It's small and Celeste is obese but we can shove her in the trunk and raise the hatchback to make room for her belly."

"Watch it, heifer," Celeste commented.

Portia positioned the rearview mirror and looked at Celeste. "Or how about we go back and get your car? Oops, my bad. You gotta share a car with your husband and it's his turn to drive today, right?"

Before Celeste could respond, Ginger chimed in. "You know what, Portia? You got a real jacked-up attitude."

Portia was offended. "*I* have an attitude? You're telling me that I have an attitude? I was fine until you and Miss My Life is Perfect and I Do Everything Right Number Two started on me."

"We're not saying that we're the perfect saints, Portia. What we're saying is that we don't set out to purposely hurt others just to get ahead."

Portia frowned and shrugged her shoulders. "Celeste, what do you mean by that? Who do I purposely set out to hurt?"

"How about the wives of the men you screw? Does the name Tamara ring a bell?" Ginger asked.

"Ding, ding, ding, ding," Celeste chimed from the back seat.

"Aw, heck, here we go down memory lane again." Portia sighed. "Look, I can understand how some folks may think of me as a self-centered, arrogant, and egotistical witch, but—"

"Uh, correction," Celeste interrupted. "That would be a self-centered, arrogant, and egotistical bi—"

Ginger hollered out to drown out Celeste's expletive.

"Y'all know what?" Portia started. "I ain't gotta be subjected to this abuse. I will be perfectly fine with driving the two of you back to your homes. That way you can enjoy the rest of this day without having to be in my presence."

"Oh, stop being so dramatic, Portia."

"You stop being so dramatic, Ginger!" she yelled.

"Don't yell at her."

Portia looked in the rearview mirror. "Who died and left you in charge of what I do? You ain't the boss of me."

"Clearly," Celeste said. "Because if I was, you would be driving a vehicle that you could afford yourself and not enjoying the luxuries of men who are in matrimony with other women." Celeste was careful not to say "holy matrimony."

"Right is right and wrong is wrong," Ginger added.

Portia had enough of their self-righteous attitudes. It was about time she put both Ginger and Celeste in their places. If they thought it was "gang up on Portia" day, they had another think coming. Portia needed to remind her best friends that they were not perfect and that all three of them were rotten apples that had fallen from the same tree.

She pulled the Escalade over to the side of the street and put the gear in park. She turned her upper torso around and faced Celeste. "Was it right for you to lie and deceive Tony for years about why you couldn't have a baby?"

"That's my business." Celeste rotated her neck and gave off much attitude.

"My point exactly." Portia focused on Ginger sitting next to her. "And was it right for you to call the police and act like Ronald was trying to kill you when it was the other way around?"

"I was defending myself and you know it."

"No, you were not, Ginger. You told us that Ron was drunk and high. So you decided to eat some spinach and turn into Popeye. You took advantage and beat the crap out of Ronald because you knew that he couldn't defend himself."

Ginger folded her arms across her chest and looked forward. Her only response was, "Humph."

"Humph," Portia added.

"Humph," Celeste said.

"Humph," Portia said again.

Celeste wasn't going to allow Portia to have the last word. "Humph."

Portia put the gear in drive and pulled away from the curb. "I'm just saying that all three of us have done dirt. You two are no better than me. So, you can keep the self-righteous comments about what I do because Portia is gonna always do Portia." With that being said, the ladies rode in silence for twenty whole minutes.

"Oh, my God. Oh, my God. Pull over!" Celeste hollered hysterically from the back seat.

Ginger nearly jumped out of her skin. At Celeste's outburst, Portia's heart rose to her throat and she slammed on the brakes. She stopped the Escalade at the crossroads of Cicero Avenue and 147th Street, in the city of Midlothian. Thank God the three of them were wearing their seat belts. Ginger's and Portia's heads would have gone through the windshield had they not been.

Ginger turned around in her seat and looked at Celeste. "What in the world is wrong with you?"

Celeste ignored Ginger's question and repented frantically on Portia's behalf. "Forgive Portia, Lord. She didn't mean to do it. She doesn't know any better, Lord."

Portia looked at Celeste through the rearview mirror. "What are you talking about? Forgive me for what?"

"You drove past a Krispy Kreme!" Celeste yelled.

"What?" Portia and Ginger asked at the same time. Drivers in cars had started to blow their horns. Portia was blocking the flow of traffic. She glared at Celeste. "I know darn well you don't have us sitting in the middle of a busy street, hollering about a doughnut shop."

Celeste veered back at her. "You know doggone well that you can't drive past a Krispy Kreme without stopping in. Who does that?"

"We're gonna do it," Ginger answered irritably. "Let's go, Portia."

Portia stepped on the gas pedal and drove forward.

Celeste panicked. "What are you doing, Portia? We gotta get some doughnuts."

Portia screamed, "I'm going around the block. Would you shut up?"

Ginger looked at Portia. "You're such a pushover."

"Anything to shut her fat behind up."

"I heard that," Celeste said.

Portia pulled into the parking lot of Krispy Kreme but before the truck came to a complete stop, the back passenger door opened and Celeste hopped out and practically ran inside. Portia and Ginger saw her holding the bottom portion of her oversized belly.

"I guess the heck with us if we wanted any, huh?" Ginger asked Portia.

"Look at her run. For doughnuts. That's a darn shame."

When Celeste returned to the truck, she was already finishing the last of a glazed doughnut. She sat in the back seat and licked her fingers clean. "Y'all didn't want any doughnuts?"

"Well, heck, before we could give you our orders you were already inside standing at the counter," Ginger fussed.

"Oh, I'm sorry. You want me to go back in there?"

Portia saw two boxes that held six doughnuts each sitting on Celeste's lap. "Nah, you ain't gotta do that. We'll help you eat yours."

Celeste looked at Portia like she had two heads. "Does the devil have you thinking that? If he does, I'm here to tell you that he is a liar. Y'all ain't getting none of these. Now, if you want me to go back in there, I will. But don't think I'm sharing my doughnuts, 'cause I ain't."

Ginger turned around and looked at her. "Are you serious, Celeste? You're gonna eat a dozen doughnuts by yourself?"

Celeste cocked her head to the side and glared at Ginger. "Is English your primary language, Ginger? Aren't you a schoolteacher? What part of 'y'all ain't getting any of my doughnuts' are you not comprehending?"

"I don't believe this. Are you really that stingy?"

Celeste answered Portia's question by putting the last of a jelly-filled doughnut, her second doughnut, into her mouth and licking her fingers.

"You're gonna eat twelve doughnuts?" Ginger asked again.

"Yep. Do y'all want me to go back in there and get you some?"

Portia put the gear in drive and cruised out of the parking lot. "Don't do us any favors."

"We're gonna remember this, Celeste," Ginger said.

They could write it down, record it, or announce it on a billboard and show it to folks driving by on the highway for all Celeste cared. They could even put a message in a bottle and throw it in the Atlantic Ocean. What Ginger and Portia would remember was the least of her concerns. The only thing that mattered to Celeste, at that moment, was the fact that she got her Krispy Kremes.

When Krispy Kreme came to the Chicago area, Celeste had a dream that God made it a commandment that saints must stop in and have a filled day. She heard Jesus say, "I come that you might have life more abundantly." Celeste interpreted the dream to mean that it would be a sin to pass a Krispy Kreme and not make a purchase.

Portia and Ginger could join the devil on a group bus over some doughnuts if they wanted to, but Celeste got hers. She was obedient to God's Word and her seat at the right hand of the Father was still reserved. She buckled her seat belt, extended her legs in the roomy Escalade and bit into a lemon custard–filled doughnut. "Mmmm," she moaned. "I should've bought milk." She looked at the back of Portia's head. "Portia, can you stop at the 7-Eleven up ahead? I need milk to wash these doughnuts down."

Portia's eyes grew wide and her mouth dropped open.

Ginger looked at the expression on Portia's face and laughed out loud. "Uh-oh. Here it comes."

Portia glanced in the rearview mirror. "You got a lot of freakin' nerve, you know that? After the way you just treated me and Ginger, I wish I would stop anywhere else for you. You sit back there and choke on those twelve doughnuts."

When they arrived at Baby World Celeste refused to exit the Escalade. "The two of you can go ahead and register me. Y'all know what I like. And if you are not sure just choose one of everything."

Ginger was fit to be tied. "Oh, heck no, Celeste. This is for your baby shower."

Celeste sat in the back seat and rubbed her protruding belly. "I don't feel so good. I think I'm sick."

Portia saw that both boxes of doughnuts were nearly empty. Celeste had left a half-eaten doughnut with sprinkles. "Well, if you hadn't inhaled all the darn doughnuts, you wouldn't be sick."

Ginger wasn't having it. Sick or not, Celeste was going to register for her baby shower herself. "Let's go, Celeste. It won't take that long. The three of us can split up and go through the store much faster."

Ginger and Portia exited the Escalade. When they stepped outside and started walking toward the store, they noticed that Celeste wasn't with them.

"What the heck is she doing?" Ginger asked.

They went back and opened the rear passenger door and saw that Celeste had made herself comfortable. She was laying down on her side.

"Celeste, come on," Portia said.

"I told you that I don't feel good, Portia."

"You are faking and we know it," Ginger said.

Celeste patted the right side of her belly. "I think I'm having minor contractions."

Clearly Celeste was putting on a show. Ginger and Portia knew she was being lazy and trying real hard to not go inside and register for her baby shower.

"Well, if you are having contractions, I'm gonna drive you to the nearest hospital."

"I don't need to go to a hospital. This has happened before. The contractions will pass once I rest awhile."

"Rest? Why are you so tired? All you've done today was lie on this back seat and eat doughnuts," Ginger stated.

Portia's patience had run out. "Look, ain't nobody got time for your foolishness, Celeste. Get your behind out of this truck and in the store!"

Celeste sat up. "You and Ginger are the hosts for the shower. Why can't the two of you go into Baby World and select a crib, swing, highchair, bassinette, bottles, and Pampers?"

Ginger looked at her wristwatch. "This is ridiculous. I ain't got all day to stand here and fight with you, Celeste. I have plans with Joseph tonight."

"I'll let you and Portia in on a little secret. I'm having a baby boy," Celeste revealed. "Just go in there and select everything blue." Up until that moment Celeste had kept the gender of her baby a secret. She lay back down. "Now shut the door because it's cold."

Portia didn't just shut the door, she slammed the door.

Chapter 15

Me, You, and Everything Blue

On the Wednesday evening before Celeste's baby shower, Ginger and Portia were standing in a very long checkout line at Walmart. They were waiting their turn to pay for everything they needed for Celeste's big event.

The two of them didn't share with Celeste that they would be out shopping. Ginger and Portia decided the evening would go smoothly if Celeste wasn't with them. Had Celeste known they were out shopping for the baby shower, she would have insisted that she tag along. After the drama she caused two weeks ago in the parking lot of Baby World, Portia and Ginger vowed to do the rest of the baby shower planning on their own, in peace.

Ginger glanced through the light blue paper plates, cups, forks, and spoons, among other items, they had piled high in the shopping cart. They spent more than two hours choosing games for the guests to play. "You think we have everything, Portia?"

Portia picked up the blue party favors and examined them. "I hope so, girl. We just gotta make sure to order the large helium balloons tomorrow."

"Celeste better appreciate what we are doing for her. The closer that baby is due the more evil she gets. I don't see how Tony puts up with her."

"Girl, Tony is so excited about this baby, he ain't thinking about Celeste. He's been sleeping on the living room sofa for two months because she says his scent makes her throw up."

"Well, if you think that's cruel," Ginger started, "listen to this one. Yesterday she told Tony if he wanted any more kids, she would happily divorce him so that he can marry someone else because not a nam notha baby will pass through her vajayjay."

Portia laughed out loud. "No, she didn't say 'not a nam notha.'"

They moved forward in line when the cover of an *Essence* magazine caught Ginger's eye. On the cover was a picture of Bishop T.D. Jakes. Underneath his picture, Ginger read: A POPULAR MINISTER EXPLAINS WHY SISTERS HAVE TO LOOK IN THE MIRROR, NOT AT THEIR MAN, IF THEY WANT HEALTHY RELATIONSHIPS, BY BISHOP T.D. JAKES, PAGE 78.

Ginger picked up the magazine from its rack and turned to page seventy-eight to see what Bishop Jakes wrote. The title of the article read, NO MAN CAN MAKE YOU HAPPY.

"Listen to what Bishop Jakes wrote in *Essence* this month." She read the article to Portia. "'Many women enter into romantic relationships hoping that their partner will somehow make them happy. This is not only unrealistic, but it's also virtually impossible.'"

"I believe that to be true," Portia said.

Ginger read more from the article then looked up at Portia. "Bishop Jakes said that good men are not so much hard to find as they are hard to receive. I believe that to be true, Portia."

Portia shrugged her shoulders. "I couldn't care less."

Ginger read more in silence. She understood that Bishop Jakes was telling women to not take the trash from their pasts into the brightness of their futures. In the article, Bishop Jakes encouraged women to do an honest self-evaluation. Ginger understood that she should move ahead and trust Joseph. Then and only then she could look forward to her happily ever after.

Portia snapped her fingers in Ginger's face. "Hello?"

Ginger was so engrossed in the article she didn't notice that Portia had already taken the items out of the cart, placed them on the conveyor belt, and paid the cashier. She looked up from the magazine. "Huh?"

Portia stood with six full heavy plastic bags in her hands. "I could use your help with getting this stuff out to my truck."

Ginger wanted to finish Bishop Jakes's article. She paid for the magazine and followed Portia out of Walmart.

Outside in the parking lot they loaded all of the bags in the hatchback of Portia's Escalade. They secured themselves in their seat belts. Portia started the engine and blasted the heat.

"Man, this is the coldest winter ever." Ginger shivered while blowing into her balled-up fists.

"The seats are heated," Portia said. "Your toosh will be nice and toasty in a few seconds."

Ginger wondered if David's wife, Latricia, drove a luxury vehicle and if her seats heated up.

As if on cue Portia's cellular telephone rang through the interior speakers and Ginger saw the dashboard light up. The name **David Hall** and the number he called from appeared on Portia's display board.

Portia pressed a button on the flat-screen panel. "Hey, lover."

Ginger rolled her eyes at no one in particular.

His masculine voice filled the interior. "Whatcha gettin' into tonight?"

"Well, I'm just leaving Walmart. Had to pick up the finishing touches for Celeste's baby shower this Saturday."

Portia hadn't alerted David that she wasn't in the Escalade alone; therefore, anything he said wouldn't be a secret. Ginger took that to mean that Portia wasn't even trying to hide her affair. Apparently the word "discreet" was nowhere to be found in Portia's vocabulary. In Ginger's eyes, Portia not informing David that she was present proved that Portia was without a doubt not ashamed, almost flaunting the affair she and David were having.

"Okay. That's cool, that's cool. So, uh, you wanna get into a li'l somethin'?"

Ginger looked at Portia's face and was disgusted to see the mischievous smile.

"Where is your wife?" Portia asked.

"Bible class."

Humph, humph, humph, Ginger commented silently. She was so disappointed in Portia. David's wife was in church learning about Jesus, probably getting her praise on right then as Portia made plans to have sex with her husband.

"Wow," Ginger said but only Portia heard her.

Portia glanced at Ginger then focused on the dashboard. "Okay, well, I should be home in a half hour and you better bring that good lovin' *and* your checkbook."

Ginger almost choked.

David's laugh ricocheted all around Ginger. "I'm gonna make it do what it do, baby."

Portia pressed a button on the dashboard. David's name and number disappeared. She looked at Ginger's face and saw that she had her lips pursed as though she'd eaten a lemon. "What's your problem?"

Ginger stared straight ahead. "I ain't the one with the problem, sis." Ginger left it at that. Trying to convince Portia that she was living foul was like talking to a brick wall. The only thing Ginger could do was pray for her best friend.

Portia knew exactly what Ginger meant. Her lust for married men was indeed her problem. She put the gear in reverse and backed out of the parking space. Portia couldn't care less how Ginger felt or anyone else for that matter. The first of the month was approaching and Portia was going to make sure her rent would be paid.

On the day of Celeste's baby shower, the hours of 4:00 p.m. through 7:00 p.m. couldn't come to pass fast enough for the hostesses. She had been working on Ginger's and Portia's nerves since eight that morning. That was when Celeste had called them on the three-way and said that the shower was off because she didn't want to be bothered with a bunch of heckling hens that day.

Portia advised Celeste that she had better take a chill pill and a nap because she and Ginger had put a lot of time and money toward planning the baby shower and, without a doubt, the afternoon was going to go on as planned. Between the two of them, Portia and Ginger had spent close to seven hundred dollars for the shower's food, decorations, games, and invitations. They put their monies together and purchased the $350 crib with Big Bird accessories from Celeste's registry at Baby World. Ginger told Celeste to pull herself together because, whether she was present or not, there would definitely be a shower.

"Make sure to come to Ginger's house fashionably late at four-thirty," Portia told Celeste. She wanted the guests to arrive before Celeste so they could greet her and make a big fuss when she walked in the front door.

"I don't want anybody grinning and laughing in my face, Portia."

Portia was two seconds away from cursing at Celeste. She understood Celeste was three weeks away from her due date and miserable. And it was true what everyone said, that misery loved company. Celeste was gifted in making everyone around her miserable.

"Look, Celeste. I don't care what you want. That's what women do at baby showers. They laugh and grin in the new mother's face so you may as well get ready for it. You knew weeks ago Ginger and I were planning your shower for today so don't trip. Ain't nobody got time for your mess. Get your mind right, boo." Portia wasn't going to tolerate any of Celeste's nonsense.

"Did you get any sleep last night?" Ginger asked Celeste.

Celeste exhaled loudly into the telephone. "A little. The baby was doing somersaults all night long."

"Have you eaten anything this morning?" asked Portia.

"Tony made me a bowl of oatmeal but I could only swallow about four spoonfuls." Celeste exhaled loudly again. "And he's been getting on my nerves, y'all just don't know."

Ginger knew better. If anything, Celeste was the one getting on Anthony's nerves. "What is he doing, Celeste?"

"First of all, he woke me up at six this morning to take my medicine when he knew I had been up all night tossing and turning. He purposely waited until I was good and asleep before he woke me up for nonsense."

"That's ridiculous," Portia said. She reminded her of a very important fact. "Celeste, you have a high-risk pregnancy. You are scheduled to take your medicine every six hours, no matter when the hour falls. You should be grateful that Tony cares that much."

Celeste's emotions got the best of her. "Why are you taking his side, Portia?" she screamed into the telephone. "You're supposed to be my girl. You and Tony got something going on? Are you screwing my husband?"

Ginger sent the loudest gasp into the telephone line. "Celeste!"

Enough was enough. Right then Portia dismissed Celeste's emotions. "What the heck did you just say to me, Celeste? Are you losing your darn mind?"

Ginger heard the crap hitting the fan. "Okay, y'all, calm down. Please let's not do this. Portia, don't say another word and, Celeste, you need to apologize to her for what you said. You were way out of line."

Celeste took a moment to collect herself. Ginger was right. "Portia, I'm sorry. It was wrong of me to say something like that. Forgive me?"

Portia was pissed and was never one to hide it when she was. "Heck no, 'cause that ain't the first time you've said that. That was cruel and evil."

"Portia, Celeste has been cruel and evil for almost nine months but this is the first time she has apologized for acting crazy."

"I don't care, Ginger. The heifer was wrong and you know it."

"Oh, I'm a heifer now?" Celeste asked angrily.

"Yes, you are," Portia stated firmly. "And a big fat one, too. I'm not feeling your weak apology."

Ginger needed the baby shower to go off without a hitch. Afterward she would allow Celeste and Portia to kill each other. "She said she was sorry, Portia."

"I know what she said, Ginger. I also know what she meant. Just because you're bloated and irritated, Celeste, doesn't mean you can just say whatever the heck you wanna say. People have feelings."

Celeste was shocked at Portia's words. "As many married men you mess around with, since when do you care about people's feelings?"

"Oh, my God," Ginger said. Though she didn't disagree with Celeste and felt that her question to Portia was a good hit, that wasn't the right time.

Portia was ready for battle. "You wanna go there with me, Celeste?"

"No. No, she doesn't," Ginger interjected. "Look, Celeste. Take a bubble bath and eat something then lie down. I'll call you back in a few hours to check on you. Where's Tony?"

Portia and Ginger couldn't see Celeste shrug her shoulders. "The heck if I know, I cussed him out then he left. And I hope he stays gone."

"Well, it's probably best that he's gone so now you can rest. Is he gonna drive you to my house or are you driving yourself?"

"I don't know!" Celeste answered in a raised voice and with plenty of attitude. She massaged her temples. Ginger was asking too many questions.

Ginger was determined to not let Celeste upset her. "Okay, well just take a bath and a nap and we will check on you later."

Without saying good-bye, Celeste slammed down the telephone and left Ginger and Portia on the line.

"Portia, I know you're ticked off but let's just get through the shower. I'm sure Celeste will be a lot better to deal with after she gets some rest."

"Yeah, whatever. I won't be at the shower."

Ginger knew that after what Celeste had said to Portia she was well within her right to avoid Celeste but Ginger needed Portia. "Please don't do this. I can't pull this off by myself."

"Did you hear what she said to me?"

"Yes, and you heard me tell Celeste that she was wrong. You know she's stressed."

"I don't care about her being stressed. Celeste is no more stressed than I am when my period is late. That's real stress, honey. I get moody, I wanna cuss people out, and I get hot and cold spells, too. So, don't talk to me about her being stressed."

"She apologized."

"Ginger, you can't pacify, Celeste. She only apologized because you told her to."

"Portia, Celeste knows doggone well that you and Tony don't have anything going on. She was just talkin' crazy. Please don't abandon the shower. I need you to come over here and help me decorate. The caterer is bringing the food at two o'clock."

Portia didn't say a word.

"Okay, Portia. How about I save a huge slice of the cake and you smash it in Celeste's face? Would you like to do that?"

"Yep."

Ginger hung up from Portia and dialed Anthony's cellular number. "Hey, bro. It's Ginger. I'm calling to check on you. I just talked to Celeste and she said you two had a rough morning."

Anthony chuckled. "Rough, huh? That's putting it mildly, Ginger. I woke her up to take her medicine and she cussed me out. Then I made her a bowl of oatmeal. She told me it was too lumpy and she cussed me out for that. She went into the bathroom and saw the toilet seat up and cussed me out for that. So, I try to calm her down by massaging her neck, shoulders, and back. She tells me that rubbing on her was what got her pregnant in the first place so she cussed me out a fourth time."

And Ginger thought she and Portia had it bad. "Oh, Tony. How do you manage?"

"I just keep telling myself this will all be over in three weeks."

"Where are you now?" Ginger asked.

"I'm in River Oaks Mall. Celeste saw a platinum crucifix she liked at Macy's. So I'm here getting it for her. I'm gonna get it gift-wrapped then bring it over to your house. When she opens the gifts for the baby, I want her to open something just for her."

Ginger was impressed. "Tony, you are one in a million. Who gets cursed out four times then buys a gift for the one who cursed them?"

Anthony laughed out loud. "Me."

Chapter 16

A Shower of Blessings

Dressed in stonewashed blue jeans and a light blue short-sleeve T-shirt with the words GODMOTHER-TO-BE printed in bold black letters, Ginger looked out of her living room bay window. With only three weeks until the baby's arrival, Celeste had yet to decide who the precious bundle of joy's godmother would be. A week ago Ginger and Portia called Celeste on a three-way and put her on the spot to make a decision on which of the two of them would be graced with the title of godmother.

"The jury is still out on that," Celeste responded.

With that being said Portia decided that she and Ginger should make the decision for Celeste and appoint themselves as godmothers. It was Ginger's idea that they both have custom T-shirts made and to wear them to the baby shower.

Ginger saw Anthony's shiny, freshly waxed silver limited edition Lincoln Navigator pull up to the curb in front of her house. "She's here, she's here," she said excitedly.

About thirty-five of Celeste's closest friends and loved ones gathered in the living room to welcome her when she walked in the front door. Ginger opened the door just as Celeste and Anthony got to it. Ginger took one look at the expression on Celeste's face and knew right away that she didn't want to be there.

"Hi, mommy-to-be," Ginger greeted her with a smile, trying to encourage Celeste to put on a happy face. "Come on in."

The expecting couple stepped into the foyer. Celeste noticed Ginger's T-shirt and was about to comment when she heard shouts of, "Congratulations!" Immediately, cousins, friends, coworkers, and sisters in Christ of Celeste's rushed to hug her, kiss her cheek, or rub her big belly as they pulled her farther into the living room.

Celeste forced a fake grin and did her best to return her guests' greeting. "Hi, everybody."

The last woman to greet Celeste was a surprise guest. "Chile, you look like a beluga whale."

Celeste was stunned. *What the heck is she doing here?* Her forced, fake grin got wider. "Hello, Mother Harper. I didn't know you were in town." Celeste glanced over her shoulder at Anthony. Her fake grin turned upside down and transformed into an angry sneer.

Anthony swallowed. He purposely didn't tell Celeste that his mother had been invited to the baby shower. Anthony knew that his mother was a thorn in Celeste's side. Overbearing, overprotective, and over the top, Eugenia Harper was a force to be reckoned with. She and Celeste were like oil and water. The two didn't blend well at all. It was said that a man sought a woman who resembled his mother. Anthony could honestly say that Celeste certainly reminded him of the lady who had given birth to him. They were both bossy, controlling, and confrontational. Truth be told the reason Eugenia and Celeste didn't get along was because they were two of a kind. Their mannerisms were identical. Whenever Eugenia visited she and Celeste were in constant battle over who was the leading lady in Anthony's life.

"Tony, you better remind your mother who your wife is. This is my house. She doesn't run anything around here," was what Celeste had told Anthony during Eugenia's last visit. She and Celeste clashed when Celeste discovered that her entire kitchen had been rearranged.

Celeste had returned home, tired, achy, and sore after she, Ginger, and Portia participated in a five-mile run in support of breast cancer research. Celeste walked into her kitchen and opened the cabinet next to the refrigerator that stored the glasses.

Instead Celeste saw boxes of cereal. She frowned. "What the heck?" Celeste moved to the next cabinet where she kept her plates. She saw canned goods instead. She shook her head from side to side. "Am I crazy?" she asked herself.

When Celeste opened the third cabinet and saw spices instead of Tupperware bowls, she flipped out. "Tooooon-nnnyyyyy," she yelled.

He rushed into the kitchen and saw Celeste standing next to the stove with a distraught look on her face. "What's wrong?"

Celeste pointed to the items in the cabinets she had left opened. "Look what your mother did."

It took a moment for Anthony to understand what Celeste was talking about. He saw cereal, Tupperware bowls, plates, and spices. "What did she do?"

Celeste's eyes grew wide and she spoke through gritted teeth. "She rearranged my cabinets, Tony. She moved everything around."

Anthony didn't see why Celeste was making a fuss. He shrugged his shoulders. "So what?"

Celeste's eyeballs grew wider. "So what? Did you just say so what?"

"What's going on in here?" Eugenia asked when she appeared in the kitchen doorway. Celeste's raised voiced had brought her from the guest bedroom.

Celeste looked from her mother-in-law to Anthony. Celeste's eyes told Anthony that he had better be the one to speak to his mother. If Celeste spoke, her words would be harsh.

"Ma, why did you move everything around?"

"Because boxes of cereal belong in the cabinet next to the refrigerator and not on top of the refrigerator. And spices should be kept either in a spice rack or the cabinet closest to the stove. Plates and glasses ought to be stored together in the same cabinet. It just makes more sense."

Celeste frowned. "To whom?"

"You don't like the new arrangement?" Eugenia asked Celeste.

"No, I don't. Your setup is inconvenient. I don't want to have to walk almost to the back door to the cabinet for a glass then walk back to the refrigerator to pour myself something to drink. I like my glasses in the cabinet next to the refrigerator. And I grew up with cereal boxes on top of the refrigerator. That's where I put them and that's where I want them to stay."

Anthony didn't want his mother to respond to Celeste. "Fine, I'll move everything back to where you had it."

"Yeah, do that," Celeste said on her way out of the kitchen. "I'm gonna take a shower."

"Anthony, you need to tell your wife to stay in her place. I'm gonna always be your mother but you can very easily change wives."

"I wanted to surprise you," Eugenia said.

Celeste looked at her mother-in-law. "Mission accomplished. I am definitely surprised."

Eugenia enveloped Celeste in her overbearing arms. Celeste felt like gyro meat wrapped inside of pita bread. "How long are you staying in town?" Celeste rephrased the question she really wanted to ask her mother-in-law. She was more concerned about where she was staying.

"That all depends on when my little grandson will make his debut. I ain't in no hurry to get back to Raleigh."

Oh, my God, Celeste thought. She had one more week to go before she gave birth. Celeste knew that was more than enough time for Anthony's mother to drive her completely insane.

Once when Eugenia had visited Anthony and Celeste she had gone through Celeste's dresser drawers and thrown out all of her dainty lace lingerie and panties. She told Celeste that she needed to purchase classy underwear. "Men don't want their wives to come to bed dressed like whores," she told Celeste.

Celeste was so mad she didn't know what to do. "Well, you obviously don't know your son. He purchased all of my lingerie."

And in the kitchen, Celeste couldn't do anything correctly.

"You really should bake your chicken instead of frying it, Celeste. Why don't you have any yogurt in your fridge? All I see is ice cream. Be careful of how much sugar you put in your pound cakes. Anthony is borderline diabetic. Girl, you put way too much bleach in Anthony's boxers."

And when Celeste arrived home from work and saw that Eugenia had replaced her 3 Musketeers candy bars with granola bars she told Anthony that his mother had worn out her welcome. "It's either me or your mother. One of us has got to go."

The next morning Eugenia was on an airplane headed back home to Raleigh. Celeste told Anthony that his mother was more than welcome to visit as long as she stayed in a hotel.

With Celeste occupied with her guests, Ginger spoke to Anthony. "Getting her here was like pulling teeth, wasn't it?"

Anthony removed his black ski cap and rubbed his bald head. "I went ahead and shaved all the hair off my head since it was falling out anyway. Ginger, I won't even tell you what I had to do just to get her out of bed and dressed. But I will say this: I am in complete agreement with Celeste about not having any more kids."

Ginger chuckled. "That bad, huh?"

"One minute Celeste is hot and the next minute, she's cold. This is January but last night she had the air conditioner going in the house. I was on the sofa with three quilts so it didn't make me no never mind. This afternoon she decided to take a bath. After about thirty minutes or so I noticed that she was still in the tub. I knocked and asked if she was all right. She didn't answer me but I heard sniffles through the door. I opened it and poked my head in and saw her sitting in the tub, crying."

"What was the matter with her?" Ginger asked.

"I'm getting to that," Anthony said. "I walked in the bathroom and knelt by tub. As Celeste wiped tears from her eyes, I saw that her fingers were white and wrinkled. I glanced at her toes and they were white and wrinkled too. I dipped my hand in the water and looked at Celeste like she was crazy. I asked her why she was sitting in cold water, crying. She said, "Cause I can't get out by myself. Why the blank you think I'm sitting in cold water?"' As Anthony spoke his neck danced just as Celeste's had. He imitated her perfectly. He lowered his head and glared at Ginger. "You know she didn't say 'blank,' don't you?"

Ginger laughed out loud and patted his back. "Tony, you have my sympathy, honey. I'm pretty sure that God will have an extra crown in glory for you. How did you get her out of the tub?"

"Well, first she cussed me out because somehow or someway I'm supposed be a rocket scientist and know that she only takes fifteen-minute baths. And it shouldn't take me a half hour to figure out that she's stuck in the tub. Now, Ginger, on the inside my blood was boiling because, for the past eight and a half months, according to Celeste, I've been a cheap, good-for-nothing, inconsiderate, uncaring husband. But I forgave all of that verbal abuse and told Celeste that I was sorry. Then I had her loop her arm around my neck and I put my arm beneath her legs and lifted her out of the tub. I wrapped a big towel around her and saw that she was looking at me kind of funny. That's when she told me that I have a unibrow and my nose was off center as a result of my parents being brother and sister."

Ginger didn't mean to but she screamed out in laughter. "Ooh, Tony, no, she didn't."

"Yeah, she really said that."

Ginger looked at the women making a fuss over Celeste. "Well, now you can get about three hours of freedom unless you wanna stay."

"You must be on crack, Ginger. I'm going home and getting in my king-sized bed and crashing." He looked at all of the women doting on Celeste. "Where's Portia?"

"She's in the kitchen with an attitude. She and Celeste got into it earlier."

Anthony raised his palms in the air. "Spare me the details. Don't tell me about it, I don't want to know." Anthony had learned to leave Celeste's spats with Ginger and Portia among the three of them.

It seemed that every other day they were arguing about something. They had always referred to each other as best friends but Anthony thought the term "frenemies" would actually be a better fit. Anthony would describe the relationship that Celeste, Ginger, and Portia shared as a bipolar one. One day they couldn't live without one another, being happy, going shopping, and exchanging cake recipes. Then the next day it was, "I can't stand you,"

"Lose my number, I'm done with you," or "I can't believe you did that." Two or three days of that nonsense and they would be sitting inside a nail salon choosing nail polish colors for manicures and pedicures.

Anthony went into the living room and greeted all of the guests, kissed Celeste's cheek and walked back to the front door where Ginger stood. "Oh, I almost forgot." He pulled a small gift-wrapped box from his shirt pocket and a card from his interior jacket pocket. "Give these to Celeste after she's opened all of the baby's gifts."

Twenty minutes after Celeste's arrival, Ginger noticed that Portia was nowhere to be seen. She walked into the kitchen and saw Portia sitting at the table, alone, feasting on barbecue chicken wings, meatballs, slices of honey-baked ham, spaghetti, potato salad, and chips.

"Portia, in case you've forgotten, you and I are both hosting this baby shower. I can really use your help entertaining the women. Why are you eating in the kitchen?"

"Because there's no room in the living room."

"There's plenty of room, Portia. You're being antisocial on purpose."

Portia swallowed fruit punch from a light blue paper cup and belched loudly. "So what if I am?"

Ginger looked at her in disgust. "First of all, unleashing your internal bodily air into the atmosphere was not only rude, ignorant, and uncalled for, it was also unladylike and not at all feminine. And I had hoped you would be the more mature one and let this petty thing between you and Celeste go."

Portia shrugged her shoulders and inserted a spoonful of potato salad in her mouth. "I have let it go, I'm fine."

"Well, if that's the case, can you please get the bag of ice cubes out of the freezer and pour half of it in the punch bowl? After that please go and mingle with the guests."

Portia stood and threw her empty paper plate and cup into the trash can. She grabbed the bag of ice from the freezer and walked out of the kitchen. Just as Ginger was following Portia with a second pan of meatballs and spaghetti, the telephone on the wall rang. She set the pan on the counter top and answered the telephone. "Hello?"

"You are so beautiful."

Ginger's heart melted at the sound of his voice. She cooed, "Joseph."

"I miss you and I can't wait to see you tonight."

Somehow he knew the right things to say to set Ginger's inner core on fire. "Oh, honey. I miss you too."

"How's the shower going?" he asked.

She sighed loudly into the telephone.

Joseph understood her pause. All week long Ginger had shared with him how stressed she was about planning the baby shower and she couldn't wait until it was over and done with. "A lot of fun, huh?"

"Well, Celeste arrived a few minutes ago. In spite of the fact that I have a living room full of women showering her with beautiful gifts for her baby, she seems determined to be in a foul mood. On the other hand Miss Portia is having a moment because Celeste said something to her that she shouldn't have. So, I'm playing the hostess and the referee but you know how that goes. What are you up to?"

"Just counting down the minutes 'til I can see you again."

"Joseph, you are so good for my ego, you know that?"

"And you are so good for my life, Ginger. Do you know that?"

"See, it's when you say things like that that makes a sista wanna run down that center aisle quick, fast, and in a hurry. You better watch yourself."

"You don't even have to run down the whole aisle. I will come meet you halfway. You better watch *yourself*."

At that moment, Ginger had an out-of-body experience. She saw the heavens open up and God's ray of light shined down on her. "I wish I could clone you so that when one of you has to be away the other can be with me at all times."

"You better talk to Celeste because I'm getting ready to kill her!" Portia's loud words were like a fire hose. They doused cold water on Ginger's love chat with Joseph.

Ginger glared at Portia in disbelief. "Did you hear that, Joseph?" she asked him. "The bell rang and round one has started. The referee has to step in the boxing ring."

Joseph chuckled. "Remind them that there's no hitting below the belt."

Ginger ended the call with Joseph. "What happened?" she asked Portia.

"I'm out there waiting on Celeste hand and foot." Portia's neck danced as she spoke. "She's being a diva. She said she doesn't want to drink fruit punch; she wants grape Kool-Aid. She claims that she remembered requesting that we add it to the menu. She refuses to drink the punch."

Ginger massaged her temples. A migraine headache was forming. "Jesus, just take me now, please." She looked at Portia. "I don't have grape Kool-Aid or any other flavor Kool-Aid. Celeste will have to drink the punch like everyone else. Her only other option is bottled water."

Portia leaned against the kitchen wall and folded her arms across her chest. "Well, you tell her then, 'cause if she snaps off at me one more time, it's gonna be on and poppin'."

Ginger picked up the pan of spaghetti from the counter and gave it to Portia. "Just take this and set it on the dining room table. I'll deal with Celeste."

Ginger grabbed a sixteen-ounce bottle of drinking water from the refrigerator. She walked into the living room and saw Celeste seated next to their pastor's wife, Lady Elaine Harris. The two were chatting. Ginger sat on the opposite side of Celeste and leaned into her. She shoved the water bottle in Celeste's hand and spoke in her ear. "I don't have any grape Kool-Aid. Okay? This ain't Burger King; you can't have it your way. Either you drink the punch or the water because it's all I have." Without giving Celeste time to respond, Ginger stood and walked away.

Before Celeste had arrived Portia had given each of the women small baby blue plastic safety pins to be pinned on their blouses. Portia explained the first game to them all. Throughout the duration of the shower, if someone said the word "baby," her safety pin would be confiscated by the woman who heard her say the word. The lady who collected the most safety pins, at the end of the shower, would win a prize. It was one hour into the shower and Portia noticed many safety pins missing from blouses.

Portia was rearranging gifts on the gift table when the doorbell rang. She opened the door and was all set to greet the guest until she saw who stood before her.

Latricia Hall gasped. "Oh, my God. Portia Dunn, is that you?" She stepped into the foyer and enveloped Portia. "It's been like what, fifteen years?"

Portia's bladder leaked urine. She became chilled to the bone. She didn't know if it was the cold January wind that blew inside or the mere fact that she had just come face to face with her married lover's wife.

Latricia released Portia and looked at her. "Girl, you still look the same," she said with a smile.

Portia's heart raced. Her teeth chattered. "How are you doing, Latricia?"

"I am great. It is so good to see you, girl."

Portia couldn't look Latricia in her eyes. She looked beyond her, out the front door for something, anything to focus on. "Yeah, it's been awhile. Come on in."

Latricia gave Portia the gift she'd brought. "This is for Celeste and the baby."

Portia took the gift-wrapped box from her. "Thank you. Give me your coat."

Latricia took off her coat and gave it to Portia then looked at her from head to toe. Portia wore skinny-leg blue jeans and a T-shirt that matched Ginger's.

"Awe, that's so cute," Latricia said about Portia's shirt. Latricia admired her black thigh-high boots that laced up the front. She had no clue that Portia's entire outfit, including the lingerie she wore beneath, had been funded from her own bank account. "You look fabulous, Portia. Still a fashionista with that Coke-bottle shape. You had all the boys in high school chasing after you. Remember that?"

Portia shrugged her shoulders. "That was a long time ago."

Latricia looked at Portia's ring finger. "You're not married?"

Portia wished she could have been anywhere else but where she was right then. The position she was in took being uncomfortable to another level. "Not yet."

Latricia's eyebrows rose. "Really? Portia, I remember, during our senior year of high school, that you had the entire football team fighting over which one would be your husband after graduation."

Portia chuckled but only to humor Latricia. She didn't have time for small talk. She wasn't interested in walking down memory lane with Latricia. She wanted answers to questions like why Latricia was there, and why she wasn't informed that Latricia had been invited.

She hung Latricia's coat in the closet in the foyer then set the gift she had brought on the table next to the front door. Portia pointed toward the living room where Celeste and her other guests were mingling. "Celeste is over by the fireplace."

Portia guided Latricia directly to Celeste and stood in front of her. "Look who's here, Celeste."

Celeste's eyes grew wide when she saw Latricia. She paused a few moments before she stood from her chair and hugged her. "Hi, Latricia. I'm glad you could make it."

Latricia returned Celeste's hug. "I was so excited when I got your invitation in the mail. I thought you may have forgotten about me from when I saw you at the bank a few months ago."

Portia frowned and glared at Celeste. *A few months ago?* If looks could kill, Celeste would have been six feet under right then. She wondered why Celeste never mentioned that she had run into Latricia. Portia hastily walked away from them and went to search for Ginger. She found her in her bedroom slipping into a more comfortable pair of shoes.

Portia walked in and slammed the door shut.

The loud noise startled Ginger. "What's wrong with you?"

Portia folded her arms across her chest. "You will never guess, in a million years, who is out there talking to Celeste."

Ginger saw her folded arms rise and fall with every breath she took. "Considering the fact that I don't have a million years, why don't you just tell me and save us both a lot of time."

"Come here," Portia demanded. She opened Ginger's bedroom door a bit and pointed Latricia out. "You see that woman talking to Celeste? Do you know who that is?"

Ginger squinted her eyes and looked at the woman. She couldn't place her face. "Uh-uh. Who is she?"

"That's Latricia Jenkins from high school," Portia said. "Her last name is Hall now."

Ginger gasped. "That's David's wife? I couldn't put a face with the name when Celeste told me Latricia came into the bank to cash . . ." Ginger stopped talking because she realized that neither she nor Celeste had mentioned to Portia that Latricia had been invited to the baby shower.

Portia caught Ginger's hesitation. "Well, don't stop talking now. Spill it, Ginger."

Ginger was not going to endure the wrath of Portia alone. She opened the bedroom door wider and called for Celeste to come into her bedroom. Celeste pointed Latricia toward the buffet table in the dining room then excused herself. She walked into Ginger's bedroom and closed the door behind her. Celeste saw the disturbed look on Portia's face and knew immediately that she was heated. And Celeste knew exactly why. Latricia Hall. She asked the question she already knew the answer to. "What's going on?"

Portia fired off, "What the heck is David's wife doing here and why didn't either one of you backstabbing skanks inform me that she had been invited?"

Ginger sat down on her bed and allowed Celeste the floor. "It's on you, Celeste. I didn't invite Latricia."

Portia looked at Celeste with raised eyebrows. Her neck rotated. "Well?"

Celeste knew the moment would come when she would have to explain to Portia why her lover's wife was on her baby shower guest list. "Latricia came into the bank a few months ago to cash a check and—"

Portia interrupted Celeste. "Yeah, I heard her say that."

Celeste continued. "We got to talking and catching up on old times. I figured out she was married to David when

I saw their names and address on the check. We talked about my pregnancy and before Latricia walked away from my window she asked me to send her an invitation to my baby shower." Celeste shrugged her shoulders. "What was I supposed to do?"

Portia's eyebrows rose. *Did she really just ask me that stupid question?* "What were you supposed to do?" She answered Celeste's question with a question. Portia looked at Ginger. She needed clarity. "Did she just ask me what she was supposed to do?"

Ginger nodded her head. "That was her question."

"How about tell me?" Portia stated to Celeste. "I addressed and mailed out thirty-five invitations. You failed to tell me that an additional invitation was secretly sent to the wife of one of my men."

"Wowwwwww," Ginger said.

Celeste repeated Portia's words out loud. "The wife of one of my men." She couldn't believe Portia's gall. "How do you say that with such ease?"

"It's like she was telling you what time of day it was," Ginger commented.

Celeste chuckled. "I mean seriously. We need to get somebody who speaks Hennessy in here." Celeste looked at Portia. "Are you drunk?"

Portia didn't answer.

Celeste leaned against the chest of drawers and looked at Ginger sitting on the bed. "Do you want to tell her how stupid she sounds or should I?"

"It's your world, Celeste. I'm just living in it."

Celeste looked at Portia. "You know, Portia, it's a shame to have all of that beauty and no brains. You've said some stupid things in your day but I've got to give you your props today, girlfriend. What you just said was the most stupidest of the stupids. If I had on a top hat, I'd tip it to you because you have outdone yourself."

"Touché," Ginger commented.

Portia looked at them both. "Oh, I see. Y'all in this together, huh?"

"In what?" Celeste asked.

"We've always had each other's backs, Celeste. You call what you did having my back?"

"I do have your back, Portia. But I'm not gonna condone your wrongdoing. Yeah, I could've told you that I sent Latricia an invitation but thought better of it. Truth be told, I didn't think she was gonna show up but now that she's here, oh well."

Portia frowned at Celeste's words. "Oh well? That's all you gotta say to me? Oh well?"

Ginger spoke up. "Portia, the three of us have done some crazy things in our lifetimes but we're grown now. We're not kids anymore. You know the scripture that reads, 'When I was a child I spoke as a child and played as a child but when I became a man, I put away childish things'? That scripture is not only referring to men but women also. We all did our dirt back in the day but it's time out for playing church. Latricia is in what I'm sure she believes is holy matrimony with a man you're sleeping with and you need to stop it."

Portia unfolded her arms and pointed her finger at Ginger. "You're preaching to me? Since you've stopped shacking up and playing house, you figure you can preach to me now?"

"I'm not perfect, Portia. And I don't pretend to be. It took me four long years to realize that Ronald was never gonna amount to anything. But when I made up my mind to get him out of my life, look what God did for me. He placed the man of my dreams right in my path. And look what God did for Celeste. It was when she confessed to Tony about keeping her secret that He planted the seed in her womb. I'm trying to get you to understand that you're prolonging your own blessings. You know you're living foul."

"What Latricia doesn't know won't hurt her," Portia stated nonchalantly.

"This ain't got nothing to do with Latricia!" Ginger shouted. "We're talking about your actions, Portia. This is about you." Ginger was frustrated. She would've bet one hundred dollars that if anyone had gotten her frazzled that day it would have been Celeste for sure. She threw her hands in the air and stood from the bed. "Look, I've said my piece. We've been in this bedroom long enough. Portia, you're grown and you're gonna do what you wanna do." She looked at Celeste. "It's time to open your gifts." Ginger followed Celeste out of the bedroom.

Portia sat down on Ginger's bed and exhaled loudly. "This really can't be happening," she said. She picked up the telephone on Ginger's nightstand and dialed David's cellular number.

"This is David," he answered.

"It's me. I'm calling from Ginger's house. Where's your wife?"

He frowned. "What?"

Portia spaced her words apart and spoke clearly. "Where . . . is . . . your . . . wife?"

"I think she mentioned something about going to a bridal shower. Why?"

"Try a baby shower, David."

"What are you talking about?"

"You called me three days ago and asked if we could get together today. Remember that?"

"And you said we couldn't because you were giving Celeste a baby shower."

Portia chuckled sarcastically. "It's the same baby shower Latricia got an invitation to."

David got quiet on the other end.

"Did you hear what I said, David?"

"Are you saying that Latricia is at Celeste's baby shower?"

"Ding, ding, ding, ding," Portia chimed out of frustration. "That's exactly what I'm saying."

"How did that happen?"

"Apparently, you store your money in the bank where Celeste works. Latricia came to the bank to cash a check. She and Celeste chatted a bit and she asked Celeste to send her an invitation to her baby shower. Fast forward a few months, Latricia's here, I'm here, and this whole situation is uncomfortable and a big freakin' mess."

"Oh, wow. What are the chances? It really is a small world."

Portia ran her fingers through her hair and exhaled loudly again. "Tell me about it. I opened the door and got the shock of my life. I darn near peed on myself. Latricia remembered me right away."

"Last night Latricia told me she was going to a shower of somebody she went to high school with but she didn't mention the woman's name."

Portia exhaled again. "This changes everything."

"What do you mean?"

Portia paused before she spoke. "I don't think we should see each other again, David."

David knew Portia was headed there. "Portia, Latricia doesn't know about us."

"She reached out and hugged me today. Can you imagine how that made me feel? Latricia was happy to see me and here I am screwing her husband."

The first time Portia had sex with David was at the home he shared with Latricia. David had told Portia up front that he was married. Portia saw photographs of Latricia and David hanging on the living room walls.

"I know her," Portia stated when she saw a photograph of David and Latricia on their wedding day. "Is your wife's name Latricia?"

David was taken aback. "Um, yeah. How do you know her?"

"We went to high school together."

"Really?" David asked.

"Yeah, but we lost touch shortly after graduation. I haven't spoken with Latricia in years."

David became worried that Portia would have a change of heart now that she knew who his wife was. "Soooooo, what happens now?"

Portia stepped to David and kissed him seductively. "Let's go to your bedroom."

It made all the difference that Portia had reconnected with Latricia. Having not met a wife or not being in contact with any of her married lover's wives gave Portia the guts she needed to be the other woman. Portia had no ties or connections to the wives of the men she slept with.

"Why you gotta make it sound like that?" David asked.

"Like what? Disgusting?"

"Yeah, disgusting. We don't screw, Portia. We make love."

"Really, David? Let's be serious. We have sex. There's no love in it at all. I'm ending it."

"Baby, you're being paranoid. Calm down."

"No, David," Portia shouted out. "I can't do this."

"Can we at least get together and talk about it?"

David couldn't see Portia shaking her head. "No. Uh-uh." She knew once she got in David's presence all of her newfound common sense would leave her brain. Portia was weak. It would only take one kiss or the warmth of David's breath on her neck and Portia would be naked instantly. "There's nothing left to talk about."

"What about the Escalade?"

Portia chuckled. *That didn't take long.* "Wow. Is it like that?"

"You know what time it is," he said calmly.

Portia knew she had to give it up. The Escalade was a conditional gift and she understood that when she had accepted it from David. She could drive the truck as long as she kept her legs open for him. She didn't want to do it but she had no choice. Portia exhaled a third time then recited Ginger's address. "It's parked outside. Come and get it."

Chapter 17

A Blast from the Past

Ginger walked over to Latricia just as she was helping herself to a second cup of fruit punch. "Hi, Latricia. Do you know who I am?"

Latricia looked at Ginger, smiled broadly, and set the cup of punch on the table. "Of course, Ginger. I would know you anywhere. I could never forget that cocoa-brown smooth skin of yours. I use to envy your complexion back in high school. How are you doing, girl?"

Ginger took Latricia in her arms and embraced her. "I'm wonderful. Life is good." Ginger could honestly say that. Had Latricia asked that same question a year ago, Ginger's answer would have been completely different.

"I think it's wonderful that you, Celeste, and Portia are still close after all these years."

"Yeah, we're soul sistas. We always will be. So, how has life been treating you since high school?"

"I don't have any complaints, Ginger. I've got good health and strength, I'm married to a wonderful man who worships the ground I walk on and I don't have to work. I'm able to stay at home and enjoy life."

Just as Ginger thought; Latricia was clueless. She really thought David worshiped the ground she walked on. David should have been ashamed of himself for making Latricia look stupid. "All right, Latricia. Sounds like you got it going on."

"God has been extra good to me, Ginger. I wouldn't trade my life for anything."

Yeah, that's what every wife says when she's in the dark. The fact that Latricia mentioned how good God had been to her, Ginger assumed she was a regular church attendee. "Where do you and your husband worship?" Ginger was careful to not mention David's name.

"Well, I worship at Progressive Life-Giving Word Cathedral, right off of Interstate 290. You can't miss it. I'm working on getting my husband more active in the church. But it's hard. David always seems to have something else to do on Sunday mornings."

He does Portia, Ginger thought. She knew of Progressive Ministries or "Gress," which was what the church was affectionately called. Ginger remembered reading an article in the *Chicago Sun-Times* that the members of Progressive had purchased a movie theater in the city of Hillside and turned it into a house of worship. The article stated that over 200 cars had traffic jammed from the cities of Maywood to Hillside. The church members had driven their cars from the old church on Thirteenth Avenue west on Washington Street to their new church home on Wolf Road.

"Apostle Donald Lawrence Alford is the pastor, right?" Ginger asked.

Latricia nodded. "That man has an anointing on him something fierce."

"How's Sunday morning service?"

"It's fire. I can't even describe it. You have to be there to experience it for yourself. But morning service ain't got nothin' on Sunday night broadcast. It's a different kind of crowd and a different kind of anointing. The Holy Ghost is straight-up ghetto."

Ginger laughed. "I listen to the broadcast often. I know all about it."

"You should meet me there tomorrow night," Latricia suggested.

Ginger smiled. "You know what, Latricia? I might just do that."

"Elder DeAndre Patterson is over there, too."

Ginger's eyes lit up. "The *He's Alive* DeAndre Patterson? I listen to him on the gospel radio station when he deejays on Saturday afternoons."

"Yes, he's really good on the radio."

"Okay, I'm sold, Latricia. I'll definitely be at the broadcast tomorrow night and I'll bring Joseph along."

"Good, I'll look for you. I always apologize to people in advance when I invite them to my church. You're gonna see some wild stuff. We leap over pews, run the aisle, do cartwheels and it's the norm for Apostle Alford to lay holy hands and the folks pass out. So, if someone accidentally steps on your feet, just excuse them and move to the side. By the way, who's Joseph?"

Ginger smiled again. "He's my sunshine. But we'll have to talk about him later. It's time for Celeste to open these gifts so I can get these women out of my house. Don't leave without giving me the directions to your church."

Ginger went into the kitchen and saw Portia leaning against the sink drinking from a bottle of water. "Celeste is gonna start opening her gifts. Get me a large garbage bag from beneath the sink for the gift-wrap paper. And I really wanna thank you for helping me host this baby shower, Portia. You're doing a fine job staying in the kitchen," Ginger said sarcastically.

"I broke it off with David."

Ginger looked at her in disbelief. "Say what?"

Portia exhaled. "David and I are done. I just talked to him."

Ginger came and stood in front of her. "What did you say to him?"

"I told him that Latricia was here and she's claiming to be happy. I told him I think she's beautiful and a wonderful woman and I couldn't keep betraying her. Then I told him to come and get his truck and to never call me again."

Ginger saw tears streaming down Portia's face and pulled her into her arms. "Oh, honey. You did the right thing. God is pleased with your decision."

Portia wiped her tears. "But I love my Escalade, Ginger. I think he's really gonna come and get it."

Ginger let go of the embrace and looked into Portia's eyes. "He needs to come and get it. Sever all ties with David. You work at a car dealership, Portia. Don't you get an employee discount? You can afford to buy your own car. I'm glad you're giving David back the truck. It's time for you to stop depending on men to make you happy. You can make yourself happy. Now what are you gonna do about the other married men? I can't keep waking up every morning wondering if it's the day I'll get another call that one of your married lovers flipped out. "

"I'm done with married men, period. When I get home, I'll call all of them and put an end to this crap."

"Whoop, gotta cut a step." Ginger teased Portia by pretending to do a holy dance and speaking in tongues in the middle of the kitchen.

Portia laughed at Ginger. It was just like her to locate the silver lining in any dark cloud. "You are so silly. You better stop playing before the Holy Ghost gets a hold of you for real."

"I want the Holy Ghost to get a hold of me." Ginger took off and ran around the kitchen table three times.

Portia looked at her acting a fool. "I'm glad you're having a good time at my expense. Now let's get real for a minute. I wanna thank you and Celeste for not turning your backs on me."

"You are our sista, no matter what. It was meant for Latricia to come to this baby shower. Look at the result of it."

Just then Latricia came into the kitchen. "Celeste sent me for a trash bag." She saw Portia's tears. "What happened, Portia? You okay?"

She could hardly stand to look at Latricia. Her guilt was eating at her. "Yeah. I'll be all right."

Ginger spoke. "She made a decision to do something that wasn't easy but it will work for her good."

Latricia came and stood before Portia. She grabbed both of her hands and closed her eyes. "Father, in the name of Jesus, I come to you on behalf of my friend."

Portia's body stiffened. Latricia praying and referring to her as a friend made Portia want to run and hide.

"I lift her up to you as she faces this challenge in her life," Latricia prayed. "It is my request that you guide her, walk with her, and show her the righteous way to go. I ask, Lord, that you crown her head with the knowledge and wisdom she needs to carry the anointing that you're about to bestow upon her shoulders. And, Lord, as she walks in your glory, whoever comes into her presence, let your light so shine in her that people will see you. Amen."

Latricia opened her eyes to see waterfalls cascading down Portia's cheeks. She embraced Portia and held her tight. She let go of Portia and turned to Ginger. "I better get that garbage bag out to the living room. It's getting messy out there."

Ginger got a single trash bag from beneath the kitchen sink and gave it to her. Latricia squeezed Portia's hand, gave her an assuring smile, and walked out of the kitchen.

Portia looked at Ginger. "Can you believe that?"

"If I hadn't witnessed it, I wouldn't have believed it."

"You think she knows?" Portia asked.

Ginger frowned. "Heck no. I don't care how sanctified a person may be. There is not a black woman on this earth who will love, hug, and pray for her husband's mistress the way Latricia just did. Trust me, she doesn't know about you and David. I will say this though, come tomorrow night at nine o'clock, I'm gonna be sitting at Progressive. I gotta get me some of that anointing power. Whatever the Holy Ghost is pouring on Latricia, I'm gonna make sure my cup gets filled with it."

When Ginger and Portia walked into the living room, they saw that Celeste had unwrapped the crib the two of them had purchased. Celeste sat in a chair in the middle of the room surrounded by a highchair, bassinette, swing, a baby bouncer, many boxes of newborn diapers, baby bottles, and so many blankets, bibs, and onesies. Someone had taken all of the bows that Celeste had removed from the gifts and put them in her hair.

Celeste opened her last gift. She held up a yellow knit sweater and pants set with booties and a cap to match. The living room filled with oohs and aahs.

"Thank you, Lady Elaine," Celeste said. "This will be his homecoming outfit."

Celeste looked at all of the gifts she received. "I wanna thank everyone for coming. Tony and I appreciate all of you and we can't wait to welcome our son. All of your gifts will come in handy and will be put to good use."

"There's one more gift," Ginger stated. She gave Celeste the small gift-wrapped box and card. "This one is from Tony. He wanted you to open something just for you."

Before Celeste unwrapped the box, she opened the card and read the words out loud: "'My darling CeeCee, you are the love of my life and the woman of my dreams. I have truly found my virtuous woman. I asked God what gift I could buy for the mother of my seed and He told me that the one true gift has already been given. It was when

He gave you to me. You are my very special gift. Inside this box is a token of my love and appreciation for having you in my life. I thank God for you. You are amazing. And I'm thankful that no one but you is my baby's momma. Love, Anthony.'"

The entire living room was quiet as Celeste opened the box and held up the $850 platinum crucifix she had been admiring for months. "Oh, my God," she cried out.

The crucifix sparkled. More oohs and aahs came from every direction.

Ginger made frappes with ginger ale and ice cream sherbet. Portia sliced the cake and served all of the guests. The women sat around the living room, listened to music, and offered boy names to Celeste.

Chapter 18

Let the Good Times Roll

After the shower, Celeste lay across Ginger's bed to wait for Anthony to arrive. She was exhausted and needed a nap after so much excitement from the baby shower. Portia vacuumed Ginger's area rug in the living room and Ginger put away what was left of the food. Portia placed the vacuum in the linen closet then went into the kitchen and sat down at the table to enjoy another slice of cake. "Ginger, do you remember what you said I could do with this cake?"

Ginger had hoped that Portia would have forgotten. "Remind me. What did I say?"

"You said I could smash cake in Celeste's face."

"I said that?"

"Yes, you did. And I can get her good while she's lying down."

"No, Portia. I paid good money for that comforter set. And smashing cake in someone's face is childish."

"But you promised me I could do this," Portia whined. "I was looking forward to it."

"I lied."

The doorbell rang and Portia jumped up to answer it. "Hey, Tony."

Anthony walked in and greeted Portia with a hug. He saw many boxes of baby clothes, a huge box that held a swing, a bassinette, a playpen, a Diaper Genie, a three-month supply of Playtex bottles, five cases of newborn Pampers, and a crib. "Wow, y'all women don't be playin' at these showers."

Before Portia closed the door, she noticed the empty parking spot where she had parked the Escalade. *Darn. David really came and got it.* For just a brief moment Portia thought about reconsidering getting back together with David. "Nope, I'm not gonna do it," she mumbled to herself. She closed the door.

"Where are Celeste and Ginger?" Anthony asked.

"Celeste is lying down; she's probably asleep by now. Ginger is in the kitchen putting the food away. You want something to eat?"

"Nah, I'm cool." Anthony proceeded to stack boxes on top of boxes.

Portia went into the kitchen and spoke to Ginger. "Tony is here and my truck is gone. I can't believe that fool actually came and got it."

Ginger wiped her countertops with a wet dish towel. "Good-bye and good riddance is what you should be saying, Portia. Go and wake up Celeste. And be careful; Tony says she wakes up swinging."

The doorbell rang again.

"I got it," Anthony yelled. He opened the door and greeted Joseph. "What's up, dude?"

Joseph entered the foyer and shook Anthony's hand. "What's going on, Tony?"

Anthony sighed. "Man, look at all of this stuff."

Joseph walked into the living room and looked all around. "All of this is for one baby?"

"One baby." Anthony sighed.

Ginger came into the living room all smiles and went directly into Joseph's arms. "There's my sunshine."

Joseph lifted Ginger and set her back on her feet but held on to her. They were wrapped around each other like pigs in a blanket. In Joseph's arms Ginger felt warmth, comfort, and complete. If she had a wish it would be to stay in his arms forever. She smiled then exhaled loudly.

Clearly Ginger and Joseph had forgotten about Anthony. He decided to make his presence known. "Get a room, will ya?"

Ginger looked at him. "I have a room, three of them as a matter of fact, but we ain't going there, okay?" She looked at Joseph. "I missed you, did you miss me?"

Joseph nuzzled Ginger's neck. "You have no idea."

"I made you a plate. Are you hungry?"

"I could eat but I'm gonna help Tony load these boxes in his truck."

"Finally, somebody is showing me some love," Anthony joked.

Ginger kissed Joseph's lips lightly and left the men alone. In the bedroom she saw Celeste sitting up on the bed as Portia kneaded the lower part of her back.

Ginger came and sat at the end of the bed, placed Celeste's left leg on her lap, and massaged the heel of her foot. "Are you tired, momma?"

Celeste moaned loudly. "That ain't the word. I don't have any energy to do anything." She caressed the left side of her swollen belly. "This boy is already trying out for football. He hasn't stopped moving since this morning."

"Ooh, can I feel him move?" Though Ginger had been pregnant twice, she had never gotten far enough in either pregnancy to feel the fetuses move.

Celeste reached for Ginger's hand and pressed it on her belly. In only a few seconds Ginger felt movement beneath her fingers.

"I feel him moving," Ginger said excitedly. "I can really feel him."

"Okay, it's my turn," Portia said. She reached around Celeste and pressed her open palm next to Ginger's. Her mouth dropped open. "Oh, wow. He's doing somersaults."

"And he's been doing them all day long," Celeste complained. "I'm ready to go home, get under the bed, and hibernate."

Portia chuckled. "You can get under there and get stuck if you want to. I don't know who you think is gonna haul your big behind out from under there."

The three of them laughed.

"Those are cute T-shirts you're wearing. It is a little presumptuous don't you think?"

"Nope," Ginger answered.

"You couldn't make up your mind so we did it for you."

Celeste looked at Portia. "Oh, really? Well, what if I told you that Anthony and I had already decided on godparents and neither of you made the cut?"

"Celeste, you can try to pull that trick if you want to," Ginger stated. "After all the crap that Portia and I had to put up with during the last nine months we deserve the right to be the godmothers. We earned the title."

"And besides," Portia chimed in, "who, other than us, could possibly be chosen? Your parents are deceased. You can't stand your only sister and you really ain't got no other friends beside me and Ginger."

"That is not true, Portia."

"It's absolutely true, Celeste. Just face it. You are evil. You always have been and you always will be."

Celeste rolled her eyes at Portia and Ginger chuckled.

Anthony came and stood in the bedroom doorway. He saw his wife sitting on the bed getting pampered. "How much y'all charge for that? Can I have next rubdown?"

Celeste smiled at him. "Hey, baby." She caressed her necklace. "I love my cross, thank you."

He returned the smile. "You're welcome."

"You see these heifers' T-shirts?"

Anthony read the bold black letters. "I thought you weren't gonna tell them, just yet, that we had chosen them as the godmothers."

"You are so busted!" Ginger shouted out to Celeste.

"We knew it," Portia said excitedly. "Sittin' there trying to make us think we weren't your first choice." Portia waved her hand at Celeste. "Chile, please."

"Oh, shut up," Celeste said to them. Of course Portia and Ginger would be the godmothers. Celeste never thought differently. Her plan was to let her best friends sweat out the wait before she announced her decision. But Anthony's big mouth spoiled it.

Celeste extended her hand toward him. "Can you help me up?"

Anthony assisted Celeste out of the bed. Ginger slid Celeste's shoes on her swollen feet and Portia placed Celeste's purse on her shoulder. Celeste hugged and kissed her friends, thanked them for a wonderful shower, and followed Anthony out of the bedroom.

"You wanna stay in my guest room tonight?" Ginger asked Portia.

"No. Give me the keys to your car. I'll swing by and get you for church in the morning."

"Don't bother," Ginger said, rotating her aching neck and shoulders. "I don't plan on waking up until the afternoon. I'm saving my energy for Progressive's broadcast tomorrow night."

With Portia finally gone, Ginger's living room was empty and clean, just the way she liked it. She found Joseph at the kitchen table eating.

"I see you found your plate. Did you warm it in the microwave?"

He shook his head from side to side and stuffed a forkful of cold spaghetti in his mouth. "I was too hungry for that. These barbecue wings are the bomb."

Ginger sat on Joseph's lap and fed him a forkful of potato salad. Then she took a napkin and wiped the corners of his mouth.

"I get the royal treatment, huh?" he asked.

"I know how to treat my king."

"I can get use to this."

"You might as well," Ginger said.

When Joseph confessed that his belly was full, Ginger opted to take a shower. Joseph sat on the sofa in the living room and watched a basketball game and waited for her.

Fifteen minutes later, Ginger stood in front of the television wearing a long white silk nightgown. "I'm exhausted. I'm going to bed." She pressed the power button on the television and went toward the bedroom. "You coming with me?" she asked over her shoulder.

Joseph rose from the sofa and followed her. Ginger lay on the bed and turned onto her right side. Joseph pulled his shoes off and lay behind Ginger and wrapped his arm around her waist and held her. Within moments he felt Ginger's head go limp against his chest; then he knew she was asleep.

Chapter 19

Let the Church Say Amen

Ginger read the directions that Latricia had given her to Joseph as he exited off of Interstate 290 and turned left onto Wolf Road. "Latricia said go to the stop sign and make a right and we should see the church straight ahead."

When Joseph arrived in the church's parking lot, he parked his car, exited, and came around to the passenger side and opened Ginger's door. She placed her hand in Joseph's and stepped out. Chivalry was not dead and Ginger was happy about that.

An usher greeted Joseph and Ginger with a smile as they approached the door of the main sanctuary. "Welcome to Progressive Ministries."

"Thank you," Ginger responded. "We're guests of Latricia Hall's."

Joseph and Ginger were escorted to the second row from the front of the church. Latricia sat on the end seat. She saw Ginger and stood to hug her. "You came," she said excitedly. "I don't believe it."

"Why not?" Ginger asked her. "I told you I would be here." Ginger placed her hand in Joseph's. "Latricia, this is Joseph, my sunshine."

Latricia shook his hand. "Hello, sunshine. It's nice to meet you, and welcome to Progressive." Latricia stepped out into the aisle and allowed Joseph and Ginger to enter the row. They sat in the two empty seats next to Latricia.

Ginger looked all around the sanctuary. She couldn't tell that she sat in an old movie theater. The entire building had been gutted, rehabilitated, remodeled, and redecorated. She whispered in Latricia's ear, "This is absolutely beautiful."

It was exactly 9:00 p.m. Elder DeAndre Patterson stood in front of the Radio Choir. The music started and Latricia leaned into Ginger and said, "I hope you're ready to get your praise on."

Ginger saw that already the saints were on their feet encouraging the choir to go forth and do their thing.

"Sang, choir. Y'all better sang tonight," the people encouraged them.

"You know, Lord, whether I'm right," the Radio Choir sang. "You know, Lord, whether I'm wrong. You know, Lord, whether I'm right or wrong. Whether I'm right or wrong."

Latricia stood and joined the rest of the congregation in song. "While I'm down here praying, Lord search my heart. Search meeeeeee, search me, Lord. Search meeeeeee, search me, Lord."

The energy inside the church was electric. Both Ginger and Joseph stood and blended in. "Search me, Lord. Search me, Lord. Search me, Lord. You know Lord, whether I'm right or wrong. Whether I'm right or wrong."

When the song had ended the people sat. The announcing clerk walked to the podium to tell all of the radio listeners about the good news the Lord was doing at Progressive Life-Giving Word Cathedral.

Ginger looked to her left and saw Apostle Donald L. Alford walking up the steps to the pulpit, followed by an entourage of deacons and armor bearers. Apostle Alford knelt to pray before taking his seat.

Ginger leaned into Latricia. "Where is his wife?"

Latricia pointed toward the soprano section in the choir. "She's the third one from the left on the front row."

Ginger sought out the first lady and saw blond shoulder-length hair, a petite nose, and small lips. She sat with poise. Without even trying the first lady exuded class.

"She's beautiful," Ginger commented.

"That's Gloria but we call her Lady Glo 'cause she shines."

After the Radio Choir sang the last song, Apostle Alford took his place behind the podium. "Everybody stand to your feet and let's begin to worship the Lord."

The congregation obeyed their leader. The saints stood, raised their hands, and closed their eyes. The musicians played soft praise and worship music as Apostle Alford encouraged the people to open their mouths and talk to God. He sang, "I just want to praise you. I lift my hands and say, 'I love you.' You are everything to me and I exalt your holy name on high."

Ginger opened her eyes. She saw heads thrown back and mouths open crying out to God. A man and woman ran down to the front of the church and threw themselves on the altar.

Apostle Alford spoke to the people from the pulpit. "Take your neighbor by the hand and say, 'Neighbor, nay in all of these things, we are more than conquerors through Him who love us.'"

The congregation obeyed their leader. Ginger and Joseph held hands and looked at each other. They repeated what Apostle Alford had just said. "Neighbor, nay in all of these things, we are more than conquerors through Him that love us."

A choir member ran out of the pulpit, down the aisle, out into the vestibule, shouting out praises. A man standing behind Joseph began jumping up and down thanking God for saving his life.

Don, don, don, don. Ginger heard the drums and organ. Don, don, don, don. The music was a prelude to what was getting ready to happen. Latricia leaned into Ginger and said, "Here we go. It only takes one person to set it off and it becomes a chain reaction."

Don, don, don, don. The atmosphere was thick. The air was heavy. The saints were ready to praise.

Apostle Alford loosened his tie. "I see y'all ain't come to play. Come on and take twenty seconds and get your praise on. Go on and give God His due."

The music and drums took over the service. The sanctuary sounded like a basketball stadium at playoff time. The entire church lost themselves in the Lord.

Suddenly, Ginger reflected back on the two babies she lost at the hands of Ronald. Then she thought about the bruises and broken ribs she suffered. She remembered having to ask him for permission to go to church. Ginger looked to her right and saw Joseph standing next to her, with his eyes closed, speaking to God in the unknown tongue. Tears were running down his face. Not only was Joseph saved; he was anointed and sanctified.

Ginger remembered the five dozen roses he sent to her job. She remembered the time Joseph had come to the school, on his day off, and gotten the keys to her car. He had it detailed, washed, and waxed, then brought it back to her. She remembered Joseph coming into the beauty shop to pay her beautician. She remembered Joseph spending last night, in her bed, next to her without touching her sexually.

Joseph had accepted Ginger's terms. If he wanted to be with her he needed to understand that she lived a celibate life and was waiting for marriage. Everything that Ronald wasn't, Joseph was and more. Ginger recalled him marrying her in her driveway. Joseph was a true man of God who adored her and gave her anything she wanted. He encouraged her, prayed with her, and not only supported her going to church but he escorted her there. Joseph was a man after God's own heart and, for that, Ginger was truly thankful.

Amid the drums, the music, the electricity that ran through her body, and the tall and handsome blessing who stood next to her, Ginger couldn't keep still. Her blood ran warm through her veins. She opened her mouth and let out a loud, "Thank yaaaa." Ginger started jumping and turning around. "Thank ya, Jesus. Thank yaaaa."

Joseph saw tears of joy running down Ginger's face. Latricia stepped into the aisle to give Ginger room.

Apostle Alford came out of the pulpit, followed by his armor bearers, and stood in front of Ginger. He whispered in Latricia's ear and asked if Ginger and Joseph were together. Latricia nodded her head.

Apostle Alford gently grabbed Ginger's hand and pulled her toward him, then motioned for Joseph to stand next to her in the aisle. The armor bearers stood behind them as Apostle Alford laid holy hands on Joseph and Ginger's foreheads. He closed his eyes and blessed them both. Seconds later Joseph and Ginger were lying on the floor.

They were slain in the spirit of God.

Chapter 20

Straddling the Fence

Portia was so determined to leave married men alone that she changed her home and cellular telephone numbers. She repented to God and asked for His forgiveness but Portia didn't vow to live a celibate lifestyle. She felt that she needed to take baby steps.

"I need to be weaned like a baby getting off the bottle." Portia tried to explain her actions to Celeste and Ginger. She had called them on a three-way.

"Why can't you keep your legs closed altogether?" Ginger asked her.

Portia loved sex. It made her feel good. "It's difficult."

"Difficult may take a day. Impossible may take a week but you can do this, Portia," Celeste advised.

"Oh, sure. This coming from a woman who lies next to a man every night. What do you know about giving up sex?"

"I did it," Ginger stated matter-of-factly.

Portia exhaled into the telephone line. "I don't believe you ain't breaking Joseph off, Ginger. You can't tell me that man has been with you all this time, spends all kinds of money, and ain't getting nothing in return. I just don't believe it."

"I'm telling the truth."

"Well, heck, since you ain't using your vajayjay, can you please loan it to me? I can certainly use another one."

Celeste screamed out in laughter. "Girl, your behind is crazy."

Ginger didn't find Portia to be comical at all. The fact that Portia didn't believe that she was celibate angered Ginger. She had come full circle since she rid Ronald from her life. Ginger was proud that she was able to turn her life around and live a celibate lifestyle. The benefit was God placing Joseph, her true soul mate, in her life. "That's the difference between you and me. I don't have to whore around to get nice things."

"Okay. Hold on now, Ginger," Celeste interjected. Their telephone conversation was taking the wrong turn. She and Ginger were supposed to encourage Portia to do the right thing, not call her names and point fingers. Celeste didn't want the three of them screaming at each other and saying things that would separate them. Celeste remembered not too long ago when words had almost caused them to lose each other for good.

"Is that what you think I do, Ginger? Whore around?" Portia asked.

"You have sex with men and they pay you for it. I don't know any other name for it. Do you, Celeste?"

"Oh, my God. Are we really gonna do this again?" Celeste wanted to just hang up the telephone and let Ginger and Portia have at it.

"She needs to understand," Ginger started, "that having sex, whether the man is married or not, is still a sin. And receiving money for it is downright degrading and whorish."

There goes that nasty word again, Celeste thought. "Okay, y'all know what, I'm hanging up. I'm not going to do this again with you two. I'm in a happy place and I'm choosing to stay there. You two can continue this conversation without me." Celeste disconnected the line and so did Ginger and Portia.

***

At the car dealership, where she worked, Portia presented a bill of sale to a gentleman who was interested in purchasing a car. When she gave it to the man, he grabbed her wrist instead of the paper. He looked at Portia and smiled. "Thank you, beautiful."

The man was handsome; Portia couldn't deny the fact that he was extremely good-looking. She smiled back at him. "You're welcome. Is there anything else I can do for you, Mr. . . ." Portia looked at the bill of sale for the man's name. When she saw it, she glanced up at him. "Michael Jackson?"

He chuckled. Portia's reaction to his name was no different from anyone else's reaction. He answered Portia's next question before she even asked it. The same question he had been answering his entire life. Whether Michael was applying for a job, signing a receipt, or standing in line at the DMV waiting for his name to be called. "Yes. My real name is Michael Jackson."

"Do you sing?"

Michael chuckled again. "Uh, no. I don't sing."

"Can you dance?"

Having the same name as the King of Pop, Michael was constantly asked if he was in the entertainment business.

"I'm afraid not. I don't sing or dance. I build highways."

Portia was intrigued. In her mind she heard a cash register ring. Construction workers earned a great living. The Michael Jackson who stood before her didn't have the cash flow of the famous silver-gloved one but Portia knew that mixing, pouring, and laying concrete came with great pay and even greater benefits.

She extended her hand toward him. "My name is Portia."

Michael shook Portia's hand. "As in Porsche?"

"Something like that." She smiled.

Out of habit, Portia looked at his left hand for a wedding band but didn't see one. "I don't see a wedding ring. Are you married, Michael?"

"I've been divorced for six years."

"Any children?"

He nodded his head. "I have an eight-year-old and a four-year-old."

Portia was curious about the second child. "Four-year-old? You said you've been divorced for six years."

"After my divorce, I met someone whom I thought I would be with forever but fate didn't see it that way. However, I got a beautiful daughter out of the deal."

Portia's eyebrows rose. "You have two kids with two different women?"

"Apparently." Michael answered.

Portia's wheels were turning. "So, you have the letters CHISUP on your check stub, right?"

Michael didn't understand. He frowned at Portia. "What's CHISUP?"

"Child support."

Michael laughed. Portia wasn't letting up. He was uncomfortable. "Yes, I take care of both of my children."

"What about your ex-wife? Are you paying alimony, too?" Portia knew the deal. With child support and alimony payments, there may not be any funds left over from Michael's paycheck for her to enjoy any of it.

Michael smiled because he knew where Portia was headed with her interrogation and the chances of her dating him were slim to none. "At the risk of you never wanting to see me again, Portia, I'm going to be honest. Yes, I pay alimony as well."

Portia shook Michael's hand again and walked back to her desk. "It was nice meeting you, Mr. Jackson," she said over her shoulder. She got to her desk and sat down.

"Seriously, Lord? You got jokes today? I gave up married men but is that really the best you can do for me? I mean, can a sista at least get her hair and nails done?"

Chapter 21

And Baby Makes Three

"Tooooonnnnnnyyyyyy!"

Anthony was in his home office checking his e-mails when Celeste bellowed for him. He rushed into the bathroom. "What is it?"

Celeste bent over the sink and panted for air. "It hurts so bad. I think I'm in labor."

Anthony's eyes lit up. He became excited. "It's time?"

She winced in pain. "I don't know."

"How far apart are the attractions?"

She looked at him shamefully. "It's *contractions,* you fool, and this is the first one."

As soon as Celeste finished her sentence she felt a liquid stream run down her legs. She looked at Anthony with a horrid expression. "Uh-oh."

Squoosh. Amniotic fluid gushed to the bathroom floor with the same force as waves rushing against the shoreline.

At three o'clock in the afternoon, on the last Saturday in January, Portia, Ginger, and Joseph sat in the maternity ward at Little Company of Mary Hospital, listening to Celeste scream and act a fool. The three of them were in the waiting room anticipating the arrival of their nephew. They had been there since eleven-thirty that morning.

Before they arrived at the maternity ward Joseph, Ginger, and Portia had stopped by the gift shop and purchased a large blue stuffed teddy bear and balloons that read HAPPY BIRTHDAY and CONGRATULATIONS.

Anthony, dressed in teal-green scrubs and wearing a surgical mask, came and sat with them. He was exhausted from coaching Celeste to breathe and relax during the contractions.

"How's it going?" Joseph asked him.

Anthony leaned his head back against the wall and pulled the mask down from over his nose and mouth. "Man, I don't think I can go through this with her. Every contraction Celeste gets, she cusses me out. I was showing her how to breathe and she told me to get the heck out of her face 'cause my breath stinks. One contraction made Celeste sit up on the bed and I swear that I actually saw her head do a 360-degree rotation on her shoulders."

Portia, Ginger, and Joseph laughed. "Man, I wouldn't wanna be in your shoes for anything," Joseph said.

Ginger tapped his shoulder. "Excuse me? You wouldn't wanna support your wife while she's giving birth to your child?"

"I didn't mean it like that."

"Well, how did you mean it, Joseph?" Portia asked.

Ginger turned her whole body toward Joseph to face him and looked directly into his eyes as he tried to get his foot out of his mouth. "Answer her question. Inquiring minds want to know."

Joseph looked to Anthony for help. Anthony shook his head from side to side. "Sorry, you're on your own. I got my own dilemma down the hall."

Joseph looked at Ginger. "What I meant was I wouldn't wanna be in Tony's shoes right now because I'm not married. But when I do get married, I will look forward to supporting my wife in the delivery room one hundred percent."

Ginger and Portia commented at the same time. "Mmm, hmm."

Anthony shook Joseph's hand. "Nice save."

A nurse came into the waiting room. "Mr. Harper, your wife is asking for you. She told me tell you to bring your narrow behind back into the delivery room."

Anthony stood and looked at Portia, Joseph, and Ginger with pity in his eyes. "Pray for me y'all."

Ginger opened her purse and gave Anthony a small bottle of blessed oil. "Take this and sprinkle it on Celeste's forehead. If it sizzles, I suggest you haul your behind out of there and call an exorcist."

Portia and Joseph laughed as Anthony took the oil and kissed it up to God then followed the nurse back to Celeste's delivery room.

Forty-five minutes later, Anthony returned to the waiting room with a blue bundle of joy in his arms. Portia, Ginger, and Joseph rushed to him. From the three of them, Anthony heard, "Oh, my God," "Let me see, let me see," and "Congratulations."

Anthony pulled back the blanket to reveal a mini him. "I want y'all to meet Anthony James Harper II, weighing in at six pounds, seven ounces. He's got eight fingers, two thumbs, ten toes and one wee-wee."

"How is Celeste doing?" Ginger asked.

"She's good. Tired but good."

Ginger and Portia took turns making a fuss over their nephew.

Anthony stood with tears in his eyes. He couldn't take his eyes off of his son. "I waited seven years for this moment. I can't even describe how it feels."

Joseph patted his back. "That's because there are no words to describe it, man. Some things you just have to experience."

"I gotta get him to the incubator. He's gonna be circumcised later on this evening. If Celeste knew that I had him out here she'd kill me."

"Why?" Ginger asked.

"Because she said she didn't want nobody's contagious lips on him. Especially yours, Portia. Celeste says there's no telling where your lips been. She made me rub my hands with alcohol before I could touch him and I'm his father."

Just for that Ginger and Portia kissed the baby on separate cheeks. "Now, go and tell Celeste that," Portia said.

The first Sunday in March, after morning service, Anthony and Celeste stood at the altar. Portia, Ginger, and Joseph stood with them. Pastor Ricky Harris held baby Anthony and sprinkled holy water on his forehead and blessed him. "Father, we surrender little Anthony to you. We ask that you guide him, teach him, and lead him." He gave little Anthony to his father and looked at him and Celeste. "God has blessed you with a miracle. Do you promise to protect little Anthony and train him in the way that he should go, so when he is grown he will not depart from it?"

Celeste and Anthony responded, "We do."

Pastor Ricky Harris turned to Portia, Celeste, and Joseph. "As godparents do you accept the responsibility to see after little Anthony, to make sure he is safe and cared for? Do you promise to step in and become parents if Anthony and Celeste can no longer be there for him?"

"We do," Portia, Joseph, and Ginger stated.

Over the past months Anthony and Joseph had become good friends. They spent a great deal of time together bowling, shooting a game of pool, and washing their cars.

Anthony had warned Joseph that a relationship with Ginger meant that he would be subjected to the fights she had with Portia and Celeste on a regular basis.

"Just stay out of it and mind your business, man," he advised.

Joseph took Anthony's advice and ran with it. It was the following day that Ginger complained to him that she had gotten in to a fight with Portia and Celeste and she was never speaking to either of them again. Four hours later Joseph answered Ginger's doorbell. Portia and Celeste had come to pick her up. They were going to the mall.

Both Celeste and Anthony agreed that Joseph was a good man and they thought he would make an excellent godfather for their son.

The day they brought their son home from the hospital, Joseph, Ginger, and Celeste came over and brought dinner for everyone. After they had eaten, they all went into the living room.

Ginger was feeding baby Anthony when he started to squirm and make a fuss. "Why is he frowning?"

"That's a booboo face," Celeste said. "I'll check his diaper."

"That's something his godfather should do."

Ginger, Portia, and Joseph all looked at Anthony.

Anthony didn't say a word. He took the baby from Ginger's arms and placed him in Joseph's arms.

Joseph was flabbergasted. He looked from Anthony to Celeste. They were both smiling. Joseph looked down into the eyes of baby Anthony and smiled. "Wow. I'm your godfather."

"That's a wonderful thing," Ginger said with tears in her eyes. She was happy that Celeste and Anthony gave Joseph the responsibility. It would prepare him for when she and Joseph had a baby of their own.

Portia looked at the baby resting in Joseph's arms. "That's a good fit."

Joseph looked at Celeste and Anthony. "I don't know what to say."

"Do you accept?" Anthony asked him.

"I'm honored," he said proudly.

Little Anthony started to squirm and frown. "Uh-oh. He's making that face again," Anthony said.

"The diapers, baby wipes, and baby powder are all on the changing table. So, have at it," Celeste stated.

Joseph carefully stood with the baby. "It would be my pleasure."

Ginger followed him. "I better assist. It could get messy."

Epilogue

What God Has Joined Together

A month later, Ginger walked into the teacher's lounge and found a message in her mailbox:

Ginger, call me, at the studio, as soon as you get this message, Joseph

Ginger called Joseph from the telephone on the conference table.

"WGN News. How may I direct your call?" a receptionist answered.

"Hi, this is Ginger Brown. I'm returning Joseph Bank's call."

"Yes, Miss Brown, he was expecting your call but he had to leave the studio urgently. He left a message that he'll give you a ring this evening."

"Okay, thank you." Ginger disconnected the call and dialed Joseph's cellular number. Her call was sent directly to his voicemail. She didn't leave a message. Ginger went back to her class.

That evening Ginger answered her doorbell and saw Joseph down on bended knee. Her heart skipped a beat. She looked at him curiously. "What are you doing?"

"Didn't the receptionist give you my message?" he asked.

Ginger thought about the phone call. "She said you were gonna give me a ring this evening."

"It's six o'clock in the evening," Joseph said.

She was even more curious. Ginger wondered what he was up to. "Okay. And?"

Joseph reached in his shirt pocket and presented Ginger with a two-carat platinum pear-shaped diamond ring. "What are you doing for the rest of your life?"

THE END

Coming Soon

Lady Arykah Reigns

The clock on the nightstand displayed 3:53 a.m. Arykah tossed and turned in her sleep. She was dreaming.

Praise and worship was in full swing. Bishop Lance Howell sat in the pulpit. Mother Pansie Bowak sat on the second pew. She clapped her hands and swayed as the choir sang.

"Come on in where the table is spread and the feast of the Lord is going on."

Arykah fidgeted. She turned to her side not knowing that she had thrown the covers from her body.

The sanctuary doors opened. Arykah appeared at the entrance. Myrtle and Monique stood on opposite sides of her. Darlita, Chelsea, and Gladys were behind her. Arykah took the first step and all of the ladies followed her.

At Mother Pansie's house two policemen forced Clyde's hands behind his back and locked cuffs on his wrists.

"Clyde Trumbull, you're under arrest for the rape of Arykah Miles and second-degree murder in the death of her unborn child," an officer stated as he read Clyde the Miranda rights. As they escorted Clyde up the basement stairs, they saw a huge collage of photographs, taken of Arykah, along the staircase wall.

Arykah turned onto her back. Tears ran from the sides of her closed eyelids, past her temples, and into her hair.

Mother Gussie stood in the middle of her living room. Dressed in a light blue terrycloth robe and curlers in her hair, Mother Gussie was visibly frightened. She shook her head from side to side when questioned by the police.

Arykah twitched then mumbled in her sleep.

At Freedom Temple Church of God in Christ, Arykah and the ladies slowly made their way down the center aisle. The congregation lost interest in praise and worship. Everyone stopped singing and clapping. They focused on her battered face. Arykah heard many gasps.

"Is that Lady Arykah? Oh, my God. What happened to her?"

Mother Pansie turned around and looked up the aisle to see what had captured the choir's and musicians' attention. Her eyes filled with disbelief when she saw Arykah and her posse making their way in her direction. She turned back around and sat on the pew, frozen. She stared straight ahead.

When Arykah had arrived at Mother Pansie's side, she looked up at her and then looked away.

The entire church was quiet. Everyone watched.

"You tried to break me, didn't you?"

Mother Pansie didn't respond to Arykah. She sat stoic on the pew.

Arykah knelt down and placed her bruised face directly in Mother Pansie's view. "Look at me!" she yelled.

Again Arykah twitched and mumbled, "No, no." Sweat beads formed on her forehead. She pressed the rear of her head down into the pillow.

Mother Pansie flinched. She hastily grabbed her purse and Bible from the pew and stood. She maneuvered past Arykah and collided with Monique, Chelsea, Myrtle, Darlita, and Gladys as they blocked her exit. She brushed passed the ladies and hurried down the center aisle but stopped in her tracks when she saw Detective Cortney Rogers and two female officers walking up the aisle. Nervously, Mother Pansie turned around and saw Arykah and her gang closing in on her. She was trapped. She had been caught.

Detective Rogers grabbed Mother Pansie's arms and pulled them behind her. Her Bible and purse fell to the floor as she was placed in handcuffs.

The church was in total shock. Many congregants looked on as their beloved Mother Pansie was arrested. "What's going on? What's happening?"

Arykah approached Mother Pansie and stood toe to toe with her. "Did you really think that you could keep me away from this church?" She clenched her teeth and poked herself in the chest. "I am Lady Arykah Miles-Howell."

Mother Pansie held no expression on her face.

"You tried to destroy me but it didn't work," Arykah continued. "You came after my marriage but that plan failed too." As tears ran down her face, Arykah's words broke. "You stole my baby from my womb but guess what, Pansie. God is still holding my hand. That weapon you formed didn't prosper. It will never prosper."

"Oh, my God, not Mother Pansie," Arykah heard many folks say out loud.

Arykah laughed emotionally. "You know what I'm gonna do for you, Pansie? As the first lady of this church, I'm gonna ask the Lord to have mercy on your soul."

Detective Rogers escorted Mother Pansie out of the sanctuary. Lance came from the pulpit and stood in front of Arykah. "You did it, Cheeks. I'm so proud of you."

Gladys, Myrtle, Chelsea, Monique, and Darlita all gathered around Arykah and hugged her. A young woman left the fourth pew, walked up to Arykah, and stood before her. She removed a pearl necklace from her neck and placed it around Arykah's neck. She hugged Arykah and walked away. Another lady came and placed a shawl around Arykah's shoulders, hugged her, and walked away. One by one all of the ladies at Freedom Temple Church of God in Christ stood in line and gave Arykah jewelry, money, articles of their own clothing, and many hugs. Finally, Arykah was accepted. She had earned the title of Lady Elect.

Arykah turned onto her side and exhaled. She slept peacefully for the remainder of the night. But once she would awaken, she would realize it had all been just a dream.

Book Club Discussion Questions

1. Celeste, Portia and Ginger had been best friends since high school. What happened that caused them to turn on each other?
2. Why did Ginger endure an abusive relationship for so long? Why did she finally end it?
3. What was Portia's attraction to married men?
4. Celeste kept a dark secret from her husband. What was it?
5. Anthony walked out on Celeste when he learned that she had deceived him. Do you think he overreacted?
6. Joseph Banks entered Ginger's life and turned it upside down. Why was it so difficult for her to accept him?
7. Why and when did Portia end her adulterous affair with David Hall?
8. In chapter three the damsels got into an argument and didn't speak for weeks. What happened that brought them back together?
9. Do you think Portia will ever get over her attraction to men with lots of money?
10. Ginger tried to kill Ronald when she knew he couldn't defend himself. Did she do the wrong thing?

UC HIS GLORY BOOK CLUB!

www.uchisglorybookclub.net

UC His Glory Book Club is the spirit-inspired brain-child of Joylynn Jossel, Author and Acquisitions Editor of Urban Christian, and Kendra Norman-Bellamy, Author for Urban Christian. This is an online book club that hosts authors of Urban Christian. We welcome as members all men and women who have a passion for reading Christian-based fiction.

UC His Glory Book Club pledges our commitment to provide support, positive feedback, encouragement, and a forum whereby members can openly discuss and review the literary works of Urban Christian authors.

There is no membership fee associated with UC His Glory Book Club; however, we do ask that you support the authors through purchasing, encouraging, providing book reviews, and of course, your prayers. We also ask that you respect our beliefs and follow the guidelines of the book club. We hope to receive your valuable input, opinions, and reviews that build up, rather than tear down our authors.

What We Believe:

—We believe that Jesus is the Christ, Son of the Living God.

—We believe the Bible is the true, living Word of God.

—We believe all Urban Christian authors should use their God-given writing abilities to honor God and share the message of the written word God has given to each of them uniquely.

—We believe in supporting Urban Christian authors in their literary endeavors by reading, purchasing and sharing their titles with our online community.

—We believe that in everything we do in our literary arena should be done in a manner that will lead to God being glorified and honored.

We look forward to the online fellowship with you.

Please visit us often at *www.uchisglorybookclub.net*.

Many Blessing to You!

Shelia E. Lipsey,
President, UC His Glory Book Club

ORDER FORM
URBAN BOOKS, LLC
97 N18th Street
Wyandanch, NY 11798

Name (please print):_____

Address: _____

City/State: _____

Zip: _____

QTY	TITLES	PRICE
	16 On The Block	$14.95
	A Girl From Flint	$14.95
	A Pimp's Life	$14.95
	Baltimore Chronicles	$14.95
	Baltimore Chronicles 2	$14.95
	Betrayal	$14.95
	Bi-Curious	$14.95
	Bi-Curious 2: Life After Sadie	$14.95
	Bi-Curious 3: Trapped	$14.95
	Both Sides Of The Fence	$14.95
	Both Sides Of The Fence 2	$14.95
	California Connection	$14.95

Shipping and handling: add $3.50 for 1st book, then $1.75 for each additional book.

Please send a check payable to:

Urban Books, LLC

Please allow 4-6 weeks for delivery

ORDER FORM
URBAN BOOKS, LLC
97 N18th Street
Wyandanch, NY 11798

Name (please print):_____

Address: _____

City/State: _____

Zip: _____

QTY	TITLES	PRICE
	California Connection 2	$14.95
	Cheesecake And Teardrops	$14.95
	Congratulations	$14.95
	Crazy In Love	$14.95
	Cyber Case	$14.95
	Denim Diaries	$14.95
	Diary Of A Mad First Lady	$14.95
	Diary Of A Stalker	$14.95
	Diary Of A Street Diva	$14.95
	Diary Of A Young Girl	$14.95
	Dirty Money	$14.95
	Dirty To The Grave	$14.95

Shipping and handling: add $3.50 for 1st book, then $1.75 for each additional book.

Please send a check payable to:

Urban Books, LLC

Please allow 4-6 weeks for delivery